The Urbana Free Library

To renew: call 217-367-4057
or go to "*urbanafreelibrary.org*"
and select "Renew/Request Items"

GIRL ABOUT TOWN

GIRL ABOUT TOWN

PART ONE

NEW YORK CITY
1931

ONE

It was never quiet where Lucille lived. Sometimes, in rare free moments away from the monotony of a washerwoman's steam and scalding water, her mother, Ida, would lovingly read aloud from one of the few precious books that hadn't been pawned. Shakespeare's arcadian visions or poems about sylvan greenery, where thoughts were never interrupted by anything more jarring than birdsong and the baaing of sheep . . . Lucille would close her eyes, listening to her mother's gentle schoolteacher voice, and dream about a place like that. Though maybe without the sheep. She'd seen raw wool loaded into the textile factory, and from what she witnessed, sheep must be as filthcrusted and degenerate as any Lower East Side bum. How clean things are in poetry, how dirty in real life.

In their tiny tenement, eight people lived in two small rooms. Her father, in a steady decline since an injury in the Great War, was now practically bedridden, unable to work, or do much more than sleep or beg for the morphine that helped that sleep come when they could afford it. They could rarely afford *anything* beyond bare sustenance, but sometimes even that was denied to give her father the gift of dreamless slumber. Cabbage or peace, it came to. A holiday was cabbage *and* peace.

Her two older brothers jauntily ran the streets most of the day and half the night, coming home drunk, grunting, and penniless—but they'd *had* money at some point every day, to get the liquor, so why didn't they ever bring any of it home? The three youngest, two girls and a boy, were in school for part of the day. But even when the tiny apartment was half empty, it was still tumultuous. People were on every side of them, roaring through the cardboard-thin walls, stomping on the ceiling, brawling below their feet, bickering at their doorstep. Life in a Lower East Side tenement was a constant cacophony of the worst sounds mankind could make.

Lucille should have been in school, but she'd dropped out a few months ago to help her mother in their small, struggling laundry business. Truant officers didn't seem to care whether a poor girl in the slums got a proper education. Now Lucille spent her days dashing through the city, picking up dirty clothes and delivering them again the next day, pristine.

Her mother specialized in dainty items—the lace shawls of proud old women, the undergarments of flighty young women—and had amassed a small but devoted clientele. The tubs of boiling water and lye took up half of their living space, but she washed only small precious things and could charge more, since the delicate furbelows required special care. Sometimes she spent an hour coaxing the frills on a fine set of knickers into place. A young woman rich enough to wear such undergarments could easily find someone to pay for their expert cleaning.

But as the Depression deepened, her clientele was dwindling. People's investments weren't so secure anymore, and in times of financial crisis, married men leave their mistresses for their wives.

"Mother," Lucille said that evening, as she'd said many evenings before, "you could *try* again, couldn't you? Just try? Maybe someone needs a teacher now."

But her mother only shook her head and rubbed tallow into her red, cracked hands. "It's too late for me," she said, her voice weary. "This is my life, and I accept it. Yes, it's difficult, and perhaps not very . . . well . . . pretty. But I have you and your brothers and sisters, and you all bring more beauty into my life than I could have ever hoped for." Then, seeing her daughter's creased brow, she caught her in her arms. "It's not *all* bad, is it?" she asked Lucille. "We've got each other." She took her daughter's smooth hands in her work-roughened ones and pulled her into a swaying motion. "And remember, you don't need money to dance."

Suddenly, miraculously, her despondency was gone. She sang a Gershwin tune and spun her daughter. Both of them were giggling as they tried the modern steps. But her mother had grown up with ragtime, and a moment later she abandoned the jazz hit for the music of her own teen years, humming and tapping out the syncopated rhythms of Scott Joplin.

They didn't happen often, these moments of abandon and sheer fun. When they did, they were a tonic for all that was wrong with their lives. Her mother's sweet lilting voice, the energy of their dancing, seemed to drive away every worry. Lucille and her mother had been dancing together almost since she could walk, perfecting their little routines of everything from waltzes and tangos to their take on modern fox-trots and swing.

But they never had more than a few moments of joy. Loutish reality, like a drunken boor, inevitably tapped on her shoulder and cut into their dance. Now their gaiety was interrupted by a low groan from Lucille's father. They stopped abruptly, looking guiltily toward the sound. Lucille pressed her lips together, waiting to see if he might go back to sleep.

His fit came on him strongly. It started with moans that rose and rose until they crescendoed in agonized cries. Lucille never knew if it was the pain that drove him mad at times or the memories of trench warfare. He never meant to be violent, she was sure, but every one of them had been bruised when they'd tried to hold him down during his fits.

Their reprieve was over. "I'll stay and help you," Lucille told her mother.

"No, Lucille, you go, or Mrs. Fahntille and Mr. Rosen will be cross." She handed over a small packet of knickers and slips wrapped in white paper and gave her a kiss on the cheek. Lucille watched her mother's careworn eyes turn to the lumpy bed in the corner of the room.

Lucille bit her lip. She pitied her father, of course, but she wondered if he would be in the same state whether he was rich or poor. Would the nightmares chase him on the softest feather bed, the old pains bite him through the finest patent coil-spring mattress? In his throes, would he strike out at the nation's finest physicians as indiscriminately as he unconsciously struck his own wife when she lay a cooling compress on his fevered brow?

No, the one she really felt sorry for was her mother. At times—frequently when Lucille was a child, less often now—she could see in her mother the vital spark of youth. It came when she danced, when she read some favorite poem aloud. Within her still, though buried deep, were all the hopes of her girlhood, giddy and free, and also the more domestic hopes of her young womanhood as a new bride and mother. Now, Lucille could see, the weight of seven people pressed heavily on her shoulders. Every morsel of food that passed their lips came from her labor. What if she should get sick? The loss of only a few days' income would be enough to put them on the streets and cast them all, particularly the girls, into a degradation from which there would be no escape.

Every second of every day, this fear hid in her mother's eyes. Yet there was still, Lucille could see, an almost childlike hope, little more than a wish made on a lucky clover, that things might change. What Lucille wouldn't do to feed that tiny hopeful spark in her mother's breast until it burst into a flame that would engulf all their wretchedness and poverty!

Lucille's dreams were undoubtedly fresher than her mother's, but to her they seemed no more possible. What could she, a sixteen-year-old girl with no skills and hardly any education, do to save her family?

"Skedaddle!" Her mother sighed again and gave her a pat on the rump, sending her out into the world.

And so, feeling guiltily relieved, Lucille left, stepping over a familiar drunk in the hallway, skirting half-naked children on the stoop, and ignoring the wolf whistle.

But I have *to get ahead, somehow*, she thought desperately. *Ahead, and* out, *away from this filth.*

On that evening Lucille would have done anything to escape her situation—if only she'd known how. . . .

Then she saw what she saw, that terrible thing—and did what she did, that terrible thing—and her entire life changed.

TWO

Isn't that like you? Late to your own birthday party." Violet Ambrose leaned into Frederick's shoulder, crushing the soft fur of her snow-leopard capelet against his sleeve. "And in morning dress, too. Oh, Frederick."

Frederick Preston Aloysius van der Waals looked down indulgently at the angelic face that regarded him with proprietary affection. She had earned the right to lovingly criticize him when he'd proposed to her in the cab half an hour before. It wasn't the most romantic setting, he knew, but the jewelry box from Black, Starr, and Frost, with its outsized diamond ring, had made such an uncomfortable lump in his pocket, particularly considering the other bodily agitations caused by the press of her leg in the back of the cab, that he'd found he couldn't wait. Coming home from a matinee of the comic play *As Husbands Go*, he was unable to contain his enthusiasm any longer. She was sweet. She was clever. She was beautiful. She made him happy.

But then, just about everything made Frederick happy. His life, almost without exception, had been ideal. Violet was the cherry on top.

Of course she'd said yes. "We're perfect for each other," she'd murmured against his lips as they'd sealed the deal. For just a second that word filled him with foreboding. Perfect, like a sharp-cut diamond, cold and unchanging. Could anything be truly perfect? And if that grand expectation should fail to be realized, what would become of their lives? What kind of facade would they erect to maintain the illusion of perfection? What lies would they tell each other?

Then she'd kissed him, and he'd breathed in the scent she always wore, Patou's Joy, and the dark premonitions wafted away like so much cigarette smoke when the cocktail party has broken up. What on earth was wrong with perfect?

They might really have been made for each other. Frederick had grown up with all of the elite bright young things whose daddies were New York millionaires. Cream had mingled with cream for so long that the current crop had gotten too used to one another. The same stories, the same jokes, the same liaisons were repeated over and over. Certainly some of them would pair off in the end, but Frederick had been thrilled one night to see a new face across the room at one of his father's many parties, a face like a mischievous seraph haloed in auburn hair.

Violet, of old Philadelphia stock, was novel and exciting, a refreshing change from the friends he had known all his life. They'd clicked instantly, magically, and if Frederick had a suspicion that their fathers—newly business partners—had thrown them together, he didn't care.

Now, nearly a year after their first meeting, they were officially engaged and on their way to Frederick's seventeenth birthday party. Like everything his father touched, it promised to be an affair of Babylonian extravagance.

"Shall we tell everyone tonight?" Frederick asked as the cab pulled up in front of the Pierre Hotel. The driver waited patiently, certain of a generous tip. Since falling in love, Frederick had taken to hailing public cabs instead of relying on his father's small fleet of chauffeured cars. Not that he necessarily got up to anything he didn't want his father to know about, but the kisses, the petting, were precious to him, and felt more so when they were at least a little bit secret.

Oh, who was he kidding? he thought as he saw the doorman eyeballing him. His father's spy network rivaled the U.S. government's, and though he mostly used it to unearth business secrets, Frederick wouldn't be surprised if his father already knew, somehow, about his engagement. He caught the cabbie's eye, imagining him flashing secret hand signals to a shabby towheaded girl scurrying by carrying a paper-wrapped bundle, who would relay the gossip directly to Mr. van der Waals's office. Frederick didn't mind. His father was his idol. If he had more time for his son, Frederick might even have considered him his best friend.

"What's so funny?" Violet asked when he chuckled, looking slightly piqued not to be in on the joke.

"Oh . . . nothing. Do you think my father will give his consent?"

"I am rather a bounder," she said, lowering her eyelashes and giving him a beguiling sidelong glance. "Maybe I'm only marrying you for your money."

They both laughed at this. Though neither paid particularly close attention to their fathers' businesses, they knew that their respective funds were almost limitless and that, as only children, their wealth, even if not joined in holy matrimony, was extravagant.

"Would you marry me even if I were a pauper?" he asked, still joking, knowing her answer without a doubt.

To his amazement, she cocked her head, considering him. "No," she said at last, and his face fell. "Well, you see," she went on, light and careless as a meringue, "we wouldn't have met if you were poor, would we? I'm only being practical. How would I have gotten to know all your lovely qualities if you were a busboy or an elevator operator?"

He supposed that made sense, but still, how easy it would have been for her to say, *Of course, darling.* . . .

"And what exactly are my loveliest qualities?" he asked, nuzzling her cheek.

"Oh, Frederick, you're so very . . . Oh, look, there's Maybelle and Fritzie." She rolled down the window.

"Yoo-hoo, darlings. Here we are!" She turned to Frederick. "Come on, everyone is waiting for you."

The cabbie opened the door, and Violet rested her hand indifferently on his arm as she flashed one slim silk-clad leg and stood, beaming at her friends, a spectacle even to those passersby not lucky enough to know her. People actually stopped and stared, as if she were a movie star.

Or even, Frederick thought with another disturbing flash of introspection that was utterly unlike him, *as if she were actually important: a president, a diplomat, an arbiter of the world's fate instead of merely its fashion.*

I must be getting old, he decided with a wry twist to his mouth. Engagement could age a man, he'd heard.

He rose beside her, and she nestled her hand in the crook of his arm. For a moment they stood thus, bound together, she looking at the adoring world, he gazing not at her beauty, but up at the facade of the fabulous Pierre Hotel, where he and his father lived. The creamy limestone base merged into an elegant tower of blond brickwork topped with a slanting copper roof and winking stylized dormers.

"Beautiful, isn't it?" he breathed.

"Thank you. . . . Oh, the Pierre, you mean? Ye-es . . . But, darling, that reminds me of what I meant to talk to you about. What do you think of One Beekman Place when we marry? This is all very well and good, but the Beekman is infinitely more chic. Oh, Frederick, I cannot tell you how I long to escape from Park Avenue, with all those dreary grandparents! Do you know, I don't think there is a single person under thirty within a block of Daddy's house. When we marry, we can get one of those darling suites at the Beek, or why not an entire floor, like you have here?"

"Two floors," he said absently. Her idea about One Beekman Place was something of a shock. Having spent the better part of his life living in hotels—first the Ritz-Carlton, and lately the Pierre—he was anxious for something more intimate, less public. He was tired of running into everyone under the sun in the elevator, of having chats forced on him in the lobby, of eating nearly every meal in the hotel restaurant. He'd prefer one of New York's cozier little mansions. Well, as cozy as ten thousand square feet could be and as little as several million dollars could buy. But still, a home of their own, without neighbors on the stairs and busybody busboys gossiping about his affairs.

"Yes, of course. What *does* he do with the other floor, anyway?"

"It's his office."

"How dreary. I'm so glad you won't have to work." Fredrick tried to interrupt, to tell her that he had every intention of working alongside his father just as soon as he went to college and his father thought he was ready to be initiated into all the secrets of the family businesses. But, excited in her golden vision of her future—*their* future— she talked right over him. "Just think of the parties we'll have! Let's get two floors at the Beek, just like you have here. Only we can use one entire level for our ballroom. Our own personal ballroom—imagine! Oh, Frederick, how I love you!" But her dreamy eyes didn't seem to be *quite* looking into his. Was it the ballroom-to-be she loved?

Violet started walking toward the lobby, beneath the cream and gold canopy where a doorman waited as if the sole purpose of his existence were to open the door for her. "What do you think about a spring wedding?"

Frederick could find no flaw with spring.

"Do you think that will give me time to get ready?" She counted up on her slender fingers. "Yes, I should just be able to assemble a proper trousseau in time, and as for my wedding gown, well, I've had the lace since I was twelve, so we won't have to send off to the French convents. That just leaves the dress itself. Madame Grès, do you think, or Vionnet? I'll have to go to Paris either way. So much to do!" She walked on, oblivious, content to carry on her own conversation, while Frederick lingered behind her.

Funny how girls are, Frederick thought. When he considered their marriage, the wedding played such a small part. Instead, he looked forward to the intimacy, physical and otherwise. His dreams were more domestic. *How nice it will be,* he thought, *to eat toast and marmalade with Violet sitting across from me at the breakfast table.*

He realized, suddenly, exactly what she was saying, and surged ahead to catch her. "*This* spring? Violet, dear, that's quite impossible. I'll be starting Harvard next fall. We can't be married until after I graduate. I know it's a dreadfully long wait, but time will fly, you'll see, and I promise I won't look at a single Radcliffe girl. . . ."

Violet pressed her lips together for a moment. Then she said, very low but quite distinctly, "I can't wait that long." Another woman might have whispered it with irrepressible longing. Violet's words were as determined and cold as a steel blade.

THREE

Lucille carried her parcel of impeccably washed unmentionables out of the dirt and stench of her own life and into another world. Almost magically, from one block to the next, the tenor of the city changed. The gray boxes of despairing tenements gave way to magnificent, thoughtful architecture, to stonework and brick that seemed to be designed for no other purpose than to delight the eye. She couldn't imagine living in one of those grand Fifth Avenue hotels. They seemed to be museum pieces, to be seen and not touched . . . or perhaps huge statues, monuments to mankind's greatness.

Well, she amended, the greatness of *some* of mankind.

She came upon the Pierre, which she thought was one of the most beautiful buildings in the city . . . from the outside at least. She'd never mustered the courage to test the benevolence of the uniformed doorman keeping close watch over the main entrance.

Lucille instinctively cringed out of the way when a small, merry group of young men and women passed her. The men were impeccably dressed, the women almost shockingly so. Their frocks, in midnight and pale gold and *eau de nil*, clung so tantalizingly and draped so low down their backs that it was obvious they were wearing absolutely nothing underneath. Lucille remembered her mother telling her once (probably in reference to their scanty supply of furniture) that less is more. She rather thought in this case that *more* might be more. She tried to picture herself in such a gown and achieved nothing more than feeling slightly chilly.

When the doors opened, she caught a glimpse of black and white decor, the huge squares of onyx- and alabaster-colored marble on the floor. It was startling after her own dim world of gray grime and dirty dun browns, startling in a way a field of color could not be. She realized that she'd stopped walking, and with a little embarrassed shake, she set off once more down Fifth Avenue, clutching her parcel to her chest. Why think about places like that? That wasn't her world and would never, *could* never, be.

She headed for the Sherry-Netherland, where Mrs. Fahntille shared a suite with her rarely seen husband. As Lucille left the Pierre behind her, something caught her eye. A cab was pulling up to the curb. A vagrant ray of the setting sun glazed the window golden, and she couldn't get a clear view of whoever was inside. All she could see, darkly intense against a nebulous form, was a pair of eyes looking in her direction. For a second, no more, she met them uneasily. Then she turned abruptly away and walked with renewed vigor. It was just another rich person. What did she care about him? What did he care about her?

The doorman at the Sherry-Netherland let her in immediately, for Lucille was there nearly every week. She rode the elevator to the eleventh floor and knocked at Mrs. Fahntille's door.

"Hello, darling," drawled a theatrical voice from the bedroom after the maid had let her in. Mrs. Fahntille had been one of the lesser grande dames of the stage for twenty years now, and if directors and audiences were beginning to forget about her, she would never forget herself. She spent countless hours on her appearance. Lucille had never seen her outside of her boudoir; she peregrinated between her lavish bed and her three-mirrored vanity, always with a cut-crystal highball glass and a faint juniper perfume of gin floating around her.

"Have you got them? Oh, do hurry. I desperately need my powder-blue lingerie set. He will be here soon!" As Mrs. Fahntille was still lounging in the downy white nest of her bed, Lucille could not at first imagine what kind of caller the woman might be expecting. Then, a second later, she could, and blushed pink.

Mrs. Fahntille flung back the covers with a flourish and leaped to her feet, her gaunt body bare. Lucille tried to both look and not look, an endeavor that left her even more flustered. In the end she managed to unfocus her eyes and hand over the pale blue lacy set. Mrs. Fahntille, unabashed, wiggled her way into it and posed. "How do I look? Will he eat me up?"

The lingerie seemed to echo and enhance the blue blood vessels that showed through her pale, taut skin, and her unfortunate turn of phrase made Lucille think of a veiny Roquefort cheese. But she only said, "You look lovely, ma'am," and waited patiently for her payment.

Mrs. Fahntille, though, loved an audience, however humble, and glided about the room, twittering about past roles and speculating about new ones. "The *quality* of the theater has declined since I was in my heyday," she opined, fixing a cigarette in a long, slim mother-of-pearl holder. "Now all the talent . . . most of the talent, that is," she amended as she peered at herself in the mirror, "has fled to Hollywood. I grieve for the future of acting if we must depend on those cheap celluloid starlets for our thespian passions. They have no life! No *presence*!" She snatched up a pile of movie magazines—*Photoplay, Motion Picture, Film Fun*—and piled them into Lucille's arms. "Take them away, darling. I can't stand the sight of them. Oh, all but this one." She snatched back the topmost. "I haven't finished reading a dishy little story about Claudette Colbert."

"Thank you, ma'am. But . . . my payment?"

"Of course, of course. Here you are." She thrust a jumble of money into Lucille's hand, more than she was owed. Mr. Fahntille must be doing well . . . wherever he was. "Scurry along now. We don't want my guest to run into anything as fetching as you, my dear. He might just eat *you* up!"

Lucille clamped her Hollywood magazines under her arm and set off to a shabbier part of town with the packet of lace cravats. Mr. Rosen, who ran a little movie theater, was as much of a dandy as he could afford to be and had a weakness for a bit of finery around his throat. He was what her mother mysteriously referred to as an "Ethel."

Lucille always tried to schedule her deliveries there for the end of the day. While she waited in the projection room for her payment, she could catch a free glimpse of the movie screen, where she watched gods and goddesses in gray scale act out their impossibly interesting lives. She lived in their faraway worlds for no more than fifteen minutes at a time, so she rarely knew how a picture ended, but like the rest of America, she was completely enamored of the movies.

That evening, Lucille watched breathlessly as the bug-eyed Peter Lorre somehow contrived to create in her the most minuscule morsel of sympathy for the role of a ruthless child killer in the movie *M*. How did he do it? She could tell from his face that he must be a nice man in real life, and yet he managed to become utterly reprehensible on the screen . . . save for that tiny touch of human sympathy he evoked in her against her will. What made her feel for such a terrible character? Was that the power of his acting? she wondered. Or was it some weakness in her? It left her shaken and baffled, that perplexing manipulation.

☆ ☆ ☆

It was nearly dark by the time Lucille left Mr. Rosen's theater. Encumbered by her stack of Hollywood magazines, she hurried as fast as she could. A girl alone as evening fell might be mistaken for a loose woman and was likely to be propositioned. As night deepened, there was the added danger that they wouldn't care what her profession was and the propositions would be replaced by demands. With no protector, she had to be home by full dark. Should she take her usual route, much longer but safe and well lit for now, or should she slip down an alleyway and cut her journey in half?

She chose the shortcut. The shadowy half dark of the alley made the crates and garbage bins lining the walls loom like leering ogres. But Lucille had no fear of mythic things; her vivid imagination painted far more probable dangers.

She heard footsteps from up ahead and shrank back, chiding herself as she did. Her mother always told her that she should walk straight and tall and confident through any situation on the street, past any vice or crime the bad neighborhoods would throw at her. *Look like a good girl who doesn't have anything to fear, and they'll never think to mess with you*, she'd told her daughter. *Look like a victim, and you'll become one.*

Instinct, though, told Lucille something entirely different. Alone in a dim, isolated place, faced with an approaching stranger, she had the prey's impulse to hide and freeze.

Leaning against the bricks behind a stack of crates, she couldn't see the interloper, but he had heavy footfalls and panted as if he'd run a long way. *He's just resting to catch his breath*, she thought, relaxing against the wall. *He'll go away soon.* She decided to wait him out. By now it would be awkward for her to emerge.

Then she heard another set of feet, soft and slow.

Lucille felt her heart begin to race. How could there be such menace in footsteps? Their steady deliberateness chilled her.

"You bastard." The voice was as soft as the step, quiet and dangerous as the whisper of a snake's belly on dry leaves.

"You don't know what you're talking about, you stupid mug," said the other man, still gulping for air. "Go home and take care of your mama."

Lucille peeked around the crates and saw a paunchy man in his forties holding himself up against the wall, his face contorted in angry contempt.

"My mother is a widow tonight," the quiet man said. He was a little older than Lucille, in his early twenties perhaps, well dressed, tall, broad shouldered. His mouth was full, and his brilliantined, slicked-back black hair gleamed faintly in the dim light.

The older man hissed something about the handsome young man's mother that Lucille suspected was not the wisest thing to say.

The younger man laughed. "Right about now I'm supposed to tell you that if you utter one more word about my mother, I'll fill your dirty brain full of lead. But really, we both know that isn't necessary. You're getting yours no matter what you say."

The other man sneered and said, "You don't have the *coglioni*."

Maybe if he'd trembled it would have gone otherwise, but even from her quick glance, Lucille knew that the young man in the beautiful suit would never, ever let anyone defy him. From inside his pin-striped jacket he pulled a gun and pointed it at the other man's head.

"Because of you, I have everything that was once my father's. The business. The money. And the *coglioni* to blow your ugly head off."

He squeezed the trigger. And he smiled while he did it.

Lucille's Hollywood magazines slid from her numbed arms, and the gunman turned, finally noticing the pale wraith in the shadows. Slowly, he raised the gun until the barrel's dark and deadly eye locked her in its gaze. Her eyes widened and her mouth parted in a soft gasp. A little voice whispered that she should run, scream, do anything other than look pleadingly at a killer. But all she could do was watch him and hope.

He watched her, too, his head cocked to the side. His eyes traced her lingeringly up and down, the gun following his eyes. She swallowed hard, and her lips moved to form a single, almost soundless word: "Please."

The shrill whine of a police siren from a few blocks away pierced the stillness. He raised the gun higher, holding it level with her head.

"Damn," he whispered a long moment later, and lowered the gun. Then he knelt by the gory corpse and put the running laundry around town all day, sick of seeing her beautiful, smart mother work her fingers to nubbins washing rich ladies' underthings when she should be teaching, sick of seeing her sisters dressed in rags, her brothers turn into number-running hoodlums. . . .

Lucille widened her luminous eyes guilelessly and looked at the police officers. But even when she opened her mouth, she didn't quite know what would come out.

gun in its hand, curling a dead finger around the trigger.

"You didn't see anything," he told her, standing and brushing his hands on his trousers.

She nodded, and that might have been the end, but th patrol car cruised by the alley at that moment, passed, the stopped with a screech of brakes. In the time it took for th car to back up, the young man had crossed the distanc between them in a few quick steps and gripped her arm.

"He shot himself," he told Lucille, low and savage, a the police car backed to the mouth of the alleyway and tw officers shone lights into their faces. "Stick to that story an I'll make you rich. Say anything else, and I'll make you dead You and all your family. My boys will kill them slowly in fron of your eyes." His grip tightened. "Then they'll carve tha pretty face off with a bowie knife."

When the two policemen approached them, the youn man raised his arms and said, perfectly calmly, "I am Salvator Benedetto. This poor man has just confessed to murderin my father, Cosimo Benedetto. In the madness of guilt, he ha shot himself after begging for my forgiveness."

Lucille looked up into Salvatore's dark eyes and sav absolute honesty there.

It was the first time she truly understood the power o acting. It could alter reality.

"Is that right, miss?" one of the officers asked.

She squinted into the glare of his flashlight. Unlike s many girls in this downtrodden neighborhood, her mothe had raised her to a high moral code. But she was sick o

FOUR

With the love of his life on his arm, Frederick strolled into the Pierre's spacious black and white lobby. It was rarely very crowded—usually only a few graying gentlemen lounging in obscure club chairs, perusing the *Financial Times*; perhaps a woman not as young as she'd like people to think, just underdressed and overly made-up enough to be conspicuous, hoping to snag a customer who was out of her league before security hustled her out. Today, though, in honor of the lavish van der Waals affair, it was much more lively.

Frederick heard laughter and the scuff and slide of soft-shoe tap. He looked around, delighted, for the young man he knew to be its source. There he was, Frederick's best friend since the summer they were quarantined together in an Adirondacks cabin with severe cases of the mumps. Over misery, cold compresses, and chicken soup, they had bonded, and when they'd left camp, it had never occurred to them that the fact they were from different social strata meant they shouldn't really be friends.

It wasn't that Duncan Shaw's family was poor, exactly. The father was a midlevel banker, the mother an artist who occasionally exhibited at the smaller galleries. They were well educated and amusingly worldly; in all respects they were a decent, upper-middle-class family. Still, as Frederick once heard his father remark to his mother in the year before she died, "Duncan's people are ordinary." That was one of the things that Frederick liked about them. He didn't know why that word in his father's mouth sounded somehow foul. Still, the two men had developed something of a rapport. The elder van der Waals guided Mr. Shaw in his investments, raising him a notch financially.

"What ho, old chap!" Duncan called, affecting an English accent. He caught his friend in an exuberant bear hug. "M'lady." He kissed Violet's little paw reverently, then broke into a huge grin and tapped out a few more dance steps. "As you see, I'm all limbered up and ready to tango." He dipped an imaginary partner and bestowed a smacking kiss midair. "Or maybe just shimmy like that little Joan Crawford in *Dance, Fools, Dance*. Did you see it? Trash, but that Joanie will go far, if you ask me. Anyone who can wiggle that much and not fall out of her . . . Oh, I'm sorry, Violet. What a lout I am."

He didn't look at all contrite, but Frederick didn't mind.

Duncan was the ham of the gang, and, like a playful puppy, could do no wrong. Violet gave her fiancé a slightly pained look but linked arms with both of them, and the trio jostled through the light crowd, nodding and smiling, until they reached the elevator.

"What a gleesome threesome!" said the elevator operator in greeting. Frederick winced slightly, then checked himself. His first thought—ungovernable and unwelcome—was that an elevator operator should never make such a personal comment in such a conversational tone. Following closely upon the heels of this came the thought that this cheerful young man's well-meaning impudence was bound to get him fired within the week.

Frederick wanted to warn the young man against such familiarity. *I don't mind*, he could say, *but there's some that would*. But he said nothing as they rose smoothly up the center of the Pierre's towering height. To refer to it would be to admit that he had the same class distinctions as the older generation. He felt it, true, but suddenly he felt ashamed to feel it.

The heavy ebony door to their apartment gave no hint of the jollity within. But it swung open to reveal a world of champagne bubbles and tinkling ice, of glittering jewels and sequins and slinky gold lamé. All of New York's high society had turned out to honor the scion of one of its brightest stars. Jacob van der Waals was one of the few men in the country who had not only *not* lost money in the great stock market crash of 1929, but had tripled his already considerable fortune.

Duke Ellington and his band played as two Ziegfeld girls gyrated gently on their podium clad in what appeared to be nothing more than hundreds of ropes of pearls, but everyone else fell silent when Frederick entered the room. For a breath they all looked in sheer awe at that handsome young man, fortune's favorite, heir to the world. Then they erupted in spontaneous applause. Waves of people moved in to congratulate him on the rare accomplishment of having survived seventeen years.

They parted when Jacob van der Waals walked slowly toward his son, arms wide. "Come here, my boy!" he boomed, and took Frederick in a solid embrace, pounding him on the back. Then he held him at arm's length. "Look at you. Your mother would be so proud. Congratulations and many happy returns!" He grabbed a flute of champagne from the nearest waiter and turned to the crowd, raising his glass high.

"A toast!" he cried. "To my son and heir, Frederick. May all the happiness of the world be laid in your lap."

"Hear! Hear!"

"Chin-chin!"

There was a clink of glass, tipsy sloshing, and more applause.

And Frederick thought, *If happiness is just laid in my lap, is it as good as happiness I've worked for?*

Then he was swept away in the party, and all his questions dissolved in the sheer joy of being alive, and loved, and rich.

☆ ☆ ☆

Eventually, inevitably, Mugsy found him.

The heavyset man with the squashed nose and cauli-flower ears nevertheless had a look of keen intelligence in his small dark eyes. They were filled with disapproval as they looked Frederick up and down.

"Morning dress," Mugsy said with a sigh.

"This from a man who used to spend his days in a loin-cloth," said Frederick. The cut had no sting. Mugsy wasn't ashamed of his past as a professional boxer.

"Attire should be appropriate to the setting," Mugsy countered in his thick Brooklyn accent. "If you was in the boxing ring, you'd be overdressed. Here, you're underdressed. And I wore boxing shorts, not a loincloth."

Mugsy himself was in impeccable white tie, its contours expertly tailored to fit his pianolike proportions while leaving room for the gun he carried cross-draw under his left arm.

"Go change," he ordered.

"But . . ."

"Go!"

And Frederick went, Mugsy following.

As he impassively assisted his master (or charge, or friend, or surrogate son) to change into the requisite top hat, white tie, and tails, he commented, "Miss Ambrose is looking like a real gem today." His face was inscrutable as he helped Frederick slip on his dress coat. "And speaking of, it seems to me she's sporting a new piece of jewelry."

Frederick grinned. "*Maybe* I know something about it. Aren't you going to congratulate me?"

"No."

Frederick's mouth gaped.

"Oh, all right already. May you and your Jane have years of wedded bliss and a big brood of little hoodlums, et cetera, et cetera."

"You don't approve, old man?"

Mugsy frowned. "Don't you think you ought to look around a little? It's a big greenhouse out there, with plenty of tomatoes for the pickin'."

"Oh, it will be years before we actually tie the knot."

"That's what you say now. Then before you know it, there's a spring wedding with her dress a little tight, and seven months later a big bouncing baby you try to convince everyone is *premature*." Frederick blushed at Mugsy's earthy analysis. "Don't look so shocked. It's perfectly natural for a young fella to want to rut it up a little. But why tie yourself down to the doll you happen to get a kick out of at seventeen? Go out. Sow some oats." His sweet, ugly face looked more humorless than usual. "I got a bad feeling about this. Put Violet off, why don't you? Wait till you're sure."

"Why, Mugsy, I never thought I'd see the day! You, telling me to go out and . . . have fun."

"Have *too* much fun. Live a little. If you still love her in a few years, you'll have my blessing. But marry her now and I see nothing but trouble. Marry in haste, repent in leisure, they always say."

"Who exactly is *they*?" Frederick asked.

"Oh, just they. And they is always right. *Always*."

Frederick shrugged and adjusted his bow tie. "We'll see," he said.

Mugsy's lips twitched, and he tugged the tie back the way it was. "We will, ya sap. And when you need me, I'll come running. I always have. I always will."

Back in the thick of the party, Frederick easily found Violet at the center of a cloud of silk and tulle, her bejeweled hand extended for the admiration of her friends. Duncan, though, was nowhere to be seen. Frederick had hoped to have his best friend and his best girl with him when he shared the news of his engagement with his father. Oh well. Duncan was probably living it up somewhere, canoodling with a girl, shooting dice with the waiters.

"Our engagement is the worst-kept secret of the century," Violet said as they received another congratulation. "That's what you get for buying me a diamond so big I can hardly raise my hand." All the same, she looked entirely pleased and managed to heft her encumbered hand for at least a dozen more admirers before they heard from one of the discreetly lurking maids that Jacob van der Waals had gone upstairs to his full-floor office.

"That's strange," Frederick mused. "What kind of business would he have today?"

"How would I know?" Violet shrugged her slim, lovely shoulders indifferently. "Probably the market just opened in Hong Kong. Oh, Frederick, I'm so glad you'll never have to bother with anything as bourgeois as making money. Frederick . . . Frederick . . ." She bit her lip, mulling something over. "Do you know, I've never liked the name Frederick. It's not your fault of course, darling. But it smacks of comic operetta, doesn't it? And the nicknames are just as bad. *Fred,*" she intoned heavily. "Rhymes with dead. And *Freddie's* even worse, like a little boy in a sailor suit."

"I've always rather liked Freddie. . . ."

"Darling, wouldn't you consider going by Aloysius? It is ever so much more sophisticated, isn't it? Just picture us, Mr. and Mrs. Aloysius van der Waals, dancing in our private ballroom in One Beekman Place. Won't it be just too, *too* divvy for words?"

Words certainly failed Frederick at the moment. He had a sudden urge to call for Mugsy. Mugsy would fix everything. But that would mean confessing to his bodyguard that he—and apparently the mysterious *they*—were right.

Resolutely, he offered his arm to Violet and they went up the private stairway to his father's office. Frederick expected to find him alone, most likely on the phone, or perhaps reviewing profit and loss statements (always with a great deal of profit and very little loss). But as they climbed the stairs, each silent, lost in thoughts of the future, they heard raised voices.

"You knew! You knew all along, you dirty bastard."

Frederick froze, pulling Violet closer to his side. The voice was unmistakably Duncan's.

"Darling," Violet said, "I'm going to dash back downstairs and see how my parents are doing. It sounds like man talk up there, and you know how I feel about coarse language!" And with that, she quickly turned and floated back down to the party, swallowed up by the escalating gaiety.

"Let's be reasonable, now," Frederick heard his father say. He inched forward to hear better.

"How could you, Jacob?" came an anguished voice he recognized as Duncan's father's.

Jacob van der Waals liked to work in a vast, open space. Why, exactly, Frederick wasn't sure, but he'd heard someone say that he liked an open view in case of predators, or spies. Still, the office had been a proper apartment once, and no one could see him in the shadow of the stairwell. He edged closer to what was intensifying into a heated conflict.

Duncan's voice, always ready for a joke or a song, sounded twisted, wrong, as he attacked Jacob van der Waals. "It's all too obvious," Duncan hissed. "You just needed more investors in the beginning or you would have lost what you had in there. But as soon as my dad and a few other trusting rubes made it look like the sure thing you promised them it was, you jumped ship with your money. You knew the company was going under."

"This is the nature of investment," Mr. van der Waals said, unabashed. "The market moves, and . . ."

"And where did *my* money move to?" Mr. Shaw asked quietly. "Into your pockets, Jacob?" Mr. Shaw sounded much calmer than his son. "I *trusted* you. I trusted the entire future of my family to you. Or did you plan from the beginning to ruin us? I'm aware you never could stand the idea of Frederick being close with us."

Mr. Shaw stepped forward, a new agitation creeping into his tone. "How many lives have you destroyed to accumulate your fortune? How many widows have you defrauded? Cheated out of their entire life's savings? Funny thing about having so very much money to protect you—you never have to pay for anything, do you? Well, my friend, now it is time for you to pay."

Then it was chaos.

"Are you insane?" Mr. van der Waals gasped.

"Dad, no!" Duncan shouted. "Don't!"

What happened next took less than three seconds but changed Frederick's world forever.

Downstairs the band kicked into a rousing version of Irving Berlin's hit tune "Puttin' on the Ritz," sending the partygoers into ecstatic shouts and yips, champagne corks popping like a firing squad. Around the corner Frederick heard the sound of scuffling and then another pop, almost the sound of champagne uncorking but much more terrifying.

Frederick, still hidden, moved forward enough to look into the mirrored wall that reflected the office and went pale. Both Duncan and Mr. Shaw had their hands on a small silver revolver. Mr. van der Waals stood removed and cold, his back to Frederick, focused on the sight of Mr. Shaw slumping to the ground. The gun fell with a clatter between them.

"No!" Duncan kicked the gun across the room. It spun near where Frederick stood, frozen and concealed. Duncan dropped to his knees and held his father in his arms. The sound of his sobs was drowned out by the joyous clamor of the party below.

Duncan looked up at Mr. van der Waals. "Your whole family is rotten to the core," he choked out. "You're going to pay for this. Everyone is going to know how corrupt you are. You'll rot in prison!"

Frederick felt his stomach knot, his lungs spasm so that he couldn't breathe, couldn't move, couldn't think. Downstairs, the band played on, but Frederick could hear nothing except the rush of blood in his own ears.

"This was an unfortunate accident," Mr. van der Waals said calmly. "Your father was mistaken and committed a rash criminal act. I'm very sorry that your family lost all their money." He didn't seem to be affected by the dead man in his office or the red-faced and sobbing young man threatening him.

"I am more than happy to provide any compensation necessary that may in some way mitigate this unfortunate turn of events." Mr. van der Waals retreated behind his desk. He pulled open a drawer and took out his checkbook.

For a moment Duncan was speechless. "You're trying to *buy* me?" he gasped at last. "My father is *dead* because of your greed, and you offer me money?" He took a menacing step toward Mr. van der Waals.

"I don't think you understand the precarious nature of your position, Duncan. You just shot your own father before a witness." Mr. van der Waals picked up the phone. "I can make one of two calls now. Either I call the police and tell them you just murdered your father in a fit of rage when you discovered he lost the family fortune. Or I call my lawyer, who arranges for your mother to be well provided for after your father's unfortunate accident. Which is it to be? Your mother will need you in this difficult time. You'll be no good to her in jail."

Duncan trembled with rage. "Don't you dare talk about my mother! I'm calling the police myself and telling them the truth." He moved to the phone, which Mr. van der Waals still held in his hand.

"Who do you think they'll believe—a rash young nobody or the richest man in America? You murdered your father, Duncan. That's what the world will see. I'm not interested in bad publicity. The police will not be coming. We have other ways of cleaning up messes here."

Duncan gazed at his father's lifeless body and then back to Mr. van der Waals. Then in a choked whisper he said, "You're a monster, and I will not rest until I see you and your cursed family rotting behind bars."

He turned and walked from the room, brushing past Frederick in the stairway shadows. Duncan didn't seem to see him at first. Then he whirled and took Frederick by the lapels, shoving him against the wall.

"Now I have to tell my mother that her husband is dead, that he left us penniless, all because he trusted and loved you," he growled low into Frederick's ear. "But someday I'm going to destroy your father. And then I'll be coming for you.

He's an evil man, but you're no better. You live on the blood of your father's victims." He let Frederick go and spat at his feet. Then he staggered down the stairs, his sobbing drowned out by the din of the wild party.

Frederick, gasping, turned slowly toward his father. Mr. van der Waals hadn't seen him in the shadows near the stairs. He looked astonished to find himself still alive. For a moment he gazed blankly at the phone receiver he still held in his hand. Then he began to dial. He didn't call for a doctor or an ambulance. He called his lawyer.

With his back to the carnage, he said, "I need you to fix something for me."

Frederick stumbled backward down the stairs, then turned on his heel and began to run blindly. He saw figures and shapes and knew there was noise, but it was all strange and muted and terribly, terribly wrong. As he brushed past Violet, she called out, "Aloysius . . . Frederick . . . what happened?"

But he kept running. He didn't know who either of those people was anymore.

PART TWO

HOLLYWOOD, CALIFORNIA 1931

FIVE

Several months after that fateful evening that changed her life, Lucille lay in a huge bed in the Ambassador Hotel in Los Angeles. There she huddled, feeling very small and alone as the gay sounds from the Cocoanut Grove nightclub floated up to her bed. The music made her think of dancing with her mother. Would she ever do that again?

She'd never been away from her family overnight before—the train ride didn't really count, because she'd hardly slept at all during the three-day journey. She thought it would be impossible to sleep without one little sister's elbow in her ribs, another little sister's knee in her back.

Lucille had been deposited at the hotel almost without a word, not knowing if someone would be coming for her in an hour or a day or a week. The first night she just cried into her pillow, but even the quality of her tears was mixed up and uncertain. Sometimes she wept tears of joy for having come so unbelievably far, within the reach of money and security and, maybe, greatness. Other times the tears fell out of fear for the future, that everything might slip from her grasp before she could even touch it, and she'd have to crawl home to poverty and leave her family without hope.

But mostly her tears were for the past, for the shameful thing she had done. If anyone knew . . .

They won't know, she swore to herself as she tossed in that oversized, too comfortable bed. *They* can't *know*.

On the first morning, she'd tentatively gone downstairs, thinking she could take a little walk or have breakfast somewhere quiet. But as soon as she stepped into the lobby she saw how far removed she was from all of these people, in her shabby cotton dress without the slightest trace of chic. Maybe everyone looked up only out of curiosity, but she was sure they glared with hostile rejection. She crept back to her room.

That evening there was a knock on her door, and she jumped up eagerly, but then hesitated, biting her lip, before finally opening it. It was only a member of the hotel staff.

"Will you be dining out tonight, miss, or shall I have something sent to your room?"

Lucille beamed at him with relief. She hadn't eaten since dinner on the train the night before, and she was famished, but still too afraid to go out on her own. "Yes, please," she said. Then, "Only, I'm not sure if I have enough money."

"Arrangements have already been made for your bill, miss. The specialty tonight is boneless squab with wild rice à la Roosevelt, and may I recommend the avocado supreme to start?"

"You may," she said breathlessly. Sal had done this? She'd hoped for little more than a train ticket and an introduction. Why was he putting her up in the fanciest hotel, giving her the best food money could buy?

After that, though she still didn't leave her hotel room, at least she didn't starve. Danish and rich coffee for breakfast; shrimp in aspic for lunch; more coffee; tiny, tender, pink lamb chops . . . She ate like a queen but still felt like a prisoner. When was someone going to come for her? The hotel staff would realize that she was just a kid from the street and kick her out. She couldn't really be rewarded, after what she'd done?

Sal's men had asked her what she wanted—cash, a car, jewels, furs, a flash apartment.

Instinctively, Lucille knew that she should do anything to avoid being beholden to Sal and his terrible henchmen. Her payment would be a start in a better life—far, far away from Sal. Just a boost, that's all she needed. Then she and the mobsters would be square.

"I want it all," she'd told them. "But I want to earn it for myself."

"What job, then?" they'd asked. There were only two ways for a girl to earn a lot of money for herself: marriage . . . or the other thing.

But she wanted neither of those.

When they'd asked, she had conjured up that night. Mrs. Fahntille's blue-veined body . . . Peter Lorre's eyes . . . the spill of Hollywood magazines to the blood-soaked pavement . . . A kindly officer had wiped away the gory splashes and handed the magazines back to her when they'd finished their questioning. Later, after telling her mother where she'd been (with very scant detail), she had climbed out onto the fire escape and read page after page by moonlight, her face an inch from the glamorous spreads. . . .

Sal's men had gotten impatient, and at last she'd blurted out her fantasy: "I want to go to Hollywood!" She had only blurry notions about what she might do there. Dancing, acting . . . That must be an impossible dream. But she could do something, learn shorthand and be a secretary, or perhaps serve lunch in the canteen.

"If I was you, I'd take the cash," one of them said. She shook her head, and Sal's two goons stepped away from her and conferred a moment in grunting, very audible whispers.

"Why's he going to all this trouble?" one asked. "He could have offed her for free."

The other shot Lucille a leer. "Why you think? He's got plans for this one."

That only confirmed Lucille's desire to get as far away from the mobster as possible. She remembered clearly the chill that had trickled down her spine when he'd threatened her family. If she was across the country, though, maybe Sal would forget about her . . . and her family.

Sal's men said they'd have to discuss matters with their boss, but after that, things seemed to happen very quickly. A few days later they caught her on the street corner and told her to pack and be at the train station by six. All throughout the day she'd tried to tell her mother, but there was no way it would make sense without admitting the terrible thing she'd done. And once her mother started worrying about her, Lucille feared she wouldn't have the strength to go.

So in the end she'd hidden a pillowcase full of her small possessions under a laundry delivery and left a note. Then the men had given her some cash to tide her over and ushered her onto a train, where she'd spent three days watching the countryside pass. She'd craned her neck to see the vista ahead, so she could look forward to all the things waiting for her. But the only scenery she could see was the part that had already passed. She'd cried until she thought she had no tears left, missing her mother, her brothers and sisters. But she told herself she'd bought a great chance. *Something* was waiting for her out West. She just didn't know quite what.

At the station in Los Angeles, someone picked her up so quickly she thought she was being kidnapped. The man must have been given an accurate description of her, for he took her by the arm and helped her into the front seat of a roadster, giving her pillowcase full of clothes a contemptuous sneer as he tossed it in the rumble seat. "Where are we going," she'd asked him, but he just drove her to an unmarked office where a man told her to talk, walk, sing, and dance while another man filmed her. She performed everything in a daze, but they seemed satisfied.

It was only then that she really let herself believe that she might have a future in the movies. But she still didn't know what to expect. They told her nothing, gave her no reason to hope . . . beyond the fact that she was still in California.

And so for several days, she waited in her hotel room.

Why didn't I just ask them for cash? Lucille asked herself early on the third almost sleepless morning. *What am I doing here, thousands of miles from home?*

She was jolted from bed by a knock on the door. Was it the police, armed with the truth, come to arrest her? Was it the hotel manager, kicking her out and handing her an impossible bill that no one was going to pay for after all?

Was it Sal? *He's got plans for this one.*

With her face shiny and her waist-long, fair hair hanging in an unkempt braid over her shoulder, she opened the door a crack. The slim, well-dressed young man behind it pushed it all the way open, almost knocking her over.

"Sorry," he said, hardly looking at her. "Where are your suitcases? You were supposed to be downstairs ten minutes ago, and if you don't leave now, we'll never make it in time. Swell way to start your first day." He paused abruptly. "Unless you plan to be a difficult diva? That could work as your shtick. I'll mention it to Veronica. But before she can go to work on you, we have to get to the studio and sign, sign, sign! Oh, you don't have your makeup on. Maybe that's a good idea, so the makeup artist has a fresh slate to work with. But gosh, slap some water on yourself. You look half asleep."

"Who are you?" Lucille managed to ask weakly.

"Your agent. Well, Mr. Herschel is technically your agent, but he likes to delegate the unknowns. Come on, get a move on! Why weren't you downstairs like I told you?"

"We . . . we've never met. You never told me."

"Sure I did. I sent four messages to the hotel. First one telling you that your audition reel was being shopped, second that Lux Studios decided they'd take a chance on you, third the proposed terms, and fourth, to be ready at seven sharp to get the paperwork out of the way so we can have you on set for your first part."

"My first part?" she asked, barely comprehending him.

"That's right. Someone big must be pushing for you to be moving so fast."

"I have to act this morning?"

"Oh, don't worry about that. They won't give you anything too challenging for your first role. A fainting damsel, a chorus girl, maybe someone's kid sister. But based on the terms of your contract, it looks like they want to fast-track you. Gosh, there are girls who would kill to have what you're getting."

Lucille gasped and looked up at him, alarmed. Did he know?

But he didn't seem to notice her reaction and only said, "Go wash your face and come downstairs, lickety-split."

He exited, letting the door slam. For a moment Lucille stood stock-still in the middle of her room. *It's a dream*, she told herself. *I'm still in that alley, deciding what to do, and this is all a dream of what might be if I do the wrong thing.* Or was it the right thing? She wasn't even sure anymore. Not with this glittering reward hanging like one of those jeweled fruits in Aladdin's cave, just within her reach.

She burst into motion, splashing water on her face and tugging off her nightgown, then shimmying into her cotton dress.

The young man was waiting for her downstairs, inside a big black car. A woman a little older than Lucille, with her hair in a side-parted nut-brown bob, peered curiously at her, then jumped out and half dragged her into the backseat.

"Veronica Imrie, how d'you do? And you're Lucille O'Malley? Not for long. Hmm . . . What can we do about that? Too Irish, you know. Can't be too *anything* here, unless you're a certain type, like Dolores del Río, but you don't always want to play Irish vixens, do you, and besides, then they'd dye your hair red for every movie even though of course no one could see its color." Veronica talked at breakneck speed, but her movements were deliberate, reassuring. Despite her youth, she was the most competent-looking woman Lucille had ever seen.

"What shall you be, then?" Veronica continued. "Not Lucille, but Lulu. Or two capitals, capital L-u, capital L-u? Well, I'll leave big decisions like that to my boss. Now, for your last name . . ."

"Who *are* you?" Lucille asked, feeling weak under that torrent of words.

"I told you, Veronica Imrie, junior publicist at Lux Studios."

Lucille was still fuzzy from sleep, and from lack of it. "Do I really have a job?"

"Does she have a job, she asks! We might make a comedienne out of you yet. Don't tell me you yearn for high drama. Not with that sweet little chin. Niederman liked your audition film. He's the head honcho at Lux. Yes, honey, you have a job. A contract, anyway, or you will once this fella approves it. Herschel assigned him as your personal agent."

The sharp young man with small spectacles perched on his nose and three hairs pretending to be a mustache on his upper lip twisted around from the front seat and held out his hand. "Didn't I tell you my name? David Mandel." He was instantly interrupted by Veronica.

"We call him 'Mandelbrot,' because he's sweet and nutty." She pinched his cheek, and he squirmed away.

"Quit it, Veronica. I'm a professional. What's Lulu going to think?"

"See," she said to Lucille, "Lulu has caught on already. So let's get you fixed up and then we can find out what your first part will be."

"Not so fast," David said. "She hasn't signed the contract."

"You mean *you* haven't signed it. You think a green little thing like her is going to read all the clauses? No offense, sweetie," she added in an aside to Lucille. "Besides, you have a peach of a contract here. One hundred dollars a week, a housing stipend, and guaranteed billing in the credits. I don't know who you slept with, but you must have done a heck of a job on him."

Lucille blushed to her ears. "I never! I . . . I wouldn't!"

"Okay, okay, keep your pants on, sister. You'll be a rarity in this town if you *do*. Almost every girl here tries to sleep her way to the top."

"Even you?" Lucille asked.

"I only sleep with this fella," she said, jerking her thumb toward David. "Fat lot of good it's done me. He won't even bring me home to meet his mother."

"Only because—"

"I'm a shiksa temptress."

"No. I'm just waiting for the right time."

"Oh yeah?" Veronica asked, hands on her hips. "And when is that?"

"About a week after she dies peacefully of natural causes."

Veronica turned to Lucille. "Because meeting me would kill her. Isn't that nice? I'm glad *my* mother is a bohemian painter who doesn't care if I bring home a Jew or a gerbil. But *you*. O'Malley . . . O'Malley . . . We don't want to kill the old personality entirely. Is there something reminiscent of O'Malley, maybe a little Irish, but not *too* Irish? We already have Maureen O'Sullivan filling that niche. I love all those *L*s though. La-la-la . . ."

"You wouldn't think she's so good to look at her," David

told Lucille while Veronica continued to talk to herself, "but trust me, she'll get you in every magazine from here to Honolulu to Hong Kong. Hold on. I can tell from that gleam in her eye that she's got something. Lucille O'Malley, prepare to meet the new you."

SIX

You see," Ben said, "you've got your three classifications of forgotten men."

Frederick sucked on the sweet end of a piece of timothy grass. It didn't do much to assuage his gnawing hunger, but he liked watching the cattail puff at the end bob with each unsteady jarring of the locomotive. In the past month he'd eaten charity porridge and raw potatoes grubbed out of a dusty abandoned field. He'd traded his socks for beans heated in their own can over a campfire.

"Oh yeah?" he asked Ben. "And what are they?"

Ben chewed on his snipe, the stubby end of a cigar. He was in his forties, he said, but to Frederick he looked nearer sixty. They'd met an hour ago in the deep shadows on the outskirts of an eastern Pennsylvania rail yard. "First train hop?" Ben had asked in a low whisper, wary of the rail bulls. "Stick to me, then." Frederick had thought he'd have to help the stiff, scrawny older man, but it had been the other way around. The train, just gaining speed, still moved much faster than Frederick had expected, and loomed so large, a churning metal monstrosity that threatened to grind him to a pulp. Frederick hesitated, stumbled . . . and had it not been for Ben's surprisingly strong grip, he might have been crushed beneath the wheels.

Ben had ignored Frederick's effusive thanks and sat deep in the corner of the half-empty freight car, staring at the passing blur of forest for the better part of an hour. But now, at last, he seemed to notice the scruffy young man and started up as though they'd left off in the middle of a conversation.

"It's a regular classification of men of the road," he pontificated in his slow, scratchy Southern voice, interrupted at regular intervals by a phlegmy cough. "You've got your bums. Can't stand them myself, though I've been called one a time or three. Your bums, now, they're scared stiff of work. They'll walk ten miles for a free meal sooner than work an hour to buy one. Your tramp, on the other hand, he's a step up." Ben squinted at Frederick. "You might just be a tramp, come to look at you."

Frederick still didn't quite know what he was. A month on the road without a cent beyond what he earned with his own labor, without his name, had changed him, certainly, but sometimes he still felt like that spoiled, stupid, selfish rich boy, waiting for someone to hand him something. And the funny thing was, occasionally—more often than he would have ever thought—people *did* hand him things. Farmer's wives would give him a glass of milk still warm from the cow. A small-town banker on his lunch break tore his sandwich in two and gave half to Frederick. People were kinder than he'd ever dreamed they would be.

But not always. He'd been chased by dogs, shot at with rock salt, and hustled away by innumerable cops. Still, those shining kindnesses glowed through the hardest days.

"What's a tramp, then?" he asked Ben.

"Tramps are nature's wanderers. Might call them explorers, if there was anything left to discover. They've got the wanderlust in them. Ain't that a splendid word?" He said it again, dreamily. "*Wanderlust.* Is that you, young feller?"

"I had to get away. I didn't much care where to." He fought back the image of Mr. Shaw lying dead, of Duncan's hate-filled eyes.

Ben looked at him sharply. "But you're not a criminal. Are you? No, I don't think you are."

Frederick was glad Ben had answered his own question. *My entire life has been built on crime*, he thought.

Ben resumed his recitation. "A tramp will work if he has to, but it's the journey that really drives him, not his next meal. Not getting from Kalamazoo to Tupelo, exactly, but getting from *somewhere* to *somewhere else* and then setting off again. Can't see it myself. If I ever strike it big, I aim to settle down. Hell, even if I strike it small. All this traveling is hard on the bones." He shifted uncomfortably on the metal freight car.

"You must be the third kind, then," Frederick said.

"Yup. I'm a hobo through and through. A hobo, he wants to work. When the work dries up, though, he turns into a vagabond. I worked hard all my life. Tobacco fields when I was a nipper in Kentucky. Lord, how I wish I had some of those fields and fields of tobacco now." He chewed thoughtfully on his cigar stub. "After that I must have got a bit of the wanderlust myself. I headed north and worked in a chemical plant. But the company folded and, well, there just aren't as many jobs as there used to be. We got this here Depression going on now, hear tell, and there's a million men, all younger and stronger and smarter than me, looking for jobs. But I know *somewhere* there's a job for me." He gave another hacking cough. "And when I find it, won't I just send half of what I make back to Nellie!"

"Who is Nellie?"

"She's . . . well, she *was* my little girl. What she is today I don't rightly know." He closed his eyes for a moment. "Must be nigh on twenty. Haven't seen her since she was in ringlets. Pretty little thing."

"Where is she now?" Frederick asked.

"Lord knows."

"How can you send her money, then?"

"Well, look on the bright side—I'll probably never find a steady job in the first place." Ben slapped his scrawny thigh and laughed until he choked. "What say we jump this cannonball just shy of Pittsburgh and see if we can't rustle up a can of mulligan?"

Clueless, Frederick asked, "Is mulligan edible?"

"Barely," Ben admitted. "You any good at catching rats, youngster?"

As it turned out, Frederick was very good at catching rats. Unfortunately, he was terrible at killing them, and got bitten by the first one he cornered in an almost-empty warehouse and grabbed bare-handed. He dropped it and it ran into a hole.

"They mostly don't have the rabies," Ben said. "But if you start foaming at the mouth, kindly let me know so I can skedaddle."

"Sorry," Frederick said. "It *looked* at me. I . . . I just couldn't."

"Don't worry about it, youngster," Ben said. He'd never asked Frederick's name, only called him "youngster" if he'd recently done something foolish, or "mister" if he looked like he was adapting to the hobo life. "You'll harden up by and by. Though I'd sleep with one eye open tonight if I was you. Now that rat has a taste of you, he'll likely come back for seconds."

While broths at home would involve his father's personal chef simmering veal bones for two days, Ben's masterpiece began with a bucket of water from a rusty tap behind the warehouse. He heated it over a fire made from scrap wood and gradually added handfuls of seeds and weeds he'd gathered from nearby lots. Frederick recognized the dandelions, but nothing else.

"This here's dock," Ben said, crumbling a cluster of seeds into the brew. "And these leaves are lamb's quarters. Lamb would be better, but lamb's quarters will do."

From one pocket of the patched coat he wore despite the heat, he drew half an onion, and from another, a bit of dried bacon. "It's been in three stews so far," Ben confessed, "but I reckon it still has a whiff of pig about it."

The coat was a veritable cabinet of wonders. An inside pocket produced a packet of salt and a handful of dried peas; a bulging outside pocket held a handkerchief, spoon, and pocketknife. Ben even had a candle stub and a few matches in a piece of oilskin. "Makes it more romantical," he said with a wink.

Frederick's mouth began to water. When the soup had cooked enough, Ben used the hem of his coat as a pot holder and hauled the bucket off the fire. Then he hunkered down and commenced eating.

Frederick's heart sank as he watched Ben shovel the steaming food into his mouth. Why had he been so foolish as to think Ben would share? Frederick hadn't contributed a single thing to it, not even a rat.

It had been a day since his last decent meal at a breadline; a wizened apple had been his breakfast. His stomach clenched in a tight knot. After a month on the road he was still naive enough to believe that people would hand him things. Now he was torn, knowing he didn't deserve a portion of Ben's meal but deeply resentful that it wasn't offered. Sure, Ben had taught him what plants to use, so maybe he could steal a pan and some matches and forage well enough to fend for himself. Maybe next time he could even harden himself enough to kill a rat that looked at him with shining, terrified eyes. Ben had already done a lot for him—he provided companionship on the road and advice about survival. He didn't owe Frederick anything else.

But Frederick wanted that soup. He *needed* it.

I'm stronger than Ben, he thought. *Younger. I can take it from him.*

No! What was happening to him? Could an empty belly really turn him into an animal?

A fragment of Latin came back to him. *Deus impeditio esuritori nullus.* No god is an impediment to a hungry man. *I stopped myself this time,* Frederick thought, *but what will happen next time? When will the animal in me take over the man?*

Ben got to his feet, setting aside the bucket. More than half of the soup remained. For a moment Frederick's heart soared.

"Back in a spell," was all Ben said, and he walked around the corner of the warehouse, carrying his spoon.

The second he was out of sight, Frederick snatched up the bucket. It smelled like heaven. He reached his hand in to scoop some out . . . and stopped.

Then he set the bucket down, the soup untouched, and started to stalk resolutely away from the camp.

"Where you off to, mister?" Ben called as he came back around the side of the warehouse. "Here, I washed off the spoon for you. Eat your share while it's hot. That's the worst of being a gentleman of the road, ain't it? When I strike it rich, first thing I'll do is buy another spoon." He laughed, then doubled over into a cough. "Won't that be livin' high on the hog?" he gasped as soon as he caught his breath.

As he ate, Frederick knuckled away the tears. He didn't want Ben to see and start calling him "youngster" again.

SEVEN

Lulu Kelly!" Veronica all but shrieked as the big black car pulled away from the Ambassador, carrying Lucille to her first role. "Irish but not *too*, cute but not *too*, lady of the evening but not *too*. Short, snappy, memorable, will look great in every typeface known to man." She pulled a compact out of her clutch and held up the mirror to Lucille's face. "Lucille, I'd like you to meet Lulu Kelly, It Girl and latest thing." Veronica's forehead crumpled in a sympathetic frown, and she shook her head. "*So* much work to be done. And really, we shouldn't leave it all for the studio makeup artists, no matter what David says. Lucky for you I carry an emergency kit with me at all times. Here, hold perfectly still."

Lucille—Lulu now—watched, cross-eyed, as Veronica

closed on her with a vampiric grin, pressing her head back firmly against the seat with one hand and advancing on her eyebrows with a pair of brass tweezers.

"Ouch!" Lulu gasped as the junior publicist plucked out the first hair with a brisk yank.

"Beauty is pain, darling," Veronica said. "Which is why I opt for plainness."

"You're not—" Lulu began, but the brusque publicist cut her off.

"Okay, so I'm easy enough on the eyes," Veronica admitted, "but I don't make my money from my face and figure, so I'm not about to torture myself any more than is absolutely necessary to keep people from laughing and pointing when I walk down the street. I fluff my hair, invest in a decent skirt suit, and I pass muster. You, on the other hand, must look eighteen for the next thirty years, come hell or high water. You must submit to the treadmill, the knife, the monkey gland—whatever it takes. Poor you."

Lulu thought Veronica looked like she meant it.

"Ouch!"

"A sacrifice on the altar of Hollywood," Veronica said kindly. "Get used to it."

Two dozen "ouches" later, Veronica proclaimed herself satisfied. "Let me darken them up a bit, or the studio might be tempted to wax them out and paint on black caterpillars." She dusted on some fawn-colored powder. "Let's see . . . What else can we do in another half mile?" She dug in her reticule and clutched something Lulu couldn't see. Suddenly, she pointed out the far window. "Will you look at that—it's Gary Cooper on that street corner!"

Lulu, starstruck, whipped her head around, and almost at the same instant felt a gentle tug and a metallic snip. When she turned back to Veronica, Lulu's neck felt cool, her head . . . *lighter.*

Veronica cranked the window open and tossed two feet of silvery hair into the car's slipstream, where it writhed for an instant like a flurry of snow before falling into the gutter.

"Sorry, dear. It's just that some girls take it so hard they start to cry in the hairdresser's chair. Not a good first impression, and makes eye bags that even an army of cucumbers can't cure. Tresses are terribly unchic. Most of the time they'll want you in a bob, and if they need long hair for a period number, you'll have a wig—for which, believe me, you'll want short hair."

Lulu's hand reached up to feel the place where her long silky hair most emphatically *wasn't,* and felt her eyes get hot.

"No!" Veronica told her sharply. "You will *not* cry." Then, to Lulu's shock, she pinched her, hard, on the thigh. "Sorry. A new pain to make you forget about the old one for a while. You'll learn to do it to yourself before long. Just keep it where the camera can't see—bite your tongue or dig your nails into your palms." She cocked her head and sighed. "Lulu—Lucille—are you sure this is what you want to do? It's a wonderful life, for some actresses, but a terrible life for *all* actresses. You could just go home. . . ."

"I can't," Lulu said after a long silence. "The price I paid to get here was too high."

"Oh, well, I could always loan you a few bucks."

"That isn't what I meant."

"Right," Veronica said sadly. "It never is."

Lulu's first gig was a blur of boredom and terror. She could barely take in the mountain of paperwork she'd just signed, and now she was surrounded by people and bustle and lights that swiveled around to periodically blind her. "We'll have to do something about your accent—which admittedly isn't as bad as some. Don't talk if you can help it," Veronica whispered to her as she sat her down in an obscure corner of the beehive-active studio. "Elocution lessons can start tomorrow, but for now, don't say anything except whatever lines they give you. They'll assume you're just trying out different accents and coach you until you find the right one. I wonder what you'll be playing. I see top hats—that could be anything from a contemporary opera scene to a Victorian street scene. Oh, there's another client of mine. Back in a jiffy."

Left alone in her corner, Lulu watched a slim, hatchet-faced older woman declaim about her erring niece as a giant camera hovered like a glaring watchful insect close to her head and a trio of overhead lights illuminated and shadowed the crags of her face. *Not everyone has to look eighteen forever*, Lulu thought. The crew took a break so an assistant could dab off the character actress's sheen of sweat. Then they did the same lines again, eight or ten times. It was not nearly as glamorous as Lulu had imagined.

At last the director decided the actress had performed her few lines acceptably, and the scene changed. Crew members rolled in brick walls on wheels, a fog machine began to gasp out heavy mist that hovered at ankle level, and the male lead emerged from some secret luxurious Xanadu, impeccably dressed, obviously made-up . . . and with the imprint of scarlet lips on the side of his throat.

"Extras to their places!" someone called, and a slew of picturesque poor shambled onto the scene. There was a rather dapper shoeshine boy in knickers, a beggar in artfully torn rags, two pretty women dressed in black, warming hands in fingerless gloves at a chestnut vendor's cart.

"Where's the flower seller?"

Lulu looked around with everyone else. No one appeared.

"Clock's ticking! Find her, or find someone else."

Just then Veronica dashed up. "That's you, darling! Hurry!" She hauled Lulu to her feet and escorted her to the incongruous street scene. "Here she is. I only just found out what her part is, and they told me she'd be shooting much later in the day. Isn't she perfect?"

The director looked her up and down quickly. The lead actor looked her up and down too—much more slowly.

"They put her in a ratty enough dress," the director said, squinting at the cotton frock Lulu had brought from home, hand-washed and lovingly mended, if admittedly faded and ragged. "But I don't think it's Victorian." He considered a moment. "What the hell—the audience won't know the difference. Get her some flowers and a little dewy shine on her cheeks and eyelids." He finally made eye contact with Lulu. "Do you have your lines?" She shook her head, and he gave a huge sigh. "Just go like this." He clasped an imaginary posy, batted his eyelashes, and said in the worst cockney imaginable, "'Oi beg yer pardon, sir, but oi've got loverly violets fer the missus. Can ye spare a ha'penny, kind sir?' Like that, with big eyes like an angel about to fall. Got it? And . . . action!"

She said her lines, the leading man patted her on the head and gave her a golden sovereign, and her job was done in one take.

"That's a great story to tell," Veronica said as she collected her charge. "I know it's just because the director is out of time, and your scene will probably end up on the cutting-room floor anyway, but still, one take on your very first scene—impressive."

"That was acting?" Lulu asked.

"Yup, that's all there is to it. Follow directions and look pretty. Well, maybe there *is* more to it, but that's enough for now. The last thing a new girl needs is thespian pretensions. The theater this is *not*. Now, off to Starlet University."

Lulu felt like she was floating after the success of her first performance. She had no idea whether she'd actually done well, but everyone seemed pleased with her, and that was enough to have her on cloud nine.

Veronica must have forgotten that Lulu's "costume" was

actually the shabby frock she'd arrived in, her humble best. She hustled her down a hallway labeled WARDROBE and handed her over to the care of one of the wardrobe mistresses, who proceeded to strip off Lulu's clothes. Despite Lulu's protests, she even tugged off her shabby cotton drawers.

"*Tch*," the woman said through a mouthful of pins. "They didn't have to make you so authentically poor. The audience won't see your undergarments. Directors!" she spat in derision, and tossed Lulu's drawers in the trash. "Where are your own clothes, miss?" she asked.

Before Lulu could answer, Veronica came in with a pale lavender silk chemise and a smart lemon-colored skirt suit with oversized onyx buttons down both the jacket and the skirt. "Some assistant moved your things to another room." She rolled her eyes to the wardrobe mistress as if assistants were the bane of both of their existences.

"But, Veronica, I . . . ," Lulu began.

"I know, you don't want to wear something so crumpled. But it will never happen again, I'm sure." She raised her eyebrows at the wardrobe mistress, who nodded emphatically. Some assistant was about to get severely chewed out. "Hurry up. We have an appointment with Mrs. Wilberforce in twenty minutes."

This seemed to impress the wardrobe mistress, and she hurried Lulu into her new suit. Veronica handed over a pair of black pumps. They fit loosely on Lulu's feet, and she had to shuffle as her publicist took her arm and led her out the door before her honesty could quite make it out of her mouth.

As soon as they exited the studio, Lulu blurted out, "But these aren't my clothes!"

"Oh, girls borrow from wardrobe all the time. As long as you don't hit up cold storage for the furs, or try to smuggle jewelry, no one minds too much. We'll return it all once you've had a chance to go shopping. Once *we've* had a chance, I mean. No offense, but I don't think I'll trust you alone in a boutique with a wad of bills. You're wiggling like you never had silk against your skin before."

"I haven't," Lulu admitted. "At least, not against *that* part of my body." She told Veronica how her mother ran a small-scale laundry for garments as fine as the lavender confection she was wearing now.

"You *have* come a long way," Veronica said with a whistle. "I wonder . . . No, people never like the truth out here, no matter how admirable it is. Do me a favor, and until we concoct your story, don't tell anyone about your mother's laundry, or anything about where you come from. Be silent and mysterious."

Lulu thought she could be silent. She didn't have nearly as much confidence in her ability to be mysterious.

One of the Lux cars drove them to a Spanish-style house with brick-colored tile and purple and pink bougainvillea crawling over the walls. A crisply dressed maid opened the door. "Mrs. Wilberforce is expecting you," she said with a curtsy and no smile.

"Go on," Veronica said. "I'll be back in two hours to

take you to lunch and do some shopping. Then tonight you'll have your first acting class. Have fun!"

There was something in the way she said those last words that made Lulu suspicious. But when the maid led her through the house to an elegantly appointed parlor, she found only a comfortable-looking elderly woman in a floral silk dress cut to show off an ample bosom and slender ankles but disguise a rather too-full midsection. In one hand she held a pair of gold wire spectacles on top of a long, jewel-encrusted handle. She placed this to her eyes and examined Lulu casually.

"Two hours," she proclaimed, "will not be nearly enough."

Then the torture began.

It began innocently enough. "Stand up straight," Mrs. Wilberforce said in a voice of quiet authority.

Lulu did. Or at least, she thought she did.

"It resembles nothing more than a jellyfish. Has it no spine? Again!"

Lulu took a deep breath and did her best to elongate herself. "Now it looks like a constipated cobra. The cords in its neck are bulging. Relax. Again!"

She relaxed too much, and the whip came out.

It was a riding crop, about two and a half feet long. Without warning, Mrs. Wilberforce snatched it from a vase full of peacock feathers and with a smart flick of her wrist slapped Lulu on the hip. Lulu shrieked and jumped away.

"It will not flinch," Mrs. Wilberforce said sternly. "It will do as it is told if it wants to be a lady. Stand up straight!"

Lulu tried, and failed, for half an hour, being compared to various invertebrates and receiving a good many taps with the riding crop, which, while they might not actually hurt, stung her pride nonetheless.

Eventually, though Mrs. Wilberforce still wasn't satisfied, Lulu was allowed to walk instead of simply stand. "It will glide," the old woman said. "It will not wiggle its hips like a common trollop. It may be a trollop, but when I am finished, it will at least be an *uncommon* one."

Mrs. Wilberforce put a book on Lulu's head. Lulu was familiar with this posture-perfecting technique. She had once seen Mrs. Fahntille strut across her bedroom wearing a volume of *Lady Chatterley's Lover* and nothing else.

But then Mrs. Wilberforce added another book, and another—all large, heavy volumes—until Lulu thought her neck would snap.

"I can't walk with these on my head," she said, the first words of protest she'd dared to utter. "I can hardly stand with them on!"

Mrs. Wilberforce glared at her. "It will stand, and it will walk. Again!"

Lulu took a tentative step. The books slid off and landed in a heap on the floor. Mrs. Wilberforce grabbed Lulu's hand and slapped her across the palm with the riding crop.

Lulu gasped, and tears came to her eyes. No one had ever hurt her before. Not on purpose, anyway. "I'm trying my best," she moaned, rubbing the red mark on her palm.

"Its best, it says? Does it know that there are thousands

of young women arriving in this town every month? One of them will be a star. Nine hundred and ninety-nine of them will go home or end up in the gutter. Its best is not nearly good enough. It must aspire to *my* best if it wants to survive."

Mrs. Wilberforce used the supple end of the crop to lift up Lulu's desolate chin. "Did you think being a star would be easy?" she asked, her voice softening. "No great thing can be accomplished without hard work."

Why am I putting up with this? Lulu asked herself. *I don't have to tolerate this kind of treatment. I can leave anytime.*

But she didn't. She thought about how she had let a murderer walk free. She thought about the money her contract promised her, the apartment that Veronica told her would be hers. For all her sins and all her gains there had to be a price. And so she let this old woman berate her and beat her and did her best to stand up straight.

Mrs. Wilberforce cleared her throat and slapped the crop against her own thigh. Her momentary softness was gone. She placed a single book on Lulu's head. "Now! Head up, back straight, chest out . . . No, not so much. It is not a pouter pigeon. And . . . walk!"

With fifteen minutes left, Lulu managed to keep three books on her head. Mrs. Wilberforce still said she walked like an adolescent giraffe, but at last the maid announced that Veronica had come to collect her.

"Good-bye, my dear," Mrs. Wilberforce said at the end, all pleasantness now. "I look forward to seeing you again on Wednesday. I have recommended you attend three times per week. Next time we will learn how to smile."

Lulu managed a pained grimace. Mrs. Wilberforce closed her eyes briefly. "So much work to do . . ."

When Veronica met her at the door, Lulu gave her an accusatory look.

"I know. I know," Veronica said with an apologetic shrug. "I could have warned you. But in this business, it's better to have some things sprung on you. Otherwise you might run away screaming."

EIGHT

From that moment of openhearted generosity that both broke and mended Frederick's heart, he and Ben were friends and brothers of the road. They cast their lot together as they traveled, share and share alike. "Through the fat times and the lean," Ben said as he spit on his hand and offered it to Frederick to shake to seal the deal.

"More like from the lean times to the leaner," Frederick said.

But with Ben's knowledge of the hobo life to guide them, they didn't fare too badly. Ben could find edible plants on every roadside and even in the cracks on city sidewalks. And they didn't always have to live off the land. Many of the larger towns had soup kitchens and breadlines.

"They're so kind to feed us," Frederick said at one charity

kitchen at the edge of a prosperous neighborhood.

"It ain't kindness—it's a kind of bribe," Ben told him. "Poor people are scary. Rich folks think if they give us a little food, we won't break into their homes."

Frederick gulped. "You never did that, did you?"

"No need," Ben assured him. "Plenty of people will invite you into their houses if you know how to ask the right way."

And so, Ben taught Frederick the noble art of the grift.

"It's a funny thing about folks," Ben said. "They won't be satisfied with a true sad story, no matter how pathetic it might be. Riding the rails for months, hacking my lungs up, not a soul to give me the honest work I ask for? Not good enough. But if I concoct a story of starving babies, or a father who lost his legs in the war, or pretend to be blind and cry that my seeing eye dog was just hit by a car, why, there's a mess of suckers who will fork over cash or food. Just for the story."

"But it isn't right to lie to them!"

"Why not? Anyway, it's not a lie—it's entertainment. These farm folks, they can't get to the movies. Give them a humdinger of a sob story and they'll be talking about it for weeks."

Frederick wasn't sure he believed Ben and vowed he'd stick to the truth. Well, maybe not the entire truth. He had to hide his real identity. Still, the truth of his current circumstances should be enough to persuade someone to give him a chance, or a meal.

They'd left the city behind and were walking along a dry, dusty road heading roughly westward. They didn't have an actual destination in mind, but like so many that year, they found themselves traveling toward the sunset. Dreams had died and hope had been crushed in the East, so now the West beckoned, singing its siren song.

"Why don't you try that one?" Ben suggested, pointing to a lone farmhouse set back from the road. It was a ramshackle place, but there was a lush garden along the side filled with carrots and cabbages. A cow with a heavy udder paced slowly in a movable pen of stakes and barbed wire.

Frederick had never actually asked for a handout before. He'd approached similar farmhouses to ask for work, and sometimes even if there was no work to be had, a farmer—or more often the farmer's wife or comely young daughter—would invite him in for a sandwich and a cup of milk. But Ben told him they had to be on the move. This middle part of the country was dangerous, he said. Drought and dust and despair; no jobs, no hope. They needed one coast or the other. They didn't want to stop for work along the way if they could help it.

Frederick walked up to the farmhouse. His back was straight from years of dancing and fencing lessons and from the pride and confidence in himself that had been instilled from birth. It was not the bearing of a beaten man, whatever his shabby seams, dirt, and leanness might say otherwise.

He knocked at the door, and after a time a woman in a faded cotton dress answered. She gave him a quick once-over and declared, "I don't want no insurance."

"Wait!" he said as she tried to slam the door in his face. "I'm not selling insurance."

"Whatever it is you're selling, I don't want any."

"I'm afraid I don't have anything to sell, ma'am. That's the problem. You see, I've lost all my money. . . ." That was one way of putting it. " And I'm heading to California, looking for work."

"No work for you, neither."

"No, you don't understand. I'm *hungry*. I don't have any money, but I was hoping that you might, out of kindness, you know . . ."

"If you aim to rob me, there ain't nothing left to rob."

"No, I only need food. Please, anything will do. The merest crust of bread. A stale canapé. A questionable oyster."

She squinted at him, and he was struck with the absurdity of it. Why, without a thought he could buy this woman's house. All of her possessions would cost less than his last pair of shoes. He looked at the scrawny woman, middle-aged with graying hair springing out of its makeshift bun. He could leave all this hunger and poverty behind and reclaim his vast fortune. Wouldn't that be better? He could give this poor, suspicious woman a thousand dollars without feeling it. He could give ten thousand such women a thousand dollars each, and it would still be less than his father gave to the Metropolitan Opera Company last year. She could buy a pump for her well and expand her garden, buy more cows. . . .

He'd left his home, his father, his fortune in disgust. But had he cut off his nose to spite his own face, as that horrible expression went? If the money had been earned through greed and evil, couldn't he redeem the filthy lucre by putting it to charitable use?

"I know what you are," the woman snapped suddenly. "You're a bank agent, aren't you? Come to see if I'm hiding any money. Tell your manager I done gave him all I can. I don't have a cent nor a crumb of food for nary man nor beast. If he means to take the farm, he can take it, but I swear I gave him all I can." Her anger dissolved and she started to weep, her tears making faint tracks in the layer of dust on her cheeks. "If he can just wait a bit, the cabbages are getting bigger, and . . . I can sell Bessie, what I raised from a calf. Please tell him I'm trying. Please ask him to give me just a little more time."

How many women like this had his father destroyed? Oh, not directly. He'd never been asked for mercy and refused it. He'd never bulldozed a house or led away a milk cow with his own hands. But he owned the banks that took back farms the minute a person got a little behind on payments.

Dirty money can't be cleaned, can't be saved, Frederick decided. *All I can save is my own soul.*

He bent down and slipped off his shoe, realizing only now that his clothes, however worn, were still better than any she might see in a year. No wonder she'd thought he was a salesman, a banker, an enemy.

"Here," he said, handing her the Morgan silver dollar that had been nestling in his arch for the last few weeks. A rich child out shopping with his mother, a regular Little Lord

Fauntleroy in velvet and curls, had dropped it, and Frederick had retrieved it and run after them. After her initial alarm, thinking he meant to rob them, the mother was so surprised by his honesty that she told him to keep it. The child had gotten a dozen shining silver dollars for his birthday, and this would be a lesson for him to be more careful.

Frederick had kept it safe all the while, partly in case of dire need, but also to remind himself that however hungry he might get, he was still a gentleman. He'd never steal, not even from the rich.

Now he pressed the warm silver dollar into the woman's hand. She tried to give it back.

"It's for you," Frederick said. "I wish it could be more."

"I won't do nothin' unnatural for it," the woman protested hotly. "I'm a good woman, I am!"

"No, I didn't mean . . . Never mind. Have a pleasant morning, ma'am."

"How'd you make out, mister?" Ben asked as Frederick rejoined him on the road. "Did she give you any food?"

"No."

"What happened, then?"

"I gave her my life savings."

"Hoo-boy!" Ben doubled over, slapping his thigh. "You do beat all, youngster. Here, I see a chimney a piece up. Follow me and don't say a word. Just keep a grin on your face."

At the next house, if anything, poorer than the last, Ben told a pitiful tale about how his wife died of consumption, leaving him with a half-wit son who had been kicked in the head by a mule as a boy. "Say hello to the pretty lady, youngster."

Frederick just smiled.

"Poor mite," the woman said. "Yes, you can tell he's simple just to look at him. You're a good father. Set a spell and let me get you a mess of soup. Can your son feed himself? Does he drool? Here, I have a bib for him. There's a good boy!" She patted Frederick on the head. It was mortifying . . . but the soup was delicious.

NINE

After a lunch of green turtle soup and crab gratin that came to an astonishing two dollars per person (paid for, apparently, by telling the waiter, "Lux Studios, darling"), Veronica took Lulu shopping. It was completely unlike any experience of a similar name she'd had at home. All her life, shopping had meant pawing through secondhand stores or nipping in the waist of one of her mother's old dresses. Never before had it meant having a stylish woman with a French accent say "*oui*" and "*non*" as lovely young models paraded in samples of the latest couture. A dozen items were selected for Lulu to try on.

Between them, the Frenchwoman and Veronica settled on two lightweight summer dresses, one in flirty polka dots, the other white and blue, faintly reminiscent of a sailor suit.

Both of those fit perfectly. They also selected a skirt suit in deep amethyst with exaggerated shoulders and attached gold-chain accents, and a black silk gown that made Lulu stammer and protest she could never possibly wear it.

"What would I wear under it?" she gasped.

"*Rien,*" the dressmaker said. "Nothing."

Lulu was relieved to learn that the last two outfits had to be altered. By that time, she wouldn't have been a bit surprised if Veronica had insisted she actually put on the black gown and flaunt herself in the street with absolutely nothing underneath.

"There," Veronica said as assistants bundled two big dress boxes into the Lux Studios car. "If we do that every day for two weeks, you'll have enough to wear for this season."

"We do this *again?*" Who could need so many clothes?

"You live by your looks, kiddo. Your face and figure are lovely—the men will enjoy that. But it's the women who buy the most movie tickets and give you a boost in the Hollywood and glamour mags. They can't hope to have your face and form, but they can all dream about having your clothes. You've got to be dressed to the nines every time you leave the house. Makeup, too. Even if you're just taking a walk or repotting your geraniums. Always be camera ready. And don't let them see you in the same outfit twice."

"But how will I ever pay for all those clothes?"

"You don't pay for them," Veronica said.

"Then who does?"

"Nobody does, you booby. Madame Defarge there gives you the clothes, and you wear them and do your best to be seen and photographed in them. If you're successful, in a few months you can go back and get another few suits and frocks. If you get a magazine spread and tell the world who you're wearing, you might get free clothes for life. You'll bring them business, you see. Women will want to dress like you."

"But I'm not famous yet. I might never be. I'm nobody!"

"Lulu, you've been in this town three days and you already got a contract with a big studio and a cute role with a couple of actual words. You might not be anything much yet, but you've blown into town like Marion Davies riding a hurricane. Someone wants you to win. And when certain *someones* want it that badly, it happens. I love that you're modest, honey, but face facts. You landed in the gravy and make no mistake—plenty of people are going to kiss up to you. Girls would kill for what you've got."

Lulu shuddered.

Veronica noticed, but misread her emotion. "It's a big deal, I know. If you play your cards right, you'll be the toast of the town. I mean, you still have to earn it, more or less. You can't have all the emotive skill of a potato, and a body to match. But if you have the right people behind you and a little natural talent, our studio trainers can do the rest. Here we are."

They had pulled up to a modernist home on the edge of town, a low building with unexpected angles and a lot of windows overlooking a wild landscape behind the house.

"Is this one better or worse than Mrs. Wilberforce?" Lulu asked nervously.

"Well . . . he won't hit you with a stick. But he might make you even more uncomfortable in his own way. Vasily Anoushkin is considered one of the best acting and dialogue coaches in the business. He does at least a little work with everyone Lux hires on contract, and then if you're any good, he'll keep you on for advanced classes. A good word from him to the executives and you can get the plum roles. He's the one to please. Just do whatever he says, no matter how ridiculous or unpleasant it may seem."

"What*ever* he says?" Lulu asked, her eyes wide with alarm. Was he going to be one of the men her mother warned her about?

Veronica looked at her for a long incredulous moment, then burst out laughing. "Oh, kid, plenty of people are going to try to get into your undies, but believe me, Vasily ain't one of them. Though you might wish all he wanted out of you was a quick cuddle when he has you hunched over making believe you're an old babushka for three hours, or lying on the ground until you've captured the convincing essence of a worm. Go on. I'll pick you up later for dinner and take you back to your apartment."

When Lulu knocked, the door swung open on soundless hinges. Hesitantly, she let herself in and followed the sound of a deep, compelling male voice speaking in an accent she didn't quite recognize. She'd heard many different languages and accents in polyglot New York, and this one resembled what she'd heard around the Yiddish theater district. It wasn't Yiddish or Hebrew, though. Russian, maybe?

She crept around a corner and found a tall, slender, elegant man who seemed designed to wear cashmere. He was declaiming before a small group of young men and women sprawled in decoratively serious attitudes on sofas, chairs, and even the floor.

"As my personal mentor Konstantin Stanislavsky said, you must *live* the role. Where the actor can *become* the person he is portraying, there is no need for technique." His emphatic verbal italics were accompanied by expressive hand gestures. He paced as he talked. "Even among the *greatest* actors, this may only happen in one role, or two. For the *rest* of you, you must train your body and mind and emotions until you can understand with *exactitude* the *depth* and *breadth* of the human experience. Because your audience will *know* when you lie! They will know and they will not give their dime to see you. What have we here? An ingénue?"

Though he hadn't turned to face her, he seemed to suddenly become aware of Lulu's presence. "Do you see, students, if I cast this one as a timid fawn, a dying child, a heartbroken girl, she will shine. She will win the sympathy of the audience because that is what she is—a creature designed to win our sympathy. She needs no technique for that. But when I am through with her, she can also play the vixen, the harridan, the conqueror, and the queen. She will understand what it is to have steel deep inside one's self, and she will not be lying when the script calls for her to shoot her lover and she squeezes the trigger without remorse. They will believe her!"

He turned to Lulu at last. "Come forward. Who are you?"

"Lucille . . . I mean Lulu." What was her new last name again? "Lulu Kelly."

"Lulu," he said. What a fascinating accent, the way he seemed to swallow her name. His speech was slower than she was used to, and heavy, somehow, as if each word had a gravity of its own. "Step forward, Lulu, and show us the depth of your emotional well."

Relieved, at least, that he didn't have a riding crop, she crept up to stand beside him. She felt the eyes of the other students on her, sharp and curious, and tried to smile at them. The boys all grinned at her, except for one serious fellow in the back who was making notes in a calfskin book, and some of the girls did, too. One dark-haired beauty sitting practically at Vasily's feet scowled briefly at her and then turned her adoring gaze back to Vasily.

"Although not all of us have been murderers or victims in our lives, we may play murderers or victims on-screen. An actor must draw upon similar experiences in his own life in order to capture the emotional resonance of his role. Lulu!"

She automatically stood up straighter, and some of the girls giggled.

"Suppose you had to play a woman who was menaced by a gun-wielding criminal."

Lulu felt her chest tighten, her breath come in gasps.

Control yourself, she whispered in her mind. *He doesn't know.*

"Of course this hasn't happened to you. But you have no doubt been afraid of some little thing—a mouse, a noise in the night. Recall that time now. Relive the sensation of being afraid. Feel it *utterly.*"

She saw the black hole of the gun barrel. She smelled the tang of blood, metallic and sweet in the air.

Lulu shook her head and did her best to wipe her mind clear.

"You must stand here before us until we are convinced you are feeling afraid. Do not act; do not force yourself to tremble. Just feel the fear inside you, and it will show on your face. We will know when it is true."

I can't let myself think of that, but I have to think of something. When have I been afraid? When my father has his dreams and wakes me from sound sleep with a scream? No. Her father alarmed her, but she was never afraid of him.

But she tried, closing her eyes and summoning up a safe kind of fear.

"You are lying to us," Vasily said. "You are not thinking of something that truly scares you. It must be real, inside you. If I tell you to say 'cat' and all the while you think 'dog,' then only 'woof' will be on your face."

Lulu combed her mind for another truly terrifying experience. All the while, Sal, the gun, the blood stalked her memory, waiting to pounce. Closer and closer the memory came. She couldn't fight it anymore. . . .

"She fainted!" a girl cried.

The next thing Lulu was aware of was the rushing thrum of her heartbeat in her ears, rumbling and watery like a fitful river over rocks. Then other sounds came to her, voices of the students:

"She must have thought of a doozy to faint like that."

"Her face looked like chalk!"

"Poor thing!"

Then another voice, harsh and dismissive. "The little twit just passed out from stage fright. She'll never get anywhere at that rate."

Lulu saw a pinprick of light, which slowly expanded until her vision was clear and she saw the last speaker: the dark-haired girl with bee-stung lips and cynical green eyes. She gave Lulu a superior smile.

Vasily, kneeling over Lulu, produced a little bottle of eau de toilette and dabbed it at her temples. When the room stopped spinning, he helped her to her feet. She expected a rebuke, but he looked at her with something like awe on his face. He stood behind her with his hands lightly on her shoulders, like a velvet cushion displaying a fine jewel.

"Learn from her, my students. Lulu did not just feel afraid. She became *fear itself*!"

The dark-haired girl blew a raspberry and powdered her nose ostentatiously with her compact.

Later, Vasily paired the students up to practice improvising realistic dialogue. Each pair was provided with a short script. Their task was to come up with what the characters would talk about *before* that, the period off camera.

Lulu was paired with the dark-haired girl. Up close she noticed she had a tiny heart-shaped beauty spot at the curl of her mouth, in a most disconcerting position that made Lulu keep thinking it was a crumb and longing to brush it off. She forced herself not to stare at it.

The girl introduced herself as Ruby Godfrey. After her earlier heckling, Lulu expected her to be impossible to work with, but to her surprise, Ruby buckled down and proved to be a good actress. Far better than Lulu, who stammered and couldn't think of anything to say.

"Lulu, we're supposed to be friends," Ruby said.

Lulu raised her pale eyebrows.

"In the script, I mean." Ruby laughed. "All actresses hate each other, so don't take it personally," she added with disarming frankness. "I just don't have time for amateurs, or anyone who might get in my way." She looked down her pert nose at Lulu. "Not that I think I have anything to worry about with you. What are you, fresh from a Kansas cornfield? Some two-bit businessman's tramp? Better make your way before he finds a younger, prettier model to bankroll. Town's full of 'em."

Lulu couldn't tell if Ruby was being insulting or was honestly trying to give her advice. Before she could figure it out, Ruby was back in character, pretending to be Lulu's childhood friend whom she just ran into in a café. After a while Lulu became more comfortable with the charade. For half an hour they chatted like old friends, and for that small space Lulu felt almost as if Ruby really were her chum.

It was just the power of acting. Vasily rang a little bell, and Ruby broke character midlaugh, checked her nose for shine again, and flounced off without a word.

Near dusk, when all the students had left, Lulu was still waiting for Veronica to pick her up. "You can wait in the sunroom," Vasily had told her. "I need to freshen up."

Lulu had been twiddling her thumbs when the front door opened. Ruby slipped in, a secret, soft smile on her face. She didn't notice Lulu in her darkened perch.

"Vasily," Ruby called in a sultry voice. "I have a question for you." Her voice grew fainter as she walked toward his bedroom. Lulu stood and leaned into the hallway to hear better. "A very special question only you can answer. Oh, Vasily! Come out, come out, wherever you are!"

"Who's there?" Lulu heard the acting coach ask from his room.

"You've trained me well, Vasily. I can be whomever you want me to be."

Lulu gasped and covered her mouth when she saw Ruby unbutton her blouse and let it slide to the stone tile floor. She entered his bedroom.

"Ruby!" came a startled shriek that lacked any trace of a Russian accent. "What are you doing? Put that back on at once."

"Oh, Vasily." Ruby sighed. "How I long to kiss you."

Lulu heard a muffled *mmmph* and another high-pitched cry of protest. "Ugh! Don't do that! Go away!"

"But I only want to show you how much you mean to me," Ruby said. Lulu could hear the confusion and hurt in her voice.

Vasily had recovered enough to resume his Russian accent. "My dear girl," he said, "I assure you I have no desire to kiss you. The fault lies not within you, but . . . Well, yes, it *does* lie within you, in that you're a . . . That is to say, you're not a . . ." He sighed deeply. "You are a very charming girl, Ruby. It's just that I prefer people who aren't girls."

"Oh! Why you . . . you . . . !" She scrambled out of his bedroom, scooping up her blouse and clutching it to her chest as she ran.

Lulu didn't manage to duck out of the way in time, and Ruby spied her. She stopped dead. "Lulu, what are you doing here? We . . . we were just rehearsing a part. A farce, for a new . . ." She couldn't keep up her bluff. Lulu could see tear tracks on her cheeks, silver in the dim light. "If you ever, *ever* dare breathe a word of this to anyone, I'll ruin you! I swear I will!"

She stormed off into the night.

TEN

Frederick stopped paying attention to state lines and city names. He was in a different place every night and thought of the vast interior of the continent simply as "the middle." His life had been in New York and eastward.

West was escape for Frederick. If anyone came looking for him, they might think to scour the fashionable hotels of Paris or even Prague. It would not occur to them to seek him in a place like Nebraska.

It was in Nebraska that they found the chicken.

It was the hen's opinion that she had found them. Frederick and Ben had been camping a little ways off the road in a desolate stretch of nowhere, surrounded by dry empty fields of corn stubble. There wasn't a farmstead in sight—and they could see for miles across the flat, featureless plain.

Frederick was awakened at dawn by a low, homely sound. "*Brrock-bock-bock-bock.*" He opened his eyes to find himself confronted by one beady yellow eye and an intimidatingly sharp beak inches from his face.

Frederick sat up and rubbed the sleep from his eyes, leaving grimy streaks. He hadn't had a proper bath since running away from home. But then, he hadn't seen a mirror either, so he didn't mind so much.

"Hello," he said to the hen, and immediately felt foolish. The hen cocked her head at him, then pecked at his shoe. "Sorry, I don't have any food for you."

"You don't feed it, youngster," said Ben from his bedroll. "*It* feeds *you*. Been a long time since I had a chicken all to myself. Well, half a chicken, anyway. Tarnation!"

"What?" Frederick asked.

"No wood." Ben gestured to the barren landscape. "So no fire." The corn stubble would burn, but it couldn't make a fire lasting or hot enough to roast meat. "We have to wait until we find a tree, which might not be till we hit Colorado."

"Where do you think she came from?" They hadn't seen a farm for miles.

Ben shrugged. "She's taken a shine to you."

"Maybe she misses people." The chicken seemed profoundly content to be scratching the dust near his feet. Frederick reached down to touch her and she scooted away just out of reach but didn't seem scared.

"They're sociable birds. If her people moved, she's looking for a new home. She's plump for a stray. Make for good eating, once we can cook her. Best not to kill her now, though. Might spoil before we can get fuel for a fire. Grab hold of her, youngster. We can carry our dinner with us."

She was hard to catch, but once she was tucked securely under Frederick's armpit, she settled down, making clucks and coos against his chest.

They walked along the dusty road through endless abandoned fields until dusk. They didn't see a single fellow traveler. The only sign of life was a hawk wheeling through the cloudless blue. The hen looked up at the hawk with mild interest, then closed her eyes when Frederick stroked her neck.

"Ben," he began, his brow creased. "Do we have to . . . ?"

"I knew it!" Ben shouted, whipping off his hat and slapping it against his leg. "I placed a bet with myself for a million bucks that you'd make friends with that fowl and not have the stomach to kill it. Is that what you were fixin' to say?"

Frederick admitted sheepishly that it was.

Ben sighed. "Well, my stomach doesn't have the stomach to miss another meal. Aw, don't look at me like that!"

"Like what?" Frederick asked innocently, laying on the puppy-dog eyes even thicker.

Ben considered for a while. "Tell you what," he said at last. "If you can hold on to that chicken until we find a farm, we can trade it for a meal. That way your little friend will live long enough to lay a few more eggs. Will that do you?"

Frederick just grinned and patted his hen.

Toward evening they found an abandoned barn next to the charred remains of a farmhouse. Ben gave Frederick a piece of twine to secure the hen and wandered off into the fields to forage for something to tide them over.

Frederick settled down, laying his head on his balled-up jacket with his feet propped up on a crate. His muscles, always hard from rowing, lacrosse, and fencing, had grown longer and leaner from hours of nonstop trudging and the backbreaking day labor he and Ben sometimes picked up. He was tired, but he also felt as if his body had become some new kind of machine capable of perpetual motion. In time, he knew, too much work and not enough food would break him down. But for now he felt strangely invincible.

A little while later, Frederick heard footsteps in the darkness. Good. He'd started to get a little worried about his traveling companion.

Frederick smiled at the barn door in relief. But it wasn't Ben who crossed the threshold; it was a big man in overalls, followed by another, smaller and shifty. The second man had a piece of board in his hand. Three rusty nails protruded from near the end.

"Hello, fellows," Frederick said affably, even though he had a sick feeling in his gut that he knew exactly what was coming.

He could tell it from their eyes, from the belligerent set of their bull shoulders.

"You're in my house," the biggest, meanest one said.

Frederick scrambled to his feet. "Forgive me," he said in

his drawing-room voice. "I thought this place was derelict. I didn't realize it belonged to you."

"Wherever I am, it belongs to me," the man said. "Give me your money."

Frederick smiled. "Right to the point, aren't we?" Mugsy had taught him to box, and he was pretty sure that in a fair fight he could take on one person, however big and mean. But there were two of them, and there would be nothing fair about it. Absurdly, he worried for his chicken, as if she were a damsel in distress he had to protect.

The man held out his hand. "Now."

"Sorry, old chap, I seem to be out of the ready. I'd be happy to offer you an IOU for the day when I'm in a more felicitously pecunious position, but I'm afraid today . . ."

The man slugged him in the jaw.

Frederick staggered but didn't fall. He'd managed to flinch in time to deflect the worst of it. The man was strong, but Frederick could tell he hadn't trained as a fighter.

"Do you really think I'd be squatting in a barn in the middle of nowhere if I had anything to rob? Use your head, friend."

The man seemed more inclined to use his fist again. Frederick dodged this blow but didn't strike back.

"Take off your clothes," the little man with the spiked board said.

"What!"

"They'll fetch a pretty penny in pawn."

"My good man, if you'll just wait until my friend returns,

I'm sure we can find a way to share this barn harmoniously."

"Your friend? That's a good one. Bet he's a six-foot bruiser and packing a roscoe to boot. You ain't got no friend here. Now hustle." He slapped the board against his palm, as his big partner moved closer.

Frederick's heart pounded wildly. *I can't let them get away with this. It isn't fair. It isn't right.* But he was afraid, and almost without his volition, his fingers started unbuttoning his vest.

Feeling like a helpless little boy, he stripped it off and started unbuttoning his shirt. Then the big man spied the chicken.

"Lookee here," he said. "Dinner." In an instant he'd snatched up the sleeping chicken and twisted her head clean off.

"No!" Frederick shouted, and launched himself at the big man. Rage filled him, and that, along with the surprising suddenness of his attack, gave him a momentary advantage. He bowled his opponent over and scrambled on top of him, pummeling his face. He forgot all of Mugsy's teaching. These were caveman blows, wildly swung with all the force of his fury and disillusionment in the human species. Blood spurted from the big man's nose, and Frederick had the satisfaction of seeing a second of panic on his face.

Then the smaller man hit Frederick across the head with his board, and the world pulsed with red and black pain. He managed to wrench the board out of his attacker's hand and fling it across the room, dimly aware that, whether through intent or carelessness, he'd been hit with the side without nails. Clawing his way out of the darkness of unconsciousness, he tried to block the punches and kicks that rained down on him. After a while he wished he'd just let himself pass out. When the time came that he couldn't even feel the blows anymore, he knew he was in real trouble. He could hear the wet-sounding *thwacks*, like something in a meat plant, but he was drifting away from it all. . . .

There was another *thwack*, louder and different, and the rhythm of the blows changed, then stopped. Through a red haze Frederick saw Ben with the board in his hand. The smaller man was on the ground, groaning. The next second, in horror-movie slow motion, Frederick watched Ben haul back and hit the big man with all his strength. Nails first. The board embedded in the big man's head, and he fell to his knees.

Ben pulled Frederick to his feet and snatched up the dead chicken. Then they staggered out into the night.

ELEVEN

Veronica had called Lulu's new place an apartment, but she might also have called it a dormitory. Though the ten-story building (with an elevator!) on a pleasantly bustling street was officially an apartment building that was open for public rental, the flats were all occupied by people associated with Lux Studios. Most of them were actors and actresses, young and just getting started in careers that might explode or fizzle at any moment. Like a very glamorous raven-haired girl named Dorothy Lamour, who had been crowned Miss New Orleans just the year before. There were a few older stage actors there too, trying out this relatively new way of expressing their art. The remainder of the apartments were occupied by midlevel Lux Studios staff, including, to Lulu's delight, Veronica Imrie herself.

Veronica handed Lulu the key and let her open her own door for the first time. "You're right above me. So you can just stomp if you need anything. And if your parties get too loud, I'll whack the ceiling with a broomstick. Of course, mine is just a studio. Still, it's handy on groggy mornings having the coffee percolator within three feet of my bed. You, on the other hand, have a nice little suite. Furnished, too. Everything used to belong to Jean Arthur."

"Jean Arthur!" Lulu whipped around, her heart racing. "She was so wonderful in *The Mysterious Dr. Fu Manchu*! Did she really live here? Where did she go?"

"It seems she was all wet here. Story is her little romance with David O. Selznick, the studio chief at Paramount, didn't go over so well with Mrs. Selznick, and her career took a nose dive. She packed up and is headed for Broadway. In any event, the lovely Miss Arthur's departure has opened up a charming place for you to squat for the time being!"

Lulu gulped and followed Veronica inside.

Lulu stopped in the entranceway and simply stared. It was the most beautiful place she had ever seen. The hotel had been nicely furnished, but this was different. Maybe because these thing were to be hers, at least for the time being. She had never seen furniture like this before. At home, good furniture meant heavy wood that might look ugly but could withstand the ravages of rot and was too unwieldy to easily pawn.

This room, though, had not only wood carved into delicate curves, but materials she'd never thought of for

furniture—shining chrome and verdigris copper, burnished leather, icy glass, the pelts of unknown animals,
those disparate elements all melding into an organic whole
that spoke of luxury and optimism. The room positively
shone, the surfaces reflecting light from the big windows
and the many electric fixtures.

"Art deco is already getting a little old-fashioned for my
taste," Veronica said, looking around critically. "Still, it's not
a bad place to start, and in a year, if all goes well, you can
move to your own house away from the eagle eyes of your
Lux minders. Mrs. Fox, the concierge you met downstairs,
is one of the best-paid spies in the country. Louella Parsons
alone compensated the old bird enough to buy a country
house."

"Who is Louella Parsons?" Lulu asked.

"Who is . . . ? Why, you green little innocent! She's the
head-honcho gossip columnist. If she likes you, she'll give
you good press and do anything to hide your scandals.
Louella Parsons is the one you have to impress if you want to
make it big here."

"I thought you said Vasily was the one I had to impress."

"Kid, you have to impress *everyone* out here. It's a full-
time job. Get a good night's sleep, because tomorrow we're
meeting Mrs. Parsons herself. The three of us are going to
decide exactly who you are."

"What do you mean?"

"Your persona, your back story. I'm thinking something
posh, like a Swiss finishing school, but we'll see what Louella

thinks. It's technically my job, but since realistically she's the one who decides what goes in ink about you, we might as well make her happy from the get-go."

"But then won't she know it's all made-up?" Lulu asked.

Veronica only laughed.

Alone that night, Lulu allowed herself to breathe her first small sigh of relief. It was real. Veronica had showed her her bank deposit book with a receipt for her first week's pay of one hundred dollars. She was making her own way, and that way was far, far from Sal Benedetto. People kept saying that she had to have someone big behind her, giving her a push. But that's all it was, right? Sal had gotten her safely out of the way, paid her off, and she never, ever had to see him again.

Someday, she told herself, *I won't even have to* think *of him again.*

But tonight wasn't that night, and she woke to nightmares over and over, tossing and turning until dawn.

"What a lovely little thing!" Louella Parsons exclaimed when they met the next morning, clapping her hands like an excited child given a sugary treat.

Lulu wasn't sure she liked being called a "thing." She looked shyly at the thick-boned woman with even but unexceptional features and a small but extravagant hat perched on her dark hair.

"Call me Lolly, dear," Mrs. Parsons said in her syrupy little-girl voice. "Everybody does."

Veronica gave Lulu a look behind Lolly's back that

clearly said people called her much, much worse when she wasn't listening. On the drive over to Lolly's house, Veronica had told Lulu how dangerous the gossip columnist could be. She might have made dozens of careers, but she'd ruined hundreds.

"Like whose?" Lulu had wanted to know.

"I could tell you their names, but you wouldn't know them—thanks to Louella. She's going to ask you about your past. Just make sure that if there's anything you don't want everyone to know, don't breathe a word to her. She might keep your secret for years, but if you ever cross her, your blackest deeds will come out." Veronica had laughed. Lulu could tell she didn't think the new young actress was capable of any deeds darker than pale gray.

Now Lulu held out her hand to the woman who might be an ally or adversary. Lolly didn't let her hand go, but tucked it under her arm and drew Lulu to a sofa. "Lulu and Lolly," the older woman said. "We could be sisters."

Lulu smiled, but Veronica made a choking sound she quickly covered with a loud cough.

"Now," Lolly continued, "tell me *all* about yourself."

A lie of omission wasn't really a lie, Lulu decided. She stuck scrupulously to the truth when talking about her family, telling about her shell-shocked father and hardworking mother, her no-good older brothers, and her innocent younger siblings.

"I knew I had to do something to help them," she said, beginning to veer from the righteous path. "So I did extra jobs on the side, scrimped and saved, and finally had enough money for a ticket to California." She opened her eyes wide and let her lips part softly, just as she had on the witness stand not long before. The judge had believed her. Maybe Lolly would too. "Since I got here, everyone has been so kind and helpful. Hollywood really is a magical place."

"Isn't it?" Lolly gushed. "And how clever of you to make such a fast start! Screen test to your first role in three days? I think we have a star on our hands, don't you, Veronica?" Lolly leaned in to Lulu and lowered her voice to a gooey squeak. "But tell me, just between us girls, didn't you have an eensy-weensy bit of help on the way? A girl as pretty as you has to have a boyfriend. Didn't he help you out, hmm? What's his name?"

"I . . . I don't . . . ," Lulu stammered.

"Off the record, of course." She mimed locking her lips with a key and tossing it away. Lulu noticed that even in pantomime, Lolly paid attention to where the imaginary key landed.

"I don't have a boyfriend," Lulu insisted. *All I have to do is not tell her*, she thought. *Why do I feel like a mouse under a cat's paw?*

Lolly dropped the girls-together act and narrowed her eyes. "Of course, only adolescents have *boyfriends*. Women like us have *lovers*."

"He wasn't my lover!" Lulu blurted out, then slapped her hand over her mouth . . . while Veronica slapped her forehead in exasperation.

Lolly sat back against the cushions, smug and satisfied. Strangely, she didn't seem inclined to pursue it any further. "Well, my dear, there's plenty of time for us to chitchat about that later. Now, on to business. I know who you *are*. Who do you want to be?"

There followed a conversation about Lulu's future in which Lulu herself played only a very minor role.

Veronica offered up her idea of a Swiss boarding school.

"But she can't speak French, and all Swiss-boarding-school girls speak French."

"Not Swiss?" Veronica asked.

"No, definitely French. MGM used that one for a little Cajun morsel last year, though I don't think girls from Swiss finishing schools eat crawdads with their fingers."

"We can use her real story," Veronica suggested.

Lolly cocked her head, pondering. "No. That will give young people the idea they can run away to Hollywood and save their families. It's bad enough as it is! We don't want to *give* people hope—we want to *sell* them a dream!"

In the end, the story they concocted was pure fantasy. Inspired by the Irish name and a trashy novel she'd recently read, Lolly decided to take Lulu's history back several thousand years.

"She can be a descendant of Étaín, or Isolde, or one of those old Irish beauties! Her ancestors were kings, and her great-grandfather was a chieftain, cruelly driven from his lands. Here in America her family made their fortune in . . . Oh, I don't know. That doesn't matter. Potatoes, I suppose."

"More likely they're bootleggers," Veronica interjected.

"We can hint at that. Very glamorous, very mysterious. Yes, so Lulu is a tempestuous Irish vixen. You know the type. Flashing eyes. Rides unbroken horses."

"I can't ride," Lulu said.

"Never mind that. We can tie you on an old gelding for a photo shoot. You'll be tied to plenty of old geldings in this business. Where was I? Oh yes. So your father sends you to an exclusive all-girls boarding school in Oregon, to remove you from all the temptation and fortune hunters of New York City. But you, free spirit that you are, couldn't take the uninterrupted company of your own sex and all those stodgy rules, so you stole a horse from the stables and rode all the way down to Los Angeles . . . where the head of Lux Studios spotted you, wild and lathered, on Hollywood Boulevard, and promptly offered you a contract."

"But will anyone believe that?" Lulu asked, incredulous.

"My dear," drawled Lolly, "my twenty million readers believe every damn thing I tell them."

When they left, Lulu—now expert horsewoman and Irish princess—asked Veronica if she'd done all right.

"You did fine," Veronica reassured her. "Don't worry about that slip about your boyfriend, whoever he might be. Everyone has a past."

"Will she try to find out who he is?" Lulu asked. "I mean, I don't have a boyfriend, but . . ."

Veronica laughed and held up her hand, stopping her.

"You don't have to tell me, kid. None of my business. But no, I don't think you'll have to worry. If you really get on her bad side, she might try to dig him up, but barring that, she'll assume he's just a boring banker or a fellow who owns a chain of drugstores. There's no story in that. As long as you're not shtupping Herbert Hoover or Al Capone, you should be safe from Lolly's investigations."

TWELVE

Adrenaline numbed Frederick's body and pushed him through the first mile of their escape.

"Is he dead?" Frederick asked Ben over and over again as they ran. "Did you kill him?"

"Not important," Ben answered him. "Past a certain point, it only matters that *you're* alive. Forget them. They were asking for it. They just didn't realize exactly what they were asking for."

"If he's alive and hurt, he needs help."

"You're not talking sense, boy. They was aiming to kill you. You don't have any obligation to think of their health and happiness."

Maybe Frederick had been hit in the head too hard, but he was filled with confusing and conflicting ideas of duty and obligation. Badness had to be stopped. Wrongs had to be put right. But people had to be helped too. He'd wanted to kill that man for killing his chicken . . . which he knew in his heart was foolish. The chicken was born to be eaten.

He stumbled, and Ben dragged him up again. "A little farther, youngster. Then you can rest."

Stop bad people . . . save good people . . . change bad to good . . .

It was a juvenile morality of black hats and white hats, of princes and scoundrels. Yet there was something at the heart of it, a simplicity that made it true.

At last Ben let him flop down in the tall grass. "I don't think anyone will come looking for us, but if they do, reckon they won't look here."

As soon as Frederick lay down, all the pain that had been kept at bay during his flight flooded back into him. His mind felt thick and cloudy, yet floating somehow.

"I have to fight," he muttered, rocking his head back and forth as sparks seemed to dance behind his eyelids.

"Easy there," Ben said, soothing him. "No one left to fight."

Deliriously, Frederick moaned, "Fight them all. Fight them, fight *for* them."

"Your head's still ringing, youngster. Close your eyes for a spell. Everything will be clearer come morning."

It was. When Frederick's eyes opened to the golden sun in a cloudless sky, he understood his future completely. Some-how—and he wasn't sure how—he would be a crusader.

It wasn't nearly enough to walk away from evil, as he had walked away from his father and his money. And it was wrong to let bad people get their way, even if it prevented pain, as he had tried to do when the two drifters in the barn demanded his money and his clothes. He realized it in that white-hot rage he'd felt at his hen's murder.

From now on, he decided grandiosely, *I will be a hero. I will always, always do the right thing, no matter how hard it is. I will help anyone who needs help, no matter what the consequences.*

As soon as Frederick could manage it, they wandered slowly across the desolate dusty fields, resting often, until they found another road. Ben's cough was worse, and he hobbled almost as painfully as Frederick. They were lucky enough to flag down a delivery truck, and for the price of one (almost) freshly killed chicken, the driver carried them to the next big town.

"I'm in bad shape, Ben," Frederick said when they climbed down from the truck. "I think my ribs are broken. It's getting a little hard to breathe."

"Nothing you can do for broken ribs 'cept rest them," Ben advised. "So let's find you a nice little alleyway to heal up in. I'll go look for a breadline or a job of work."

"But you can hardly walk yourself," Frederick protested.

Ben gave a wet cough but waved away his friend's objections. "You rest here. I'll bring you supper soon as I find any."

"Bless you, Ben," Frederick said weakly.

"Hogwash," Ben said, and hobbled off into the bustling city.

Frederick shifted his sore body onto a makeshift bed of newspaper in the alleyway and watched the world go by the thin wedge of his vista. It was a smartly paced town and looked like it had suffered a little less than other places. He thought he smelled the telltale pulp and sulfur scent of a paper mill. A paper factory would be enough to keep a town relatively prosperous.

Still, it was a far stretch from New York. The people he saw were all dressed in the louder, more boisterous cuts and colors of the twenties instead of the more sober hues of Depression austerity. Their clothes, slightly threadbare, still announced the promise of yesteryear—but only because they couldn't afford the clothes of the new dire reality.

Though he knew it would be a while before he was capable of hard labor, Frederick had high hopes for this town. Where were they? Colorado, maybe? From the glimpses he could catch of its citizens, it seemed like the kind of place that appreciated hard work and determination. *As soon as I don't look like one of Mugsy's opponents*, he thought, *I'll look around for a real job.*

He was still asleep when the police found him.

"What's your name, boy?" There were two of them, one hulking, one smaller with sergeant stripes, reminding him uncomfortably of the men he'd met last night. Were they here because of that? Did the man die?

He waited too long to answer, and the little one kicked his foot.

"Jack," he finally said. He should have worked out a fake

name before, but Ben hadn't pressed him, and no one else ever asked. Sonny, kid, youngster, mister . . . On the road it was like he was part of a club that welcomed you no matter who you were and didn't ask too many questions.

"You got anything to prove that, Jack?"

Of course he'd left all his identification behind: his passport, driver's license, club memberships. He thought of the cavalier way he used to whip out one of his cards, black writing with a touch of gold on heavy ivory stock. "Here you go, old man. Have your secretary call my butler and arrange a lunch."

"You answer when I'm talking to you," the sergeant said, low and dangerous. The bigger one didn't say anything, but the breadth of his shoulders spoke volumes.

"No," Frederick answered as politely as possible. "I don't have any identification."

"You a troublemaker? How'd you get so beat up? Someone catch you stealing a chicken, huh?" He spat on the ground next to Frederick's feet.

The mention of chicken riled him. He looked the sergeant defiantly in the eye. "I've never caused any trouble for anyone, sir. I'm simply looking for a job."

"Listen, boy, you get out of town, and you get out quick. This here's no place for a dirty, thieving bum like you. There ain't no work, and there ain't no breadline. There's only this." He pulled his truncheon from his belt and smacked it against his hand. *At least this one doesn't have nails in it*, Frederick thought.

"I'm just waiting for my friend," he told the sergeant. He was relieved. At least they weren't saying anything about last night's incident. "He's sick, and he needs my help. As soon as he comes back, I'll leave. I promise."

"You *promise*? You hear that, Moe? He *promises*. That's a laugh. Get walking." He shoved Frederick out of the alley-way. "Second thought, get running." He aimed a blow at Frederick's backside.

"I can't leave without my friend. He won't know where to find me."

"If you don't hightail it pronto, he'll find you in the hoosegow."

Ben was getting weaker by the day. Once Frederick's injuries healed, he planned to support Ben as best he could. "Just let me find my friend and I'll . . ."

The sergeant shoved Frederick against the wall and pressed his billy club to the side of his throat. The big one gave him a look that told him he better not dare resist. "That's it, boy," he growled, spittle flying onto Frederick's face. "A few days in chokey for you. And don't think it's all hot showers and free meals. We got us a chain gang going."

Suddenly the pressure on his throat was relieved. He saw Ben tugging at the officer's arm. "Can't you see the young-ster's hurt? Let him go!"

The big policeman didn't hesitate. He picked Ben up off the ground by the lapels of his coat and slammed him back down sideways on the pavement.

"Ben!" Frederick screamed, and lunged for his friend.

The officer rammed his truncheon into Frederick's stomach, and he doubled over.

"You want the old one too, Sarge?" Moe asked. Ben wasn't moving. He looked like a heap of rags someone had tossed out.

"Nah. He'll keel over on a chain gang. No work left in him. Throw him in the wagon and haul him to the city limits. He can be the next town's problem."

"I'll find you, Ben!" Frederick called as the officers locked cold metal handcuffs around his wrists and dragged him away. "I promise!"

Tell them, a voice screamed in Frederick's head. *Tell them!*

He longed to tell his jailers who he was. From the first humiliation, when he had been ordered to strip, was nearly drowned by a fireman's hose of freezing water, dusted with lice powder that burned his lungs, and given a set of over-sized black-and-white-striped prison clothes that smelled of mothballs, rats, and other people's sweat, to this last hour of his confinement, he had to fight himself not to win his freedom by confessing.

I'm a millionaire, he could tell them. It would be a lie, really, but only because he knew that to say "billionaire" would invite too much incredulity. *I'll give you a thousand dollars if you let me make a phone call.* Then Mugsy would fly in and set him free and he could get Ben to a proper hospital.

Frederick thought of his friend constantly. Where was Ben? Was he in trouble? His bad lungs had nearly done him in, and that attack from the policeman . . . What if Ben was unconscious? What if he was dead?

The months on the road had been hard, but his time in jail and working on the chain gang was something out of a nightmare. The random, malicious taunts and blows of the jail screws, the terrible nights lying awake on his cot, barely breathing, hearing but not seeing the things that were happening to other prisoners, hoping they wouldn't happen to him.

Now that he was free, the only thing on his mind was to find Ben. On the road he'd seemed hale and unstoppable, despite his hacking cough. But he'd looked so broken after the officer's assault. Could he have even made it to the next town? Frederick couldn't imagine traveling without Ben by his side. They were a team.

He trudged on, searching for his friend, the loose soles of his shoes slapping out a slow rhythm on the pavement. He found Ben at last in the next town. It took only a few inquiries among the street people to find out that a derelict old man spitting up blood had made camp in the lee of a trash bin behind the five-and-dime.

"Ben! What happened to you?" Frederick pulled his friend up by the shoulders from his bed of soggy newspaper. Ben groaned and tried to push him away.

"Can't . . . breathe."

Frederick eased him back gently, and Ben sucked in a shallow, wheezing gasp.

"See your ribs are healing all right, youngster," Ben

whispered. "Wish I could say the same for mine. Busted 'em when that copper tossed me. Ain't been the same since."

"One of the ribs might have punctured your lung," Frederick said. He felt Ben's forehead. It was burning hot. "You might have pneumonia. We have to get you to a doctor!"

"Can't locomote, I'm afeard."

"I'll carry you, then." But when Frederick tried to pick him up, Ben gave a thin, terrible wail of pain.

"Just leave me here, youngster. No good beating a dead horse. My days in the traces are done."

"No! You can't just give up, Ben. I'll find you a doctor. Wait right here!"

Ben managed a pathetic chuckle. "Don't aim to leave."

Ten minutes later, Frederick was pounding on a doctor's door. "Please, you have to come help my friend. He's dying!"

The doctor looked him over and started to shut the door. Frederick shoved his foot in the crack before it could close.

"Sorry," the doctor said, not unkindly. "I have five kids to support and the bank's getting antsy about my office mortgage. I can only take paying customers. You'll have to get him to the hospital in the next town. That's . . ."

"I know where it is." It was right across the street from the jail. "That's too far, and he can't walk. Can't you come look at him?"

"Do I have to call the sheriff?"

"Didn't you take an oath, Doctor? To help people?"

The doctor shoved the door harder, pinching Frederick's foot.

No, I can't do it, Frederick thought. *Not even for this.*

But it's Ben. Ben who helped me onto my first train. Ben who shared his mulligan. Ben who understood how I couldn't kill a chicken.

"I have money!" he blurted out. "A lot of money."

The doctor looked at him skeptically. "Show me," he demanded.

"I . . . I don't have it on me."

"Get out of here, boy."

"I can send all of your kids to college. I swear—anything you want. Just please help my friend."

"Did you escape from the asylum? Scram!" The doctor managed to push Frederick's foot out of the way and slammed the door shut.

Frederick pounded with both hands. "I'm rich, do you hear me?" He was screaming like a lunatic. People on the street stopped to watch. "I'm Frederick Preston Aloysius van der Waals, son of Jacob van der Waals, and I can buy this whole stinking town! Open up, damn you! I can make you a millionaire—just help my friend!" He kicked at the door.

"What are you looking at?" he screamed to the gaping pedestrians. "Someone better help my friend, or I'll buy every single one of your houses and turn them into manure farms!" He raged on, cursing and screaming at everyone he saw. Tears were running down his face as he turned and raced back to Ben.

His friend was near the end. He was still breathing, barely, but his fever was gone, and his body was growing unnaturally cold. Fleas that had been living in his beard began to hop off, believing him already dead.

"I told them who I am, Ben," Frederick wept, clutching his friend's hand. "No one believed me."

"Who *are* you, then?" Ben asked softly, his eyes cracking open with mild curiosity, showing a glint of his old self.

"I'm rich. I'm a billionaire. I told the doctor, but he wouldn't believe me. He wouldn't come help you. I could buy an entire hospital! But I can't save you." Frederick buried his face in his hands.

After a moment he felt Ben touch him on the shoulder. "Don't need . . . savin'," he gasped out. "Just need . . . a friend . . . on the journey."

His hand fell away, and his last breath escaped in a sigh.

"Ben," Frederick whispered. "Oh, Ben . . ."

PART THREE

HOLLYWOOD, CALIFORNIA 1932

THIRTEEN

L ulu! Hey, baby face! Turn that blond head of yours toward the camera," the director, Ira Sassoon, shouted into his bullhorn.

For a moment the pretty young girl in the middle of the set didn't respond. Even after a year in Hollywood, she still wasn't completely used to being either Lulu Kelly or something as exotic as a platinum blonde. At her core she was still a child of a Lower East Side tenement, a gangly girl mocked for being all elbows and knees. Back then, her silvery corn-silk hair was called "towhead," and it wasn't considered an asset. Now her coltish form had rounded in all the right places, and they called her fair hair platinum blond. If she hadn't been born with it, Hollywood would have given it to her in a bottle.

Lulu, she reminded herself. *I'm Lulu Kelly.*

The director had to yell her name again before she snapped out of her daze. "You look a little peaked," Sassoon said. "Do you need Docky to give you a little pick-me-up?"

Docky was Dr. Martin, the studio physician.

"No thanks," she said, shuddering inwardly. She'd heard stories about Docky and his pick-me-up pills. She flashed the director her megawatt smile and turned her heart-shaped face with its alluring dark blue eyes toward the camera.

Then the Hollywood machine began to whir.

Lois, her favorite makeup assistant, dabbed away the shine caused by the sweltering studio lights. A nervous new stylist named Stanley smoothed the Marcelled waves of her bobbed hair. An impatient wardrobe assistant twitched the hem of her silvery Schiaparelli gown until it hung perfectly. Then, after they'd done their work and been shooed away by the assistant director, Sassoon barked, "Action!" and the familiar hush fell over the set as Lulu transformed herself.

It took only an instant, but the change was perceptible to everyone watching. One moment she was just a girl playing dress-up. The next she was someone else. With a subtle shift somewhere inside her that reflected plainly on her face, she'd become Jezebel March, the wild society flapper tamed by the love of a good man in the film adaptation of the scandalous hit novel *Girl About Town.*

Never mind that her leading man stank like an ashtray and wore more makeup than she did. Never mind that her high heels hurt and she'd barely eaten or slept and she'd be expected to shine at a studio party that night until the wee morning hours. When filming began, she entered another world. It was a kind of ecstasy, she thought, a sort of wild abandon and ultimate control all at the same time. She became another person and in doing so became utterly *herself*, because she was the one making it happen. Lulu threw her entire soul, every ounce of her passion, into playing Jezebel.

Mostly because she loved it. But also because if *Girl About Town* wasn't a hit, Lux Studios might cancel her contract. Then—even though she'd had her picture in *Photoplay* nine times so far—she feared she'd be quickly kicked to the curb and forgotten. Veronica hadn't minced words when describing the fates of the many girls who had come (and mostly gone) before her. The astonishing amount of early publicity Lulu had been given had earned her the animosity of many of her peers, mostly the other young contract actresses, and they would ensure that if she ever fell, she'd fall hard. Every budding starlet was only one bomb away from oblivion.

A year ago everyone had assumed that she had a rich, influential backer pushing her to stardom. It had certainly looked like that. Sure, the girl had chops, they said, but doors *open* that fast only when there's funny business going on behind *closed* doors. But no sugar daddy had ever emerged; no benefactor had stepped forward to share her limelight. She'd been given a good push at the start, but now she was on her own.

At least, Lulu desperately hoped she was. The alternative

would be too terrible. She hadn't heard a word from Salvatore Benedetto since her train pulled into LA, and that's the way she wanted to keep it. He was the reason she could send five hundred dollars to her mother every month. He was the reason her name was on everyone's lips as the next It Girl. But he was also the reason she still slept with nightmares and woke up with a gnawing sense of guilt and apprehension every morning. It was no wonder she cherished every opportunity to inhabit someone else's life, if only under the camera lens.

The character Lulu played had picked up a mangy mutt from a trash heap on a dare and was going to make a pet of it. Every film had a dog or a baby—they both really brought in the crowds. In this scene she was blind drunk and braying to her costar that "life was for living!" With fire in her eyes and ice in her heart, she swore she'd live hers any way she liked. In the current script, faithfully adapted from the novel, her costar was supposed to stalk away, leaving her alone with her mangy dog and a bottle of gin, collapsing in an angry puddle of tears. Later, after the dog bit her on the face and ruined her good looks, he would ask her, "You need someone to take care of you?" Cue earnest, manly look. "You're my angel!" Then he'd take the reformed jazz baby into his arms, her eyes full of grateful tears, his full of strength and resolve. Fade-out. *The End.*

What a bunch of hooey. Why did everyone think that all a woman needed was a strong man to take care of her? It was just another great Hollywood lie. But it sold tickets, so the lie would be told over and over again as long as it was profitable.

Except the scene wasn't working. Oh, Lulu was spot-on, her tears unfeigned, her anger real, despite her problems with the script. Even her costar's overacting and annoying mannerisms didn't ruin the scene. No, the problem was that the dog was just too cute.

The audience was supposed to understand why the hero saw it as an ugly metaphor for Jezebel's compulsions and predict the dreadful consequences awaiting the distraught heroine. But every dog they tried stole the show, and though they were excellent actors, enthusiastically shaking hands or playing dead, none of them could muster up the necessary menace.

They'd auditioned all sorts of dogs, sending out a universal canine casting call. They thought a bull terrier might work, but unfortunately, he had a floppy ear that made him well-nigh irresistible. A huge German shepherd with gleaming teeth had a snarl that looked like a grin in a toothpaste commercial and was impossibly noble. The chow's blue tongue lolled as if he were tipsy, and the Samoyed resembled a fashionable muff.

Today they went for small and mean. A raffish wirehaired terrier had been rolled in the mud until he looked sufficiently disreputable. Lulu was sure he would work. The dog had this disconcerting way of cocking his head and narrowing his eyes, as if he could see into her soul and wasn't quite sure he liked what he found there.

But just as she was really getting into the part, Sassoon yelled, "Cut!" and she let the dog slither out of her arms. He nosed at her ankles hopefully but was dragged off by his handler.

Lulu heard feverish discussion around the director's chair. Sassoon was red-faced and scowling. She caught snatches of muttered conversation: "supposed to be a mangy mutt" . . . "smart aleck" . . . "those eyes."

Lulu walked over. "What's wrong this time?" she asked.

"The damned dog's a ham," Sassoon said, exasperated. "He has *eyebrows*. Are dogs supposed to have eyebrows? The whole time you're delivering your passionate speech about how no one can put a leash on you, he's waggling his eyebrows like a dirty old man lurking outside the schoolyard. He stole the scene. All of the takes are useless. Can the dog! Can *all* dogs. Harry!" A frazzled assistant rushed to the director's side. "Get the script doctors, pronto."

Lulu rubbed her temples. A rewrite. That could mean an extra week of filming, maybe more. Lulu was frustrated because a plum role was being cast this week, set to begin filming in three weeks, and if *Girl About Town* wasn't wrapped by then, Lulu didn't have a chance. And *that* wasn't going to happen.

Girl About Town was her biggest role so far. Hers was the lead name on the marquee. After her first lucky break, she had won a measure of fame playing little sisters. She'd died prettily twice. In her latest film, in quite a big role but still second fiddle, she played a coquette just out of finishing school who sets her cap at the man her sister is secretly engaged to.

Now, finally, she was the lead, a spoiled rich girl behaving badly, a million miles away from her true background. It was a good role, a fun frolic that would probably do well and give Lulu's career the boost it needed. When she first came to Hollywood, that was all she cared about—getting a good part that would pay well and lead to the next good role. But now that she'd been bitten by the acting bug, now that she knew she had real talent, good wasn't good enough anymore. She wanted *great*.

The House of Mirth was that once-in-a-lifetime part that would showcase her talent and put her on top. She felt it in her bones. Even though the country was in the terrible grip of the Depression and unemployment was at an all-time high, seventy million people each week were still willing to hand over their fifteen precious cents to escape reality in a darkened movie theater. *The House of Mirth* had it all: tortuous choices between love and money, between honor and position. It had adultery, betrayal, and tragic death—the dramatic trifecta.

When Lulu played a wealthy good-time girl, she was acting. But if she could play a girl torn between a poor but good life and filthy lucre, she wouldn't have to act. She would *be* the part. Lulu knew all about that ultimate test of morals.

The well-oiled efficiency of the set dissolved as soon as the director left. Grips rolled the lights away, and extras retreated to the corners to smoke and gossip.

Lulu's costar, Blake Tanner, sidled up to her. He was nice enough, if a bit vapid—a big man in his early twenties, with a square chin and a smooth voice, who gave good face to the movie rags. He had a habit of delivering all of his lines with an earnest wrinkle between his eyebrows, which some people mistook for good acting.

"Heard a tasty little tidbit on the rumor mill," Blake said.

"That mill never stops turning, does it?" Lulu said with annoyance.

"My dear, that's what fame is. When the rumors end, you're no longer famous. You can only keep your secrets when no one cares about them anymore."

Lulu gave a little shudder. No one would ever discover what she'd done . . . would they? No, it was impossible. Only one other person knew the truth, and there was no way he was talking.

"Who's it about?" she asked.

"You, baby face. Word is you're going to be developing a passionate romantic interest in the near future. Here's hoping it's with me. Dolly's due for a sleep cure, so she'll be in a coma for two weeks waiting for the pounds to melt off. I'll be a free agent." He winked at her. Dolly was a dancer on the Lux payroll, and Blake's official tabloid girlfriend at the moment. "If you like, I'll have a word with Sassoon and Niederman and see if we can swing it. It would be great publicity."

"No thanks. I prefer to make my own mistakes." And since she said it with a sweet smile, she was long gone before he figured out she might have insulted him.

Like I'd let that off-the-cob clown so much as pitch the woo in my direction, she thought, furious. But that was the Hollywood way—it was what she'd signed on for.

For a while they had let her be the ingénue, a wide-eyed innocent. Her fresh face had stood alone. But now, a year later—an eternity by Hollywood standards—they were ready to pair her off to add to her allure. She wasn't expected to love whomever they chose. She hardly had to see him, outside of photo opportunities. But she had to accept it or have her contract torn up. If that happened, she'd go from making a small fortune each month to living with her folks again. Despite her best efforts, the lavish lifestyle Hollywood demanded of her seemed to eat up her money. If she were to fail . . . she hoped she'd be brave enough to sink low again. But she was afraid she might have gotten too used to luxury.

No, she swore as she sought out a quiet corner of the set. *I'll make it. I swear I will.*

Her corner wasn't quiet for long.

A girl with big green eyes and a tip-tilted nose walked up to Lulu with feline elegance. "I don't think the problem is the dog," she said. "It's you, *extra*." In the acting world, that was a serious insult.

"Ruby Godfrey, you wouldn't know good acting if it socked you in the snoot." Lulu balled up her slender little hand. "And it's just about to."

She had the satisfaction of seeing Ruby back up a pace. She and Ruby had both been up for the starring role in *Girl*

About Town. But all Ruby got was the part of one of Lulu's friends, one of a gaggle of flighty, gay society frails. Lulu had to admit that Ruby was a good actress. She just had a habit of getting on the wrong side of people. And, Lulu thought grimly, of seducing the wrong men.

Lulu hadn't breathed a word about certain things she'd witnessed, but word had gotten out anyway, and Ruby considered her a sworn enemy. It seemed like losing the part was the last straw in their relationship. Now Ruby was furious, and she harassed Lulu on the set with constant digs.

"You've got a big mouth, tootsie," Ruby spat. Then the girl's eyes narrowed maliciously. "In fact, I heard your *big mouth* is what got you the part." She sniggered. "Everyone knows you're a casting-couch girl."

"Why you . . . ," Lulu fumed.

"Check your lipstick, toots," Ruby sneered, and walked off with a wiggle.

The slum child within Lulu longed to grab her rival by the hair and pull it out by the roots. *But I'm better than that,* she told herself, and took a deep breath, then another. *At least, I am now.* A couple of the extras had heard the exchange. *Peachy,* she thought. *Now the magazines will report that we're feuding.* Gossip columnist Lolly was still firmly on her side, but other tabloids would take whatever their sources gave them. What clever headline would they use? "Starlets Start Spiteful Spat?"

She watched Ruby perch on a chair, checking her face in the mirror of her ever-present compact. She'd never seen someone so in love with her own face. And in this town, that was saying something.

Just then Sassoon called them all back.

"Everyone can break for today and take the next two days off." There were groans from the extras, who were paid only for the days they worked. "We might be off another week, but keep your schedules open in case I call you all back early."

"What's the holdup?" Lulu asked, managing (thanks to Mrs. Wilberforce's deportment lessons) to sound sweet despite her impatience. She'd never have a shot at *The House of Mirth* now. True, with the days off she could make the audition more easily, but once they heard she wouldn't be finished with this dumb flick on time, they'd pick someone else. Probably Ruby Godfrey, who had only two more scenes to shoot and would be done long before Lulu.

"We nixed the dog. But the script doctors had a brilliant solution: Instead of a pooch, Jezebel will pick up a fella. A regular street rat, a down-on-his-luck petty thief whom she wants to reform."

"So now this fella will be the one to bite me?" she asked wryly.

"They're still working that out. He's blackmailing you, he's a gigolo, he tries to steal your beloved grandmother's pearls, Lord knows. But in the end, a knife comes out and you get carved up." Lulu heard Ruby snort with laughter. "Elegantly carved up, of course. Can't have our star disfigured, even with putty and paint."

"You have the story line laid out," Lulu said as persuasively as she could. "Do you really have to wait a week?"

"We have to find the fella," Sassoon said. "I figure we get someone authentic. The streets are teeming with good-looking indigents. It can be a publicity stunt—studio picks bum for bum part, changes his life, that kind of thing. So tomorrow I'll send a scouting crew out, and maybe by the end of the week we can start shooting again."

"Tomorrow?" she asked, aghast. "I could find you someone in an hour and get him coached and ready in three. Give me a loaf of bread, let them fight over it on the dole line, and the winner gets the part."

"It's not as simple as that," Sassoon said. "You can't just pluck a star out of the gutter. We have to audition them, train them. . . ."

I was plucked out of the gutter, Lulu wanted to protest. But even on the set, even with Sassoon, she was supposed to maintain the charade that she was a cheeky finishing-school runaway. "Tell you what," she said. "Don't break for the day. Break for an hour. When I come back, I'll have the perfect fella for you. You just see if I don't." She stalked off, pulling the set door violently open, letting a shocking beam of real sunlight into that artificial world. Then the door slammed behind her.

The handsome young man in the pin-striped suit missed Lulu by minutes. He strolled up to the guard shack, his meaty hands loose, his eyes hard.

"Sorry, sir," the guard said. "This is a closed set."

The man with the suspicious bulge under his exquisitely tailored jacket handed the guard a bill. It had the right number of zeros. "Nothing's closed to me," the man said, and asked where Mr. Niederman's office might be.

FOURTEEN

Frederick had been traveling nonstop ever since Ben's death. He'd abandoned the steady westward progression he and his friend had been pursuing and simply peregrinated around the continent, surviving. Shortly after Ben had been tossed ignominiously into a pauper's grave at the outskirts of town, Frederick had a scare. Needing something to stuff into his shoe to fill the hole in his sole, he'd snatched a three-day-old newspaper that had been tumbleweeding on the breeze . . . and saw his own face on the front page.

The photo had been faded by the sun, but he recognized it immediately. It had been taken at a gala benefiting the Metropolitan Opera. He stood smugly in his sleek white tie, a Young Turk with the world at his feet.

The photo disgusted him. But beneath the disgust was an ache. Would his happiness have lasted if he'd never been enlightened as to the terrible truth of his fortune? He longed for that blissful ignorance, Adam in Eden.

He read the article, and his chest began to feel tight. "Beloved son of tycoon Jacob van der Waals . . . missing, presumed endangered . . . kidnapped . . . amnesia . . ." Anything but the truth, that he had fled everything his family stood for. There was a quote from his father. "Whoever has taken my son, I promise you won't be arrested or charged if you just release him or deliver him to the nearest hospital or police station. If you come forward, you will be rewarded. If you prefer to remain anonymous, I will never hunt for you. Only return my son."

Does he really think I've been kidnapped? Frederick wondered. No, he had to know what really happened. How had Jacob van der Waals explained Mr. Shaw's death? What lawyers, what criminals had he called to sweep that blood, and guilt, under the rug? There was no mention of it in the article, of course.

The article went on to say that anyone who provided information leading to Frederick's recovery could be eligible for a reward of up to half a million dollars. That phrasing brought a rueful chuckle. It was so lawyerly that it promised nothing. "Could" be eligible . . . "up to" half a million. Even if someone caught him and brought him home, his father would never pay.

Why, now that he understood what his father was capable

of, Frederick thought he might even make anyone who helped his son simply disappear. Frederick shuddered. It had happened before, and in his innocence he hadn't realized who must have been behind it. A man who owned the corner store of a commercial block Jacob wanted to buy conveniently fell into an elevator shaft after months of refusing to sell. When city officials couldn't be bribed into razing a historic building that sat on land Jacob coveted, the building conveniently burned to the ground, along with seven residents.

Frederick skimmed the rest of the article. "Mr. van der Waals has an army of private investigators searching for his son." Frederick would expect nothing less. The next lines chilled him:

> The young man has been spotted by reliable sources at numerous points around the country. A railroad guard in Pittsburgh saw him in the company of what appeared to be a hardened criminal, possibly a drug fiend. And only yesterday, a vest bearing his initials was discovered in a decrepit barn about a hundred miles outside of Wichita, Kansas. There was blood on the floor and signs of a desperate struggle. People for miles around are being interrogated as van der Waals's private investigators swarm to the locale.

They were close! Before Frederick could even read the last paragraph, which he dimly saw had a quote from Violet, he had folded the newspaper, shoved it into his shoe, and run as fast as he could. It didn't matter where. *Away* was enough.

Only later had he wondered what Violet might have had to say about his disappearance. Late that night he had pulled the newspaper out of his shoe and tried to read the last few sentences. But they had been worn away by sweat and dirt, and the single word he could read of her statement to the press was "money."

After that scare, Frederick had never stopped moving. Even when he wasn't heading west, every step seemed to take him farther from his old home. He'd settled into a mostly solitary routine of begging, breadlines, and occasional work. It was penance for almost eighteen years of crime. The crime hadn't been his, but he'd benefited from it all the same, and in his eyes that made him just as culpable as his father.

Frederick was lonely, deeply, deeply lonely. He kept to himself as much as possible lest someone recognize him. He hadn't seen a mirror for months, but he hoped that by now nothing of his old self showed in his face or manners. Still, he couldn't risk it, and often he went for days without talking to another human being. Sometimes as he fell asleep in an alleyway or the lee of a dry stone wall, he thought he heard Duncan Shaw's irrepressible laugh. Frederick would be half on his feet before he realized it was only the call of some distant night bird and remember he'd lost Duncan's friendship forever. Then in the morning he would be jostled awake by a constable's boot and smile for that fleeting instant when his bleary brain believed it might be Ben.

I couldn't save either of them, he thought. *What good am I?*

Solitude, anonymity—that was what he thought he deserved. But his gregarious soul called out for a friend, if only so he could have another chance and prove he wouldn't let everyone down.

Almost by accident, Frederick found himself in California. Someone had told him there might be jobs in New Mexico, so he'd hopped a train, thinking he might even cross the border to *old* Mexico, continue south, and get lost among jungles and revolutionaries. But he'd slept through the unloading and had then been locked in the sweltering car until it reached California. He'd been found by one of the rare sympathetic railroad bulls, who got him a drink of water and told him he wouldn't arrest him because dehydration was enough of a punishment for train hopping.

California would do for now, but the Pacific called him. In almost every paper he scavenged from the street, he found another article about the missing van der Waals boy. They didn't seem to be getting any closer, but they were still looking. Maybe it wasn't enough to have a mere continent between him and his old life. He could strike out for China, for India. A continent *and* an ocean or two dividing them might be sufficient to convince Frederick that his father had no hold over him. Not anymore.

Frederick had exactly five cents to his name now. He was saving that in case he wanted to make a call on a pay phone one day. He still wasn't sure whom he was going to call. His father, to demand an explanation? Or maybe the

Department of Justice, to turn his father in. Or Violet, to tell her she was free to marry someone else. Maybe Mugsy, the other person his heart ached for, the man who was so much more of a father than his real father had ever been.

Frederick would never call the van der Waals's family lawyer, James Cox, Esq., to ask him to wire the latest dividends of his massive trust fund. Nothing on earth would induce him to touch that money again. There was more than a hundred million cash in his own name, safe in a bank that had never failed, and another ten million in bullion locked in an impregnable vault. He had acres of citrus groves in Florida, an oil well in Texas, grain fields and a bottling company in Canada, a house on the Hudson, a hotel in Bermuda, all his by inheritance from his mother, or placed in his name for tax purposes by his father. He hadn't touched a penny of it. Not when he'd gone two days without eating. Not even when he'd seen a train full of orphans kicked out of their car in the middle of nowhere because they hadn't been given enough fare to ship them all the way to their new orphanage in Chicago.

He'd arrived in California three weeks ago and had drifted into Los Angeles last week. In the countryside he'd found occasional day labor, and he'd scavenged for wild plants and snared rabbits for stew. But here in Los Angeles there were no rabbits, and the weeds that grew in cracks between the pavement were all unfamiliar. He'd thought California would be a paradise—that's what the other men of the road said. But where he'd hoped to find oranges free for the picking, he found only more people, less work.

In place of jobs there was charity, much more than in the nation's heartland. He wasn't sure why Los Angeles seemed to take slightly better care of its poor than other places did. Maybe, he thought with a snobbish vestige that shamed him, the poor here were of a higher class. In rural America, displaced people were farmers whose land had died under the dust bowl, or factory workers who had barely scraped by even in the best of times. They moved in search of anything, to feed themselves and their families for one more day.

The poor people in Los Angeles, though, had come full of dreams. They didn't just want to survive—they hoped for meteoric success. When Frederick found a breadline that day, he met four aspiring actors, a dancer, a piano player, an elocution instructor, and a history professor who hoped to consult for studios. There were fast-talking young men who hoped to be agents, clever women who wanted to be publicists.

As he neared the front of the line, he spied a platinum-haired woman in a three thousand dollar dress, no doubt a star or socialite come to dispense charity. Was she born into it, or had she clawed her way to the top? His money—if he'd had any—was on the latter. That was why there was so much charity here in Los Angeles, and in Hollywood in particular. All of these people knew how lucky they were. So many of them came from nothing and caught a break, so they understood the poor, the desperate. *They might enjoy their wealth, and flaunt it, just like my father does back in Manhattan, but they give it away, too.* His father could not even imagine what it must be like to have no money, no prospects. But these Hollywood people could.

FIFTEEN

*I*t *must have been Satan* *himself who invented high heels*, Lulu thought as she minced along the pavement between huge warehouselike sound stages to catch one of the many studio cars waiting to chauffeur their stars. She felt like a prisoner in her pinching, pointy—though admittedly elegant—shoes and her skintight dress of silver lamé. She was picturing a huge clock ticking down a deadline until her missed opportunity when she heard a yip, and a thud, and a whine from around the corner of the commissary.

Curiosity had gotten her into trouble before. That other time, the cry had been human, and this one was obviously canine. But they were similar, somehow, filled with the helpless knowledge that something terrible was coming and there was absolutely no hope of escape.

She hesitated at the corner of the dark alley, chewing her lip in a way that would have made her makeup artist, Max, give her a stern lecture. She heard a curse, a kick, and the unseen dog gave another yowl.

Before she even knew what she was doing, she was running down the alley—blisters be damned—and had grabbed a big man by the shoulder. "If you kick that dog again, I'll . . . I'll . . ."

She broke off. What could she do? The last time she'd cowered in the face of threats. Not this time. She lifted her chin defiantly.

"Back off, toots," the man said. "I been giving this mutt meat I could have fed to my kids, thinking he'd be a star. But ten auditions and the lazy cur ain't got one role." He aimed another kick at the little muddy shadow cringing at his feet, but Lulu used all her strength to pull him back, and he missed. "Guy sold him to me said he'd earn his weight in gold, if only I fed him right and took him to casting. Well, he's sucked down his last slice of liver. First I ax the fleabag, and then I track down the fraud who sold him to me."

"Stop! You can't do that!"

"Says who?" The man looked down at the little dog and lifted his big boot. Lulu shoved him as hard as she could, and when the man raised his arm to backhand her, she quickly slid a bracelet off her wrist.

"Here, take this. It's worth ten times what that dog costs."

"You on the level, lady?" he asked, examining the platinum links, the winking little rubies.

She nodded.

"If the pawnshop tells me this is a fake, I'm coming back to find you." He scowled at her, then glanced down at the dog. "Looks like you earned me some cash after all, pooch," he said, and reached out his hand to pat the dog's head. He retreated with a curse, blood dripping from his palm.

Lulu suppressed a titter. "Scram, before I call security," she said with fraudulent cool. Which, now that she thought of it, would have been the best thing to do in the first place.

"You scram, too," she told the dog when the man was gone. There would surely be some other sucker who would give him a good home. The dog seemed inclined to engage in a silent staring competition with her until she felt compelled to explain her situation to the animal. "I've got to find a diamond in the rough I can polish up in an hour and get back to shooting."

The dog gave a skeptical bark and cocked his head at her. She gave him a closer look. "Oh, foot! It's you." It was the ham, the wire-haired terrier with the knowing eyes. She reached down and let him sniff her knuckles, then jerked her hand away. "No sir, you aren't going to bamboozle me. I know a sharp when I see one. You need an owner. Fine. Trot off and find some other sucker, because it ain't going to be me. The last thing I need is a dog."

He barked again, plainly saying he begged to differ.

She huffed off, embarrassed at carrying on a conversation with a dog. Even one who gave every indication of listening and understanding.

As she strode away, she heard the clatter of nails on the pavement behind her and turned to see the little dog trotting after her. He plopped down on his haunches and wagged his short tail so fast it was a blur.

"I don't want a dog," she told him sternly. The golden-brown tufts of hair above his eyes twitched. Dogs might not have eyebrows, but this one sure *thought* he did.

She started walking again and sighed at the sound of little paws trotting after her. "I'll give you one thing, mutt— you're loyal. Okeydoke. I saved you and you're grateful. You can follow me if you want to. You're your own man now. Go wherever you like. But I'm not feeding you."

She leaned over and patted his fur before taking his small face in her hands. He bared his teeth at her in a canine grin. "You think I'm a softie, don't you?" she said as she fondled his ears. They flopped forward, looking like the corners of a library book that's been checked out too many times. "It's no use licking my hand. You might be with me, but you're not my dog."

But she smiled when she got into the studio fleet car and the dog hopped in beside her and lay down with his chin on her lap. Loyalty and gratitude were equally hard to come by in Hollywood. She'd better take them where she could get them.

"Where to, miss?" the driver asked.

"Where's the nearest breadline?"

He thought she was joking, but at last agreed to take her to a place where the Salvation Army handed out two meals a day. "I'll get a ticket if I park here," he said as they neared, "so I'll drive around the block. Be careful," he cautioned. "They're an unsavory crowd."

"They're just poor," Lulu said hotly. "That doesn't make them bad."

"It does, some of them," the driver countered. "It drives them to do things a comfortable person might shrink from."

Lulu hesitated, then stepped out of the car with conviction.

She was immediately greeted by an onslaught of wolf whistles. Too late, she realized that she was still wearing her costume from the set, and the slinky silver lamé clung provocatively to her curves, completely inappropriate for daylight. Coupled with her coiffed hair and her too-heavy stage makeup, it made her look like a street walker, or at best, a lost and sauced party girl.

The little dog yipped and gazed up at her questioningly as she hesitated by the car. "You're right," she told the little dog, "I should have put on a coat. I always have the best ideas too late."

The soup kitchen was well off the main strip, in a dim corner where glittering stars and tourists with money to spend didn't have to be offended. *The poor make the rich uncomfortable*, she thought. She could feel her own guilt welling as she slowly walked past the congregation of down-and-outs on the breadline. They were mostly men, but there were families, too, and old women, and ragged children. For a heartbeat Lulu thought what her income could do for them. How many could she help, if she made a few sacrifices? She could still send enough home to her folks, have a decent place to live. She'd just have to give up her maid, her rented Spanish-Revival-style house with its lovely courtyard and colorful tile work. . . .

No. I earned it, fair and square. Well, maybe not on the square, but I did something unpleasant, and here I am, successful. It was work—grueling work.

She looked them over with a critical eye, not letting herself think about how hard they might have struggled, what they might have suffered. There were plenty of young men on the breadline. They'd probably come to California full of dreams just like people had eighty years before, during the California gold rush, lured by the promise of dazzling success. Maybe a few had found it, but most had unearthed only poverty and failure, like the rest of America. There simply weren't enough jobs, no matter how hard a person was willing to work.

They were a rough lot, dirty and foul smelling. Lulu tried to see beyond the grime and despair to their faces, but it was difficult. None of them looked remotely promising on first glance. It wasn't that he had to be particularly handsome. She thought of Wallace Beery or Edward G. Robinson. No, a man didn't have to be a knockout, but he *did* have to have something else in his face—a spark, a vitality, and preferably a little bit of mystery. Something that made people look at him, and look again, and not want to stop.

None of these men had it. They only made Lulu want to look away. Their faces were gray, forgettable, all similar in their creased and grimy despondency. They were the faces of men without fight left in them.

No, wait—there was one young man who caught her eye. Near twenty, with a shock of untrimmed black hair, the prominent brow ridges of a dashing Neanderthal, and a chiseled chin made to take a punch, he positively seethed. One of the other shabby men jostled him from behind, and the fellow turned on him with a cold, fierce look, a dangerous half smile, making the man back off with a stuttered apology. Oh yes, there was fight left in this one.

Lulu considered the character Sassoon had decided on to replace the dog. He had to be young, good-looking enough to attract a society belle, with a touch of sympathy and a hefty portion of menace. This one had the looks, like Valentino with a hangover, and menace by the bucketload. If he had half an ounce of smarts, Sassoon could train him up to his part and *Girl About Town* could resume filming that afternoon. She walked up to him.

"Hey, mister," she said, gently tugging on his ragged jacket sleeve.

He shook her off roughly without looking at her. "Back of the line, muffin."

"Excuse me?" Lulu asked indignantly.

The man turned, and the way he looked her up and down made her really wish she'd remembered to grab a coat. "A hot buttered muffin, at that. But you still can't cut in the line. I haven't eaten since yesterday. Stick around, baby doll, and I might have something for you after chow." He winked at her, and though it made her feel profoundly uncomfortable, she also decided he had enough charisma to fill a seventy-foot screen with ease.

"You don't understand," Lulu began, speaking quickly and forcing herself to keep calm. "I might have a job for you. An opportunity for a . . . a man such as yourself. You'll be fed and paid, all for a little bit of work that I promise you won't find too onerous."

He took in the spangles at her wrist and throat, the clinging silver gown that flowed over her form like water. "What kind of work?" he asked in a gravelly rumble.

Her patience fled, and she felt the slum girl in her emerge. "What do you care?" she snapped at him as she would have to a fresh newsboy. "You're a bum without visible means of support!" For a second she felt horribly guilty . . . but he put a quick end to that.

He leered at her and stepped closer. "Looks to me you've got no visible means of support under that dress."

She gasped and stepped back a pace. She wanted to slap him; she wanted to run away. But she needed to get *Girl About Town* wrapped. Her whole career depended on it. Swallowing her nerves, her anger, she said, "Do you want the job or not? If you do, follow me." She stalked off with a false air of confidence, looking for her driver, and was relieved to hear not only the dog's tip-tapping claws, but the slap of the man's broken-soled shoes following. If she could just get him to the studio!

Before she got very far, she felt a gentle hand on her shoulder. She whirled, but it wasn't the man she'd hired. It was another man, no more than her own age, seventeen. He'd broken out of the queue, losing his place to trot after her. She'd considered him briefly in the lineup but had rejected him immediately. Under his filth was a handsome face, certainly, but it was soft, innocent, kind. Not at all what she was looking for.

"I wouldn't go with him if I were you," the boy said.

"Sorry," she said shortly. "I'm only hiring one, and you're not my type."

"He's not what you need," the young man said.

"I don't mean to be rude, but please mind your own beeswax. I'm a big girl, and I know what I need." The lead in *The House of Mirth*. Lulu took her new costar's arm and began to walk away again. She looked over her shoulder. The young man was still watching her, making indecisive movements, as if he meant to follow. He really was extraordinarily good-looking under his dirt. But there was no way he could ever attack someone, and that's what this new character had to do. Still, with that mug . . . "Stop by Central Casting and tell them I sent you," she called. Maybe he could get a part as an extra.

They strode away, leaving the young man behind. Where was that darned car?

Lulu dropped his arm as soon as they were alone. "Now, mister," she began.

"Rocco."

"It *would* be. Now, then, Mr. Rocco, when we get where we're going, will you please just do exactly as you're told?"

She turned up the charm as Mrs. Wilberforce had taught her and looked up at him hopefully.

He smiled at her, which she took as a good sign until she realized he was looking down her dress. She gulped and put a little more distance between them, but Rocco took her elbow and pulled her tightly against his side.

"Relax, baby. I'm a pro. I'm gonna take you somewhere you've never been before."

"What? Who's writing your dialogue?" She tried to pull away, but he turned the corner sharply, jerking her with him. "Hold it right there. You've got the wrong idea."

"I know you can't wait to get me to your place, but let me give you a little taste of what's in store for you, on the house." He pushed her against the wall of the shadowed alleyway and kissed her.

For just a second, before she realized what was happening, her body responded, filling with a thrilling warmth. She'd had film kisses galore, but she'd never been taken passionately in someone's arms for real. The length of his body pressed against hers, and his lips were fiercely sweet, demanding.

Then her brain caught up with her body, and she shoved him away and slapped him as hard as she could.

Rocco rubbed his cheek, looking more amused than angry. "I can play that game, sister," he said. "But for that I charge extra. And now that we've brought up the subject of money . . ."

Her chest rising and falling fast under the shimmering

material of her gown, she could only stare at him, uncompre-hending. Beside her, the little dog growled low in his throat.

"He's a gigolo," said a soft voice from the sunny entrance of the alleyway. It was the young man from the breadline. "I tried to warn you, but apparently you're a big girl and know what you want." Slapping Rocco had felt so good, Lulu wanted to do it to this fellow too. Imagine, throwing her words back at her like that, just because she made one teeny little misjudgment!

Rocco clenched his fists and said, "Why you little . . ."

But the young man seemed completely unperturbed. "You know, a man who sells his favors for money." He looked at Lulu with an infuriating grin.

"I *know* what a gigolo is," she said furiously. "I don't care if he is one. I need him—not for *that*, but I still need him. Rocco, come with me. And if you try to kiss me again, I'll break your beak."

"Wait a minute," Rocco said. "Is this some kind of joke? You better not be pulling a fast one on me. Pay up now, or there's trouble." He held out his beefy hand.

"Pay up for what?" Lulu asked indignantly. "You haven't done anything yet, except commit an act of public indecency. I ought to have you arrested." She wiped her lips with the back of her hand, forgetting all about her perfectly applied lipstick.

"You've already bought my time. You pulled me out of the breadline. You owe me." He advanced on her menac-ingly. The little dog got between them, growling louder.

"Stay away from her." The young man's voice was as soft and gentle as ever, but he stepped forward with his fists clenched. Lulu gave a hysterical little hiccup of a laugh. What on earth did he think he could do against huge, enraged Rocco?

Rocco looked amused. He swung a lazy punch that would have broken the young man's jaw . . . had it connected. But the young man pivoted out of reach and said, "I don't want to hurt you. Just leave the lady alone and we won't have to notify the police. I seem to have heard about an old woman whose cash and new boyfriend vanished around the same time. They were telling the story on the breadline yesterday, and apparently the boyfriend looks exactly like you. Strange, huh?"

"Shut your mouth!" Rocco gave a roar and charged at him. The young man sidestepped and landed a punch to Rocco's temple that laid him out flat.

Lulu thought the young man looked a little sad about it.

The dog gave the prostrate form a sniff, then lifted his leg over Rocco's shoe.

The young man gingerly scooped the terrier up mid-whiz and dropped him beside a trash bin to finish his business. "No point adding insult to injury," he told the dog. "That's just rude."

Lulu stood with her hands on her hips. "He doesn't understand you," she said, then added a little sheepishly, "He just looks like he does."

"What's his name?"

"He doesn't have one." Why were they talking casually

about a dog when there was an unconscious, violent gigolo lying at their feet?

"Of course he does. Don't you, boy?" He crouched down, and the dog marched up to him, his tongue lolling, his tail wagging like mad. "We just have to figure out what it is." The dog gave a sharp bark. "Yip? Is that it?" The dog sneezed. "No, not that." He scratched the dog under the chin, then stood.

"How did you do that?" Lulu asked, pointing at Rocco.

The young man shrugged. "My friend Mugsy taught me," he said, as if that explained everything. He seemed more interested in the dog than in his recent victory. Or in her, which piqued. "He's a loyal little pooch. How about Fido? That's Latin for faithful."

"You speak Latin?"

"No."

Well, that was okay then. Her world might be a little rocked by a starving bum who spoke Latin.

"I only read it. Anyway," he went on, ignoring her startled look, "he doesn't seem like a Fido."

"Why did you follow me?" Lulu asked, stamping her foot.

"For your name. You said to stop by Central Casting and tell them you sent me. Only you never told me who you are."

"Don't you watch movies?"

"Used to. Not so much anymore."

"Well, I'm a star," she said, annoyance making her arrogant.

"Let's see . . . You must be Barbara Stanwyck?"

"I wish."

"Carole Lombard? No, no scar." Carole had a scar on her cheek from a car accident, but managed to cover it up with makeup and collusion with the cameramen. How did he know about her scar? "Mae West? No, too young. Shirley Temple? No, too old. I give up. Which star are you?"

"I'm Lulu Kelly."

"Of the Lower East Side Kellys, right?"

Lulu flushed bright crimson.

"Your accent shows when you get angry. No, don't get *more* angry! Deep breaths. There you go. Now, shall I escort you to your mansion, Miss Kelly? Or is it Mrs.?"

"It's nothing to you," she huffed.

"Sorry about your gigolo. Are you sore at me? I can revive him, and you two can carry on as you were before my rude interruption."

"Don't smile at me like that," she said.

"I don't know any other way to smile."

"I needed someone for a small movie role, and I needed him fast. A poor, handsome guy with a mean streak. I figured I'd find the genuine article so we wouldn't have to waste time training him up. Now I can kiss my dream role good-bye. Unless . . ." She narrowed her eyes. This young man was an impressive boxer, but he hadn't ever looked mean or mad during the whole uneven fight. "Do you want to make some money?"

"You need a replacement gigolo?"

She tried to slap him, but he evaded her just as easily as

he had Rocco. "I'm sorry," he said. "I've forgotten some of my manners on the road. Forgive me?"

"Maybe," she said, "if you can act. *Can* you act?"

He gave a wry smile. "I'm acting now."

"Ha. Well, I suppose you'll have to do. Come with me."

But before she had gone three steps, she turned around. Rocco was slowly groaning back to consciousness. Good. At least he wasn't dead, though Veronica would no doubt be pleased with the headlines it would generate. "Femme Fatale at Fault in Fatal Fight." In Hollywood, there was no such thing as bad publicity.

Lulu crouched down beside him and slipped off her other bracelet, a twin of the one she'd given to the dog owner, except with small emeralds set in the platinum instead of rubies. She put it in Rocco's jacket pocket, stood, and walked briskly away.

"Why did you do that?" the young man asked.

"Because no one should have to sell himself," she said.

The young man stopped smiling. She looked at him as he strode beside her. His eyes, bright hazel, regarded her with something that made her feel uncomfortable in a vastly different way than Rocco's gaze had. She felt he was judging her, like maybe she'd passed one test but might not pass any of the others. He reminded her of that damned dog. The nerve of him, a boy from the gutter without a penny to his name, making her feel like that! She had half a mind to leave him here. But no, she needed *someone*. He wasn't much, but he'd do.

"Is this wag part of the deal?" the boy asked, looking

down at the dog, who regarded them attentively. "Look, doesn't his face remind you of Charlie Chaplin?"

"Charlie," Lulu said. "Now, that's a good name for him."

"You know, I think you're right."

"What about you?" she asked. "What's a good name for you?"

The young man seemed to think about it for a while. "Freddie," he said at last. "Yes, I think that's the perfect name for me. Freddie Van."

SIXTEEN

Do us both a favor and listen carefully. All you have to do is learn your lines and follow directions, and this will be the bee's knees," Lulu told Freddie as they cruised down Burbank Avenue in the backseat of the studio car. Freddie had the window rolled down, and he and Charlie were enjoying the warm California air.

"Who says I want the job?" Freddie asked.

"Of course you want the job. You're broke, right? Didn't you come to Hollywood to be a star? Everyone would give their left leg to get a speaking role."

"Yet I don't often see one-legged men in the movies," he said, managing to keep a straight face when she shot him a look.

"Are you trying to get my goat?"

"Maybe," he answered.

"Well, consider my goat got. Ugh, these shoes are even more annoying than you. I'll ruin my stockings, but I can't take it anymore. Here, hold them for me." She stooped to pull off her heels.

"Am I playing the part of a manservant? Your hands are free. You can carry them yourself, can't you?"

"Men have fought for the right to drink champagne from my slippers, you know," she informed him.

Freddie took the shoes and sniffed. "Men with no sense of smell, apparently. No, don't take offense. Feet are feet, as the philosopher once said. Rich feet smell no better than poor feet after walking all day in the California sun. Feet make us all equal. What do you think, Charlie?" He held the dainty shoes down for Charlie to smell. The dog gave a delighted whine and tried to start a game of tug-of-war.

"Well, mine are happy feet now," Lulu said, leaning against the car's warm leather interior and stretching her toes.

"Is it worth it?" he asked. "All that trouble and pain to look beautiful?"

She looked at him archly. "You tell me."

But he didn't. He only chuckled to himself and turned once more to the sun streaming through the window.

After a long moment of silence, she asked warily, "So you think I'm beautiful?"

"No. Not particularly beautiful. Your mouth is too big and your nose is too small and your eyes are too far apart and your chin is too pointed."

"Why, you . . ."

"A man's entitled to his opinion."

"A goon like you has no class," she said, forgetting everything Mrs. Wilburforce had taught her about how to be a lady. "You wouldn't know beauty if it slapped you in the face."

"It tried to."

"Ha! I thought you said . . ."

"Well, maybe some people would think you're beautiful. But you've got something better going for you."

"Yeah? What's that?"

"You're interesting," Freddie said.

Lulu opened her mouth to reply and then stopped short. She looked to Freddie like she didn't know if it was a backhanded insult or the nicest compliment she'd ever gotten in her life. Probably plenty of men had called her beautiful. He wondered if anyone had ever called her interesting.

Defensively, she said, "Nice. Next thing you'll be calling me smart. What's after that, the kiss of death—a good sense of humor?"

"Tragic, isn't it?"

"You think you know me after a few minutes?"

"I've smelled your shoes. That tells me a lot."

"Ew. Tells me plenty about you, too." She forced herself to be calm. "Listen, oddball, do a good job here and we never have to see each other again. On the level."

"Incentive for me to fail. What if I *want* to see you again?"

Lulu flushed. "Become a rich and famous star and I

might just give you the time of day." The words came out before she had time to think about them. Something about this boy made her feel fluttery in the pit of her stomach.

"What if I'm just one or the other?" Freddie asked.

"Then pick rich. It's much easier. Fame costs too much."

"So you couldn't like a poor boy?"

"I wouldn't bother trying," she said with a toss of her platinum locks.

"Sometimes you get things without trying for them, as the philosopher once said."

"Who is this philosopher you're always talking about?" she snapped.

"Murphy B. Murgatroyd, aka Mugsy."

"The one who taught you to box? A fighting philosopher?"

"More of a nursemaid. Is this the place?" They'd come to a big wrought-iron gate with the letters *LUX* twisted into the metal. The car glided to a stop. An elderly guard built like a fireplug with legs stepped out of the guardhouse.

"Hello, Gus. This is a new actor," Lulu said. "Strictly temporary. Says his name is Freddie Van. He'll be on the set today, and maybe tomorrow, but don't let him in after that. He doesn't belong here."

The door swung open, and Freddie held out his hand to the guard, who stood nonplussed a moment before shaking it. "Very pleased to make your acquaintance," Freddie said pleasantly.

Gus looked at Freddie's ragged clothes. "I've seen 'em

come and seen 'em go," he said. "And this one is more of a comer than a goer." He nodded sagely. "Listen to him, acting like a jim-dandy when he obviously ain't had a good meal in weeks. Sounds like he's got a silver spoon in his yap. You found a keeper, Lulu."

She shook her head. "I think you've been stuck in that hut too long, Gus. You don't know what you're talking about. This guy is an extra at best. He just got lucky today."

"A little luck is all this guy needs. See you around, Lu. Glad to know ya, Freddie." He tipped his cap.

"Don't let it go to your head," she said as they walked to the set of *Girl About Town*. "He thought Clark Gable would be a flop, and he told me the other day about some crazy redhead named Lucille Ball with a couple of bit parts to her name who he swears is going to make it big. No one wants to watch a kooky redhead. What does Gus know? He still thinks talkies are just a fad."

"I won't get my hopes up. About that, anyway."

Freddie looked at her shapely form and sprightly, bouncing walk. "I *might* get my hopes up about something else, though." He caught her eye for a second and smiled, which made her feel both uneasy and the tiniest bit elated.

As he followed her through the citylike streets of the lot, he thought that the last thing he wanted right now was an entanglement. This whole thing was a bad idea. A guy on the run shouldn't have his face in the movies, even if it was a small part. Freddie was definitely on the lam, as desperate as any criminal. His father would stop at nothing to bring him back. He knew the private investigators must be getting close. And Mugsy, who knew him like the back of his own hairy-knuckled hand, could probably sniff him out eventually, if Freddie's father had managed to convince him to help. Freddie was an only child, sole heir of his father's fortune. *I do all this for you,* his father used to say when he took Freddie on a tour of a refinery or steel mill. It used to make Freddie proud.

Suddenly he felt a little pang of homesickness, a lingering twinge of love for his father. *No,* he told himself severely. *Not for my father, for the man I believed him to be, once.*

"Wait here," Lulu told him, and he stood with his hands in his pockets, whistling "Brother, Can You Spare a Dime?" thinking about the peculiar girl he'd just met. What a whirlwind! What a perplexing mix of traits—vanity and self-consciousness, kindness and quick temper, frivolity and seriousness. He might have dismissed her as just another empty-headed flapper if she hadn't given Rocco that bracelet. She tried to hide her accent, but when she was upset she betrayed her lower-class origins as clearly as if she were wearing a sandwich board. She was the kind of girl he never would have talked to in his old life. Her kind probably wouldn't have made it as far as a hat-check girl, he thought. Their spheres never would have intersected.

Now look at her—a star. But one who understood what desperation could do to a poor man, who knew the value of a second chance. He wished there were more people like her in the world. He'd met some surprisingly decent folks in his travels, but he never thought he'd meet one in jaded Hollywood. Especially one so pretty.

It made Freddie ponder. He'd followed her to the studio for a lark, because he was lonely and rootless, and yes, he needed the money. As far as he was concerned, this was just another job of day labor. If he could chop wood or milk cows in exchange for food, surely he could act. If he appeared in a movie, he might earn enough cash for hammock on a ship to Hong Kong. By the time the private eyes saw the film, he'd be long gone.

But now that he'd met Lulu, he had second thoughts. Maybe he could build a new life for himself here, under a new name. He'd thought to make amends for his father's misdeeds through manual labor. It seemed nobler, somehow, to live by the sweat of his brow than by something like banking or the law. Those professions were overflowing candy stores for the dishonest and greedy.

Yet what was Hollywood but an industry based on lies? He was fully aware of the irony. Hollywood was an industry, and at the top of every industry was a man who had built his fortune on the backs of hardworking people.

No, he told himself firmly. *I'm definitely leaving the country.*

Lulu bobbed back into view, her deep blue eyes dancing, a smile playing on her lips.

Only, not quite yet.

SEVENTEEN

Lulu vehemently argued her case for casting Freddie. "I'm telling you, Ira, he's absolutely perfect. Look at him! Young, broken, sad, filthy, disgusting, and pathetic! He's the absolute gold standard of pitiful scum!"

"Coming from you, dear lady, I'll take that as a compliment," Freddie cheerfully responded.

They stood in the director's tiny on-set office, facing off with Sassoon, the producer, and the writer.

"Lulu, we're just writing the new scene. The pages haven't even gone upstairs to the studio. Sure, I get it! He's nauseating—"

"This just keeps getting better!" Freddie chimed in

"But can the bum act? Can he deliver lines? For cryin' out loud, the guy looks loaded to the muzzle!"

"Pardon me, but this *bum* would like to assure you that he isn't 'loaded to the muzzle,' and for your information, I've declaimed selections from Shakespeare, Ibsen, George Bernard Shaw, and Oscar Wilde. And, I'd like to add, I received high acclaim."

Lulu, thinking he was overplaying his role a bit, nudged him sharply in the ribs and whispered, "From whom? The garbage collectors?"

Everyone else simply stared at Freddie, momentarily dumbfounded by what had come out of the vagrant's mouth. A little smile crept over Lulu's rouged lips. This just might work.

It was at that moment that a young bespectacled production assistant knocked, stuck his head into the room, and asked, "Are we shutting down or shooting, Mr. Sassoon? We're wondering if we should release the crew or not."

Lulu gave Sassoon her most beguiling smile. "Pretty please?"

"Come on, Freddie. Let's get you to makeup. Then you can learn your lines while I shoot my next scene. You'll be up afterward." Lulu hustled along with the harried production assistant and her new costar.

"I have to wear *makeup*? What kind of role am I supposed to be playing?"

"Everyone wears makeup, kiddo. You're playing a good-looking but dirty street bum whom my character picks up on a dare."

"I'm good-looking?" he asked. He wondered if she realized he was mocking her for asking the same thing earlier. "Funny how that torturous high-heeled shoe is suddenly on the other foot."

"No, you're not, but once the makeup department gets ahold of you, you'll pass. They'll clean you up and pancake you. . . ."

"I thought I was playing a dirty bum. Don't I already look the part?"

"Oh, they don't want *real* dirt. Actual dirt doesn't look real enough on camera. You'll have greasepaint."

Freddie had to laugh. What a mythical world, where real dirt wasn't dirty enough. He didn't know whether to be disgusted or amused. Ben would have gotten a kick out of it, though.

"Here are your pages," she said as another assistant rushed up to them and handed them the rewritten scene, the letters smudged from the fresh typewriter ink. The little dog tried to follow her onto the set, but she shooed him gently back to Freddie. He walked in three circles and lay down, his tongue lolling out, surveying the cast and crew like an old pro.

A svelte man named Max, with an apron covering his impeccably tailored tan poplin suit, took charge of Freddie and directed him into a small barren dressing room. One assistant ushered him into the shower and instructed Freddie to suds himself from head to toe. Freddie was more than a little shocked at how embedded the filth on him was from the many months of vagrancy, and he luxuriated in the steaming-hot deluge. He was like an archaeological dig, and each new layer of dirt removed revealed some forgotten feature of himself.

When he'd been completely scoured and sanitized, another assistant applied an astringent, a conditioning face cream that smelled unpleasantly like stale urine, and finally a sort of slick liquid plastic that made his face stiffen. "Takes years off you, love," the assistant whispered into his ear. Freddie stared at his shining face in the mirror, trying to decide if he really did look twelve.

Only then did Max, the head of makeup, personally go to work on him. A colored cream gave him the proper complexion, powder dulled his shine, and then, with the exacting eye of a true artist, Max set about painting Freddie's face with faux dirt. He murmured to himself as he worked. "More on the left side than the right. You would sleep on your left side, yes, so that your right arm is free to fight if there is trouble on the savage streets. You wake, you rub your eyes, and the dirt smears, just so. Now for the fingernails. They are dirty, but you have a nervous habit of picking them, or perhaps you clean them with the tip of your knife, so we apply the dirt, so, and then scrape most of it away again."

By the end of the process Freddie was theatrically filthy. "I look quite dangerous," he told Max. "Except perhaps for the eyeliner. If I had you on the streets, no one would ever bother me. Thank you."

Max put his right hand over his heart and gave a little bow, then went to search Lulu's arched eyebrows for any stray hairs before her next scene. Freddie settled down to watch, and soon Max rejoined him. Though only a few people were to be in the scene, there were a slew of support crew holding lights and microphones, as well as a crowd without any identifiable purpose. Max, who adored the sound of his own voice, began to tell Freddie about some of them.

"That's Vasily Anoushkin," he said, pointing to the man in gray cashmere. "Russian acting coaches are all the rage now. Ooh, look at him scowl at Sassoon! He thinks *he* should be the director, and in my opinion he's not wrong. But the ones to watch out for are the ones who *aren't* scowling at each other." He gave an exaggerated gasp. "Speaking of, did you see that look Ruby Godfrey just gave Vasily? Butter wouldn't melt! She smiled at him like the MGM lion. And if I know her, she doesn't want to eat him up in the fun way. I don't know what their battle is, but I can tell it's brewing. Usually my money would be on Vasily, but look, he won't even make eye contact with her. I wonder . . ." Max cocked his head, lost in thought. "No, not Vasily," he decided at last.

Freddie listened with half an ear to the makeup artist's gossip. He was far more interested in watching Lulu prepare for her part. She looked so intensely serious, pacing out steps to secret marks on the floor, examining the camera and lighting angles, mouthing her lines under her breath.

"And there's Lolly—Louella Parsons to me, because I'm not quite fabulous enough to be at that level of intimate hatred yet. Wait until next year, when my new makeup line is out. She'll be kissing my . . . whatever part of my anatomy she can reach to get free samples. Like she needs another layer of pancake." Max babbled on about the most intimate secrets of everyone on set until the director called the actors and crew to their places.

"What is this scene about?" Freddie asked Max.

"The devil-may-care society girl is a little tipsy at her boyfriend's party, and to be cute she decides to play with his gun. Only she doesn't know it's loaded, and she almost shoots him by accident."

Freddie watched the prop supervisor, a ginger-haired man with a potbelly, put the weapon in a desk drawer. It looked suspiciously heavy. "Tell me that isn't a real gun."

"Oh, it's real, all right, but not loaded. Fake guns look so . . . fake. We'll dub the 'bang' in later. All very safe. We're just a bunch of kids playing dress-up and make-believe here."

"All the same," said Freddie, rising, "I'd like to check it out for myself." He'd handled plenty of guns in his life—skeet shooting by the lake, duck hunting in Connecticut—and he'd swear, from the apparent weight of the revolver in the prop man's hand, that it was loaded. Or was it just that guns had such a terrible association for him now? Once they had been playthings for an afternoon's sport. Now he knew them for the deadly weapons they really were.

While the actors were taking their places and waiting for Sassoon to be ready, Freddie took the revolver out of the drawer. His hands were shaking as he remembered the sound of the gunshot in the closed room, the sight of Mr.

Shaw slumping to the ground. But he opened the cylinder and spun it, making sure that every chamber was empty, then put it back in the drawer. He knew he was being foolishly overcautious. . . . Still, the idea of Lulu playing with a gun worried him.

The prop supervisor squinted at Freddie suspiciously as he walked back to his seat, then checked the gun again. Freddie shot him a smile, which wasn't returned, and gave a little shrug. Still eyeballing him, the prop man fished a cigarette case from his pocket, then slapped his other pockets for a match.

"Ruby, ya got a light?" the man called when his pockets turned up empty. Ruby, rolling her eyes, tossed him a matchbook. Freddie absently watched the black and gold square arc through the spotlights. It was a bad throw, though, and skidded by Freddie's feet. Ever the gentleman, he picked it up, glanced casually at the gold ram's head embossed on the cover, and pitched it the rest of the way to the prop supervisor.

His mind easy now, Freddie sat down again and waited for the show to start. He had his lines memorized in moments, and then alternated between memorizing the other parts so he'd know his cues and watching the crew members at work. They were such an efficient team, wheeling massive cameras and adjusting blazing lights to perfection, but they seemed to be having fun, too, laughing and gossiping. It seemed like a nice place to work. *I could get very used to this*, he thought. *I could stay. . . .*

Then he noticed one man who didn't look like he belonged. At first Freddie thought he might be one of the stars, handsome and aloof. He wore a dark suit, with slicked-back hair and a heavy gold ring on each forefinger. He was a little older than Freddie, maybe nineteen or twenty, yet he carried himself like the master of the world, his chin jutting and his eyes proclaiming ownership of everything he saw. Despite the suit, there was something base and physical about him, something predatory.

No one else seemed troubled by his presence. There were always executives and the like lingering in the wings to watch their dollars at work, and for the most part the actors and crew ignored them unless specifically asked to entertain them. This man watched one of the actors intently: Lulu. Freddie didn't think she'd noticed him yet, but he never took his eyes off her, until the moment he grabbed a passing assistant and whispered a question in his ear. Afterward, the man in the suit strolled nonchalantly onto the set and took the gun out of the drawer. Freddie heard the click and spin of the cylinder opening, but he couldn't see what the man was doing with it. Was he the set safety expert, checking the gun one last time?

"Who is that?" he asked Max, but the makeup artist only shrugged and said, "Another guy with money."

Before Freddie could do anything, Sassoon burst onto the set, slapped down a rolled-up copy of the script, and shouted, "Places, everyone. I want this in one take." For a moment Freddie couldn't see the set at all as everyone seemed to swarm on the actors, giving them one last piece of direction, telling them to break a leg, adding just a touch more powder. Vasily whispered something into Lulu's ear. Louella gave air kisses to half the cast. Then, after some exasperated words from Sassoon, the set cleared of everyone but the actors. "And . . . action!"

Instantly the actresses dressed as rich party girls began to talk and giggle and flirt with the actors playing wealthy young men. Ice clinked in glasses, rhinestones sparkled under bright artificial light, and Lulu, portraying Jezebel March, swallowed water posing as a martini, stage slapped her supposed beau, and pulled the real but unloaded gun from the drawer. She laughed gaily, did a little dance, playfully pointed the barrel at her friends and rivals, and—

"Cut!" Sassoon roared. "Damn it, Tanner. She didn't hit you that hard. You don't have to stagger. Let's do this again, and make it fast."

Vasily slipped to Lulu's side and took the gun from her hand. He looked like he was giving her acting tips, showing her how to point the weapon convincingly. Vasily handed it to Blake Tanner as he passed, and he took it back to the desk. Freddie saw a dark-haired vamp of a girl with a heart-shaped beauty mark near the corner of her mouth glide up to Blake and put her arms around him. She whispered something in his ear, cast a look over her shoulder at Lulu, and laughed. Then she pulled the revolver from his hands and aimed it at Lulu. Lulu just glared at her.

"Get a move on, Ruby," Sassoon barked, and the girl

made a pouty little frown before putting the gun back in the drawer and taking her unobtrusive place among the extras.

"Action!" Sassoon called again, and the process was repeated. As Lulu danced and whirled with the gun, Freddie saw her suddenly stop, a look of shock on her face as she noticed the handsome young man in the suit lounging in a corner. Her back was to the camera, though, and a half second later she caught herself and went on, but there was a new hysterical edge to her laughter.

She knows him. And she's afraid of him.

As the scene went on, Freddie could tell that Lulu was shaken. Blake Tanner lectured her character, and she snatched up the gun, aiming it at the gaggle of high-society friends, then at Blake, at her own head, at . . .

At the man in the snappy suit lurking off set. Freddie thought Lulu's maniacal look had nothing to do with acting. Or was she aiming at the dark-haired young actress, who was deliberately maneuvering to have a more prominent place in front of the camera and who now stood almost between Lulu and that man?

There was a jostling among the other actors. Lulu's male costar moved abruptly, and the dark-haired girl stumbled slightly, then recovered. Freddie barely noticed. He watched Lulu's hand tense, her finger curl and tighten. But there would be no "bang." That's what Freddie had assured himself with his last-minute inspection.

Lulu squeezed the trigger, and Freddie flinched at the explosive report of gunfire. The camera swiveled to focus on the supposed bullet hole predrilled into the wall, and for a second all eyes were either there, or on Lulu, who was supposed to faint gracefully on cue. Everyone was still acting, despite the startling boom. Everyone except for the dark-haired pretty young girl. Freddie saw a spot of red bud and blossom like a tropical flower on the décolletage of her white gown. Then, with a naturalism that would have made her acting coach proud, she sank to the ground with a *thud* in a heap of bare limbs and swiftly spreading scarlet.

More than anything, Freddie wanted to run to Lulu. But he dashed to the stricken girl instead. He was still pressing his wadded-up jacket to her wound, speaking softly into her ear, when the police arrived.

EIGHTEEN

Lying on the floor with the echo of the gunshot ringing in her ears and the chaos of people and voices all around her, Lulu was profoundly grateful to the screenwriter and Sassoon for having kept the fainting scene. She'd argued against it when she'd first read the script, saying that her character would never faint. Jezebel might scream, she might flee, but she would never simply relinquish all responsibility for her actions by slipping conveniently into unconsciousness.

To which Sassoon had brusquely told her that fainting allowed them to quickly cut to her male costar's perspective, and also show an awful lot of thigh when they panned back to Lulu sprawled decoratively on the plush ivory carpet.

Since that first day in Vasily's classroom, Lulu had hardened to the point where she would never truly faint again.

She had no natural escape from the nightmare that was unfolding, so she turned to her only real strength: acting. While girls screamed and running feet pounded around her, Lulu pretended to be out cold. She felt a warm wetness on her arm, a little dog's tongue licking her reassuringly. Good old Charlie. He was on her side, at least.

Just one more minute, she begged the universe as she squeezed her eyes closed, still feigning unconsciousness. *Please let it not be real.* The little terrier whined and licked her cheek, bringing her closer to the terrible reality. *I know it has to be real, only . . . not yet.*

Because *he* was there. And where he was, danger and death followed.

While she pretended to be unconscious, she tried to figure out what happened. Her first thought was that Sal had shot someone—had shot *her*, in fact. Then she realized that the shot had come from her gun. *But that's impossible. It's only a prop!* The smell of gunpowder hung in a cloud around her, and her hand ached from the revolver's recoil. *No. This can't be happening.*

But Lulu heard the shouting everywhere around her. "She shot Ruby!" "Is she dead?" "Medic!" "Call an ambulance!" "Call the police!" "Call the legal department!"

She let herself peek from barely cracked eyelids at the pandemonium around her. Some of the actors were still hunkered down in case more shots followed. The gun had fallen from her hand, and she saw Roger King pick it up.

"Where's security?" he barked.

"Taking care of Docky," someone answered. "The good doctor drank himself into a stupor and had to be escorted home."

"Perfect." Roger grimaced and opened the revolver's cylinder, dumping the bullets and spent shell into his palm before slipping them into his pocket. He put the gun on a table. "Nobody touch this," he ordered. Then he and the assistant directors started to herd everyone off to the side while a few people crouched over Ruby.

In the corner, Louella looked shocked but not displeased by the terrifying events that were clearly the seeds of a delicious scandal. She was frantically taking notes. Vasily, hovering nervously nearby, looked utterly stunned at first. Then Lulu thought she saw what looked like the shadow of a smile flicker across his face. Blake, pale and aghast, attempted a semblance of composure. Shakily, he ran his fingers through his hair and turned his best side to the world.

Lulu felt a presence looming over her and squeezed her eyes shut. A hand, large and warm, rested on her shoulder. *No, no, no. Not him.*

When I open my eyes, it will be . . . who?

Of all the people in the room, Lulu settled on the one she knew the least. That strange young man with his Latin and his fisticuffs, who laughed at her so maddeningly and thought she was "interesting," of all things. *Please let it be Freddie Van coming to my rescue,* she thought desperately.

She opened her eyes and . . . *Of course . . .* It was the mobster, Sal, looking down at her, still as stone in the midst of all that chaos, with hard eyes and an amused mouth.

"You've really got yourself into a scrape this time, kiddo." His voice was soft, and so was his hand on the bare skin of her shoulder. But those eyes . . . they were still the black iron she remembered. "Let's see if we can fix that."

And she knew by his tone that he could. He could fix anything. He was that kind of man. Money, power, those were important, and she knew Sal had them in spades, inherited from his father, the single most powerful crime lord in all of New York. But he had something else, too: will.

She'd heard it bandied about by people in Hollywood over cocktails, people with half-formed ideas and an exaggerated sense of their own importance. *"The will to power,"* they said knowingly, mispronouncing Nietzsche's name, spilling their cocktails, and thinking they had it because they had fast money and fickle fame. They were wraiths beside this solid man.

Sal looked at her, and she knew immediately that he could make everything all right.

But what would it cost her?

The screaming and mayhem seemed to Lulu to stretch forever. Time worked strangely, expanding and contracting. Sal helped her to her feet. She felt the warmth of his body. It seemed to draw her magnetically, and she swayed closer. She felt faint, for real this time. How easy it would be to collapse into Sal's arms and let him make all of this go away. Because even if she wasn't guilty, she knew that she appeared guilty, and that might be enough.

In the distance she heard Sassoon bark, "Give her air! Clear the area, for crying out loud!" Why was everything moving in slow motion?

People knew she and Ruby always competed for the same parts, that they had a long-standing grudge. Lulu could lose her career, her freedom. She could be cast back into the gutter, and her family along with her.

How had it happened? Who put real bullets in the gun?

I've been set up, she thought as she trembled on her feet. *Someone wanted to make me look guilty. But who?*

She knew it couldn't have been an accident. The prop master made sure of that. The guns they used were kept in a special place and checked and double-checked. If there were real bullets, it was because someone wanted them to be there.

Sal touched her cheek, gently brushing away a platinum lock that had come free from her opal hairpin. Lulu felt the temptation of small helpless things to lean on a strong protector, the desire of a kitten to curl up against a fierce dog. But the teeth that could protect her could also rip her apart. Shocked at her momentary urge, she pulled abruptly away, staggering to be on her own, unsupported.

She saw Freddie kneeling on the floor. Beneath him was . . . Oh! Red and more red . . . real blood, undeniably real in that fake world. *It's not supposed to be real,* she thought stupidly. *Not here, of all places.*

Ruby's eyes were rolled back, and her mouth hung open. The blood was everywhere, so much, too much. No one could lose all that blood and survive. A sick feeling rose in Lulu's stomach, and her knees shook. She reached out a hand, but there was only Sal nearby and she could not reach for him. For a moment her hand flailed in the empty space, looking for support. She thought, frantically, what would an innocent person say? The adrenaline of wild fear coursed through her. She *was* innocent, but she felt culpable somehow.

Because of Sal, something whispered in her ear. *Because of what you did. You're a bad person, and here's the proof.*

But now Sal was gone, melted into the background as if he'd never been there. For a confused instant she wondered if he actually had been. Was he a manifestation of her own corrupt deeds come back to even the score? The world was haywire, blurry . . . except for the vision of blood, dark and thick, pooling beneath Ruby's unmoving body.

Lulu stood alone in that crowd of actors and extras, director and crew. Vasily stared at her, blinking rapidly. Even Lolly froze for a moment, her notes forgotten. They all seemed to make a space for Lulu, a circle of loneliness, the masses, angry and afraid, collecting to judge the guilty. She stood in a spotlight. Her mouth moved, but she felt as if she'd forgotten her lines.

What happened? she wanted to say, but the words got stuck, and her lips mouthed "Wh . . . wh . . ." again and again. "What . . . ," she managed to gasp.

But another voice covered her words.

"What the hell happened?" Niederman barked as he burst from his private office. All eyes turned to Lulu as the on-call Lux emergency medical team frantically tried to revive the blood-soaked Ruby. Niederman took Lulu roughly by the elbow and hustled her away.

"I just played my part," Lulu said in a small voice after she collapsed into Niederman's office chair. "I was just acting. That's what I do. I never thought there would be real bullets in the gun. How could I? I don't know how it happened. . . . It's all a blur."

"Sure," Niederman said, mopping sweat from his fore-head and chomping on his cigar as he paced. "Stick to that. That's what you tell them."

"But that's what happened," she protested. "The script said to pick up the gun and wave it around and fire it. That's all I did. Don't you believe me?"

"Of course I do," he said. Then his entire aspect changed. His eyes became remote, his voice hard and cyni-cal. "It doesn't matter if I believe you or not. Frankly, it doesn't matter if the police believe you. The question is, does the public believe you're innocent? If they do, you're golden. If not, you go from a rising starlet and money-making machine for Lux to a temporary tabloid headline, and then next stop: box-office poison." He didn't seem to be talking to her anymore. "When the lawyers get here, we'll see if we can make this all go away. God knows we pay the police enough hush money to mop up all the messes you boozed-up, overentitled actors make in this town. With a little luck and a cooperative judge, this might all disappear.

As far as Lux is concerned, this needs to have never happened."

There was an insistent pounding on the door. Lulu's entire body began to shake.

"You just keep your mouth shut, and . . . Damn!"

"Lulu Kelly, you're under arrest for murder," bellowed one of the two uniformed police officers who barged past the hapless studio security.

It felt to Lulu as if her lungs were collapsing. The roar of blood racing through her head seemed to deafen her, and her vision kaleidoscoped.

"She's dead?" Lulu whispered. For a second it seemed like the most important thing. Then the other part hit her. "No! I didn't do anything. It was an accident! I mean—"

"Shut your mouth, Lulu," Niederman said. "Wait till the lawyers come. Gentlemen, I'm sorry, but you can't take my prize starlet away before the attorneys get here. We have an understanding with the department. You don't want to be undermining the DA's office, now, do you?"

"That understanding don't hold here," one of the policemen informed him. "An entire soundstage saw this woman shoot the victim. Everyone says these two girls had a beef. Our deal don't hold for murder."

"What, your retainer isn't enough? Five hundred—a thousand! Come on, just fill in 'accidental discharge' in the cause-of-death section and call it quits. Two thousand!"

The policemen stood Lulu up and pulled her arms behind her back. She felt cold metal and heard the slither and click of handcuffs being latched onto her wrists. "No, please! I didn't do anything!" She began to sob.

"The chief of police and the DA's office will be hearing about this!" Niederman shouted after them as they dragged Lulu away. "Don't worry, Lulu. I'll have you out in an hour."

"I didn't do it!" Lulu screamed wildly over her shoulder. "It was an accident!"

The entire cast and crew watched, silent. No one made a move to help her, and no one looked her square in the face. Freddie, Ruby's blood mingled with his fake-dirt greasepaint, met her eyes for just a moment, then looked away. Every face was almost blank with shock. Even the little terrier at Freddie's feet looked lost and confused, whimpering softly as he shifted from paw to paw. Only Sal, standing in the shadows, wore a little smile on his lips.

Niederman had promised to have her out in an hour, but the next morning Lulu was still in a cold room under the glare of a single lightbulb, sitting on a painfully uncomfortable metal chair with her hands locked behind her back. It wasn't a jail cell, quite, but despite her desperate pleas, she hadn't been allowed to visit the bathroom. Instead, a leering guard had brought her a bucket, already none too clean, and waited in the doorway, pretending not to watch, while she awkwardly hiked up her silver Schiaparelli gown.

Men had come and gone for the last sixteen hours, questioning her with varying degrees of severity until she thought she was losing her mind. No one had actually hurt her physically yet, but they'd bullied and harangued her for hours on end, denying her even a cup of water. Standing inches from her terrified face, they'd shouted and spat and paced and shouted some more, the same questions over and over.

"Why did you shoot Ruby?"

"Why did you hate Ruby?"

Or sometimes, as if they were offering her a little rope to grasp at, the better to hang her later: "Who paid you to shoot Ruby?"

Lulu felt like she was in a nightmare. This didn't make any sense. The shooting was obviously an accident. Why were they jumping to conclusions? They should have interviewed everyone on set before they even thought of arresting her. She'd seen enough crime and courthouse movies by now to know proper procedure.

Something was terribly wrong. There seemed to be no way out and no one to help her.

Shortly after dawn, a new officer came in. At least, she assumed he was an officer, though he wasn't in uniform and she didn't see a badge. He was well dressed, in a pin-striped suit with broad-cut shoulders. *Maybe he's a detective*, she thought. She composed herself to beg, to argue, to bat her eyelashes and smile sweetly, whatever it took to be believed. She turned her eyes up to him hopefully . . . and without warning, he slapped her hard across the face.

Lulu fell off the rickety stool and cried out, the white-hot sting of his open hand burning her cheek. But as soon as she hit the floor, he hauled her up roughly, his fingers digging into the soft flesh of her upper arms.

"You're going to rot in prison, Lucille," he snarled, breathing the stench of stale cigarettes into her face. "That girl's parents have got the best lawyer in town, and they're going to throw the book at you."

"I didn't . . ."

"Shut up! It's too late for a confession. Do you know what they're going to do to a pretty little thing like you in the pen?" He whispered something in her ear, and she shuddered. "You'll be *broken* when you come out. A broken little toy for any man to sweep up."

She tried to wriggle away from him, but he held her tightly, bruisingly.

"Why is this happening to me?" she whimpered.

She turned her head this way and that, trying to escape, from him, from all of it, but she could still feel his hot breath on her face.

Suddenly, the door of her interrogation chamber opened.

"Let her go!" a man's voice commanded.

In seconds, the brute was gone. When Lulu was tenderly folded into strong masculine arms, she was beyond caring that they belonged to Salvatore Benedetto.

"Don't worry, doll face. I've got you now. It's gonna be all right. I'll take care of *everything*."

NINETEEN

inutes later Lulu found herself in a private room in the police station, her handcuffs off, curled on a sofa with Sal's jacket around her shoulders.

"I'm a businessman, not a romantic," Sal said bluntly once they were alone. "I didn't come to Los Angeles just for you, but, baby, you're pretty damn high on my list. When I first met you, I thought you were a hell of a broad, full of spunk and smarts, and yeah, you're a real looker, too. But you were still a nobody, see, and Sal can't have a nobody on his arm. So I watched you. I made sure you had all the right chances to become *somebody*. And now you're shining, a star, a diamond—one I want to own. I made you, Lucille. . . ."

"I made myself," she said staunchly. He sat down next

to her, and she cringed away but managed to hold his gaze. "And I'm not Lucille anymore. I'm Lulu. *I* did that—for myself. Not you."

He looked at her indulgently and snickered. "Words, Lu—just cheap words. Lucky for you, I like a girl with a mouth on her. Listen: You got a murder rap. I can square that—for a price."

Lulu gulped, feeling sick, but she listened.

"New York is taking care of itself. California's where the future is. I'm setting up shop out here, and I want you by my side."

"Why?" she asked, frankly curious. "There are a million beautiful women out here, and most of them would say yes to you. Why me?"

He took her hand, and she didn't quite have the courage to pull away. "You're not just any girl, Lucille. Not every frail can look down the barrel of a gun and then tell a straight story to the cops afterward. Not every girl can look like an angel on the witness stand, knowing she has a signed contract with the devil in her pocketbook all the while. You're like me, doll face." He smiled smugly.

Lulu jumped to her feet, Sal's jacket pooling at her feet. "I'm nothing like you!" she shouted. But in her heart, she had her doubts. *You'll both do anything to get ahead,* a little voice whispered inside of her.

No, that's not true, she told herself. *I just did one thing,* once, *that's all. Maybe it was a mistake, but that's behind me. I've repented. I've been saved.*

"I'm not like that," she said, hanging her head miserably. "I'm a good girl."

Sal captured her hand again. "Yeah, you're that, too. Maybe that's really why I want you." His voice had softened from its demanding tone, and he stroked her palm with his thumb. There was something so compelling about him, the mix of brutality and tenderness. *He wouldn't be brutal to me,* she thought, comparing him with the man in the pin-striped suit who'd slapped and threatened her so terrifyingly. If her only choice was between a man like him in the penal system or a man like Sal in the free world, wasn't the answer obvious? If a bad man is good to the person he loves . . .

"I wasn't supposed to be a gangster," Sal said suddenly, pulling her back down to the sofa and speaking earnestly in her ear. "My pop, he didn't want me to be like him. For most of my life, I didn't even know what he did. Oh, I knew he was rich and powerful and that everyone respected him, but he said he was a businessman. I believed him. I wanted to be just like him. He was my hero. He was . . . my pop."

To her amazement, she saw tears in his eyes. He turned away for a moment, and when he looked at her again, they were gone.

"So I studied hard—math and accounting, law, trade, everything I could learn about Wall Street. I wanted to be as good a businessman as he was. When I was fifteen, he gave me my first business. It was a failing movie house. I swear, that place was so full of rats I thought maybe I should just make it a cat emporium. No one would pay to see a movie there."

"What did you do?" Lulu asked.

He gave a little shrug, but she could tell he was proud of himself. "I stopped charging for movies. I hired a couple of broads off the streets. You know, girls who will do *anything*. Then I charged triple prices for cocktails and cigarettes and served them right in the movie seats. You should have seen those floozies wiggling down the aisles."

"Those poor girls," Lulu whispered, thinking, *It could have been me, or my sisters, if I hadn't come to Hollywood.*

"Are you kidding me? Those frails were deep in the clover. They were better deal makers than I could ever be. Every night they negotiated top dollar with a dozen men, got them boiled beyond recognition, and were paid in advance for services never rendered. They made out like bandits. Before long I had a dozen girls."

"So you turned a movie theater into a whorehouse?" Lulu said incredulously.

"Everyone was happy, and profits were through the roof. And we still showed movies. I got a guy running it now as a speakeasy, and now that films have sound, we have the best sound system. A talkie speak! A talk-easy!"

He laughed at his own joke, and Lulu smiled wanly. She was trapped. Sal or prison. He could get her out of the frying pan easily enough, but there was no doubt he was just another kind of fire.

He spelled it out clearly, just in case she had any lingering uncertainty. "I want you, Lucille. I want you by my side. I'm gonna be the biggest thing to hit this town. I've already made arrangements with some of the hotshots out here—your guy Niederman, for one. I've got the connections, and the money's gonna come rolling in. I'll be at every party. My picture will be in every magazine."

Lulu's eyebrows twitched upward at this.

"Oh, Lucille, you're thinking of the old days. Crooks are celebrities now. Haven't you seen *Little Caesar, The Public Enemy, Scarface?* People love gangsters. And thanks to my business training, my graft looks so legit, no one can touch me."

He pulled her closer and took her face in his big hands. *So strong,* she thought. *Not safe, but safer than the alternative.*

Her eyes half closed. *All you have to do is say yes. Just like you did when he told you to lie for him. Saying that little word will save you. Because even if you get acquitted and don't go to jail, a murder trial will ruin you. You'll have nothing. Your family will be on the streets.*

He was looking into her eyes, searching with a peculiarly childlike hope. She couldn't say yes. But if she said nothing, he'd assume, and take what he wanted. It was easier that way.

He moved closer, his full, curving lips brushing hers lightly.

"Lucille . . . ," he murmured, and kissed her.

Lucille! He still called her that, but no one, not even her mother, ever used her old name anymore. She'd legally changed it within weeks of signing her contract. Her identification said Lulu Kelly. That was the only name the police could possibly have for her.

Yet that monster in the pin-striped suit who'd slapped her and whispered those vile things in her ear, the one who'd made her believe that anything—even Sal—was better than the fate that awaited her in the courts and jail . . . *he'd* called her Lucille.

He was one of Sal's thugs.

Sal had set all of this up! Lulu was certain of it. The real bullets weren't in the gun by accident. Sal had put them there, or paid someone to put them there, just to get her into the kind of trouble only he could dig her out of. And when the cops on his payroll weren't getting results, he told his own henchman to work her over, to make her so desperately afraid that she'd have no choice but to accept Sal's offer.

She jerked away from him, her breath coming shallow and fast.

He wasn't her savior. He was the devil who tried to trick her into worshipping him.

And he'd almost succeeded.

But she was still just as trapped as ever. Ruby had still been shot by a gun Lulu had fired. Sal or prison. Sal or scandal. Sal or poverty.

Lulu didn't think she was strong enough to make the right choice.

Before she could say a word, the door burst open and in strode a man in a uniform decorated with an impressive array of brass stars and embroidered stripes, his chest jingling with medals and a golden badge that declared in black letters: CHIEF OF POLICE.

Behind him were Veronica Imrie, David Mandel, and, still in his painted-on grime and splashes of all-too-real blood, Freddie Van.

TWENTY

What the hell is she doing here?" bellowed Walter Finnegan, the chief of police. "I come back from my day off to find that this girl's been illegally held overnight, without so much as a phone call. There ain't even been a proper arrest report. And who the hell are you?" He glared at Sal. "Jesus! Never mind. I'll get to the bottom of that part later. What a goddamn mess!" Sal looked calmly back at Finnegan, as if this official, too, was just a healthy bribe away from being in his pocket.

Finnegan turned to Lulu. "Meanwhile, miss, I sincerely apologize for the inconvenience you've been caused and hope that when you talk to the brass at Lux you point out how very swiftly I corrected the matter once it was brought to my attention. Mary and Joseph!" he muttered to himself as he strode away, rubbing a headache from his temples. "Can't a guy even take a night off for his daughter's birthday party without the whole precinct going to hell?"

Lulu, scrambling to her feet, called after him, "You mean I'm not a suspect?"

"Sure you are," the chief said, his voice receding down the hallway. "But so are about a dozen other people, including God. As in 'act of' on the insurance reports. So don't go leaving the country, or even the county. Got an aspirin?" he shouted to someone Lulu couldn't see. Then he was gone.

"Come on, Lulu," Veronica said, holding out her hand. "Let's get you home and cleaned up."

Lulu tottered across the room, almost falling when she reached her publicist. But Veronica was stronger than she looked and propped Lulu up. "No photos, please," Veronica whispered wryly.

Lulu stepped in measured paces away from Sal, trembling with the certainty of small, tasty prey that he would not let her go, that he would pounce, digging his claws into her until there was no escape. But Sal did nothing. When she reached the doorway, she couldn't help casting a glance over her shoulder.

He smiled at her, smug and supremely confident.

"I'll be seeing you, Lu."

It sounded like a threat.

But there, lingering just within sight, was the man who had already saved her once before. Rocco was a puppy compared to Sal, but Freddie had taken care of him neatly enough.

She heard an excited yip, and the little terrier bounded up to her and put his paws gently on her knees, giving her a canine grin. "Easy there," Freddie said when the dog almost knocked her down. Charlie retreated and looked adoringly up at her. Why was Freddie here? To save her again?

The door closed behind them, and she was swept up in David's and Veronica's chatter and hugs. Within a few seconds, it was almost as if her whole terrible ordeal had never happened. Almost. *I'll be seeing you, Lu.*

David and Veronica each had one of Lulu's arms. Freddie and Charlie trailed behind as they left the station.

"You poor dear. You look a fright."

"No, she doesn't, Veronica," David insisted staunchly. "Lulu couldn't look bad if she tried."

"I know, and isn't it grand I'm not the jealous type? Oh, Lulu, I had such a time getting in to see you! Do you know how much Lux *donates* to the chief to be cooperative about studio matters? No one should have laid a hand on you—a contracted employee! A star! Oy vey!"

"See, she converted while you were in the chokey."

"And his mother still won't meet me." Veronica shrugged. "*C'est la vie.* But, Lu, it's a crime. No, not what you did. Did you . . . ? No, never mind. Of course you didn't, and even if you did, you still didn't, in my book. I know which side my bread is buttered on. I mean a crime that they locked you away and interrogated you without so much as a mink to toss over your shoulders." She rubbed Lulu's goose-bumped arm briskly. "What *ought* to have happened is that the deputy chief of police should have come, hat in hand, to make an appointment. Then, in maybe a week, he could have stopped by for tea and asked the Lux lawyers a few gentle questions while you sipped oolong in the background. Then someone would write Ruby a big fat check, or her mother if, God forbid, and that would be that."

"She's still alive?" Lulu asked.

"For now," Veronica answered. "The doctors aren't saying much, but I get the impression it's a matter of wait and see. They don't sound all that hopeful, though. The bullet nicked her heart."

David pushed the door open, and there they were in the morning sunlight—free. The brightness made Lulu's eyes water.

"But for some reason, the police decided to ignore all prior arrangements and lock you away. What happened to you in there? And who was that dreamy he-man pitching the woo your way? I flirted with half the officers in this city and threatened the other half, and no one would let me in to see you. David here tried to use his muscle, but even that didn't work."

"Aw, Veronica," David said. Veronica leaned across Lulu and kissed him lightly on the cheek.

"Then around dawn this mug saunters up, still in the same old glad rags from the set, and starts talking like the love child of a Supreme Court justice." She jerked her chin at Freddie, who was still trailing behind. He smiled modestly. "He goes on about habeas corpus and I don't know what, until those coppers were quaking in their size twelves. This guy's got acting chops in spades. I could almost believe he was a millionaire with a horde of lawyers on his side. Is he on loan from another studio? Now, here we are," she said, as if all Lulu's troubles were neatly tied up.

David opened the door of a little two-seater, officially company property, though he had all but commandeered it as his star in the agency remained on the ascendant. The little dog jumped onto the driver's seat, tongue lolling, and placed one paw on the wheel. "Is this fella yours, Lulu? Max gave him to Veronica and told her to take care of him."

"He's not mine, exactly . . . ," Lulu began, then gave up once and for all. It looked like she was stuck with a dog.

"Shoot, I don't think we'll all fit, at least not comfortably."

"I can always sit on your lap, Mandelbrot, but I doubt these two want to get so lovey-dovey."

Freddie spoke up at last. "We can get a cab," he said, and offered his arm to Lulu. She took it.

Veronica gave them a look. "Or maybe they do."

Freddie almost hadn't come. After the ambulance had carried Ruby away, bloody and unconscious, he had started walking. The terrier tried to follow him, but Freddie handed him over to Max and fled while the little dog whined and barked and dug his paws into the floor, trying desperately to pull away.

A passerby told him it was about twenty miles to the Port of Los Angeles. Freddie had made a quick calculation. Five hours of brisk walking would take him to a harbor where he could go anywhere in the world. Surely he could talk his way into passage. He'd take any job, accept any destination.

By dusk he could smell the salt water, and by nightfall he was at the port. Seagulls wheeled overhead, and from out at sea came the mournful bovine lowing of ship horns as they navigated around the breakwater. Freddie had never seen the Pacific, but he felt so at home on the water. The cargo ships were ugly, utilitarian things, but they called out to him. *Come away with us! Make a new life across the sea in some exotic place where your father can never find you and the sins of your family won't haunt you.* He could farm sheep in New Zealand, teach English to merchants' sons in China. Here, at this port, the world was open to him in a way it never had been when he'd lived in a mansion with millions in the bank.

It was the right time to go, too. His father was getting closer. He could feel it. There had been another article about him in the newspaper, just a few column inches, but it ran his picture. That had never been a problem before. He was a far cry from the sleek and satisfied young man he'd been a year ago, in his white tie and tails, with his devil-may-care grin. No one would recognize the dirty ragamuffin they saw today as the scion of one of the world's richest families.

This time, though, they'd been clever enough to use a different picture. It had been taken a few months before he'd run away. Some visiting young English aristocrats had persuaded their American brethren to attempt a game of rugby. It had been violent fun, dirty and thrillingly vicious. When it was over, someone's girlfriend had taken a photo of them all, disheveled and muddy. They'd agreed to look as tough as possible, mugging hooligan faces for the camera.

That was the photo they ran this time. Freddie's hair was sticking up at odd angles, and dirt was smeared across his face. He looked hard and grim. Very much, he imagined, like he did at this very moment. Anyone could recognize him. Beside the photo was the reward: $500,000. A sum that would have people around the country scanning every face they passed, hoping against hope that they might be the ones to hit the jackpot.

Freddie passed a hobo hunkered in a doorway, a hat made of folded newspaper shading his face from the sun. Everyone in America, even the poorest, had access to a newspaper. Any one of them might become his captor. And then . . . what? Couldn't he just run away again? His father couldn't keep him a prisoner.

Of course he could. He was ruthless. He'd never let anything valuable slip from his grasp, and Freddie was his prized possession. *He'd do anything to keep me, not through love, but through pride.* God forbid the other millionaires think he couldn't handle his own son. Heaven forfend that Freddie's flight from fortune make someone doubt the perfect system of thievery and lies Jacob van der Waals and his ilk had created for themselves.

In the last year, nothing had managed to bind Freddie. Ben had been his only friend, and even then he'd kept wandering. Now, though, Freddie felt different. And it scared him.

The difference was Lulu.

Why should a girl he'd known for only a scant few hours matter to him? Sure, she was in trouble now, but was she any different from the thousand hard-luck stories he'd found on the road? Everyone had bad luck. Everyone lost their jobs. Everyone was railroaded by the law. It was bad . . . but it was a bad world. He had to look after himself.

Which, he realized with a shock, was exactly what his father would say.

That alone was almost enough to turn him around.

No, she's none of my business. Besides, she was a star. She had people on her side. They'd take care of everything. Any fool could tell she probably didn't have anything to do with the shooting. Plenty of people had handled the gun. It could have been any one of them, or even someone he hadn't seen. His eyes hadn't been on the gun the whole time, and the crowd of actors had sometimes obscured his view. *She'll be fine without me. And I'll be much better off without her.*

But that man, with his swell suit and slicked-back hair. The one Lulu was so obviously afraid of. Freddie had seen him corner the first policeman on scene. He'd witnessed money changing hands. It was a hefty stack, the kind carried by the highest level of the underworld. No one else had that kind of bankroll in their pocket. The truly rich, like Freddie's father, never carried money at all. They had credit at every store and donated to museums rather than slipping a dollar to a beggar.

That exchange was what made this situation so ominous.

Immediately afterward, Lulu had been dragged away. No one had been questioned. No witness names had been taken. It was undeniably a setup.

But still none of his business.

Freddie tried to focus on finding a job that would give him passage out of the country. The first two ships he tried simply waved him away. He'd washed the blood from his hands, and the spatter on his shirt had dried to the point where, in the darkness anyway, it could easily be rusty dirt. Still, he couldn't look too prepossessing, and apparently he didn't pass inspection with the mates. He decided to try his luck lower down on the food chain and struck up a conversation with a stevedore loading crates of live chickens.

"Where are those poor devils headed?" he asked the wiry bearded man whose skinny arms looked like bundled cords.

"Vladivostok," he said.

"How do you keep a chicken alive across the whole Pacific Ocean?" The chickens pecked testily at their cage.

The stevedore grinned. "We don't. Our captain eats them. These are personal chickens."

"No chickens for the crew, then? What do you eat?"

"Gruel and hash and borscht and vodka. Rye bread too." He shrugged and loaded another crate of uselessly protesting chickens.

"Sounds delicious," Freddie said. "Can you use another hand? I wouldn't mind a meal, and a trip."

The man looked at him skeptically.

"I'm a hard worker. Here, let me help you. For free. You

can judge for yourself." The man might not have the power to hire him, but he could put in a good word with someone higher up. Failing that, he would know the best places for a stowaway to hide aboard ship.

Freddie grabbed a stack of three crates and carried them across the gangplank. When he did so, he found himself eye to eye with a chicken. It regarded him accusingly. "*Brr-ock!*" it said, and pecked in his direction. It couldn't reach him through the bars.

You're in for a nasty ride in steerage, he thought. And then, how did they say it in *The Mikado*? "A short, sharp shock."

The hen looked at him as if she blamed him for all the world's ills.

There's nothing I can do, he told himself.

Then he remembered the other chicken and the grand proclamation he'd made after its death.

I will be a hero, he'd sworn to himself back then. *I will always, always do the right thing, no matter how hard it is.* Ben's death had driven all that out of his head. The unfairness of his friend's unnecessary passing had made Freddie bitter and isolated. Now, it took a chicken to remind him of the right thing to do.

He carried the crates back to the dock and unlatched the cages, one by one. By the time the stevedore noticed, the chickens had scattered to freedom and Freddie was gone.

"How did you get me out when no one else could?" Lulu asked as Freddie slid into the backseat of the cab beside her.

He adjusted himself so there was a bit more space between them. The little wire-haired terrier promptly filled it.

"I just told the truth."

"And what was that?"

"Don't you know?" he asked, looking at her sidelong. "And here I thought you were innocent."

"I am. But I still don't know who did it. What did you tell the police?"

"I used some of those acting skills you taught me . . ."

She made a little choking noise.

". . . and found out where the chief of police lived from the studio directory at the guard gate. I told him over breakfast that I was one of the studio attorneys who had taken a bit part for a lark and had witnessed the entire unfortunate event."

"You did what?" she asked incredulously. He just shrugged.

"So you know who shot Ruby?" Lulu asked.

"You did, of course. The question is who put the bullets in the gun. I told the police that I personally witnessed at least six people handle the gun immediately before it went off—including you and including myself."

"You!"

He looked sheepish. "I was a little worried about you, and . . ." Lulu couldn't help it. Her lips curled into a fetching smile. Freddie looked away. "And I don't like guns. When I checked, the gun was definitely not loaded. But I guess technically I'm a suspect too. Anyway, after I gave the chief my statement, he charged down to the station and released you. Simple."

"Yeah," she said bitterly. "So simple not a single person at Lux could manage it." She leaned forward and gave the cabbie her address. "I can't think straight until I've had a bath. Thanks for your help. Where can I . . . ?"

She hesitated. She was going to ask where she could drop him off, but obviously he didn't have a home. She had to reward him for his courage and kindness, but she didn't have her pocketbook with her.

"Would you mind coming home with me for a while?" she amended.

Freddie raised his eyebrows. "My, that's awfully forward. We hardly know each other. I've heard that things move fast in Hollywood, but . . ."

Lulu felt her face redden. "Why, of all the insufferable . . . I just meant that you could clean yourself up, and you could tell me what you saw on the set. Stop smiling at me like that!"

"I told you . . ."

"You don't know any other way to smile. I remember!"

"You're quoting me already? I *am* getting famous."

Frustrated, she didn't know whether to laugh or slap him. Slapping him hadn't gone so well before, but she was too tired and upset to have much of a sense of humor left. So she drew herself up regally in the taxi seat and slapped him verbally. "If you come to my house, I can pay you handsomely for your trouble," she said coldly. "Or rather, my maid can see to it. I'm sure she can find some leftovers in the kitchen too. You can be done and gone by the time I finish my bath."

She saw his face harden slightly. "I didn't do it for the money," he said, just as coldly.

"Everyone does it for the money," she snapped, feeling like a heel. He deserved better than that. He was like that ridiculous little terrier, good and brave and loyal. Lulu wanted to keep him. She wanted to keep them both. But she wasn't the kind of girl who could pick up strays.

She looked at Freddie from the corner of her eye.

But maybe . . .

TWENTY-ONE

Nice place," **Freddie said** as they pulled into Lulu's elegantly graveled circular driveway.

"Oh, this old roost?" she said lightly. "You should see my last place in New York. Twelve stories high." Of course, those twelve stories had two hundred families living in them. He'd spotted her accent, but she wasn't about to give him any more ammunition. Besides, her past had spent too much time in her present. Now she wanted Lulu Kelly and her lovely made-up life to wash it all away again.

"I'm impressed," he answered as they entered the large redbrick home. "Most people I know only have one or two stories. Did each servant have their own floor?"

She shot him a sideways look and called out, "Clara!

Oh, blast, it's her day off, and I was so looking forward to a hot bath. What am I going to do?"

"Maybe what ninety-nine percent of the world—the ones without servants—do every day. Run your own bath."

Lulu glowered at him over her shoulder as she strode up the staircase toward her master suite, leaving him on the landing. "I *know* how to run my own bath. I mean that I'd planned on Clara taking care of you while I do. Follow me. The guest suite is on the left; you can freshen up there. Or will being clean make you feel too unlike yourself?" She could have pinched herself. *Why am I behaving so awfully?* He made her nervous . . . and giddy.

"What a charming hostess you are! Don't fret. I'm positively Darwinian in my ability to adapt. And I can always keep myself busy. Where's the master bath? Through here?"

"Wait!" she cried, running after him as he darted past her and headed down the hall toward her bathroom—and bedroom. "What are you doing? Don't you dare!" Charlie followed blithely, sniffing the corners of what he plainly knew was his new home, no matter what Lulu might say.

Freddie was already bent over the huge oval tub, fiddling with the faucets. "Do you prefer scalding or merely hot? I always like my baths to almost hurt at the beginning. Soothes away life's troubles." He began picking up various bottles of liquid and shaking pots of colored crystals. "You don't strike me as a lavender girl. Oh, I mean woman, of course."

Lulu tugged at his shoulder, but it didn't seem to have any effect . . . other than to keep her closer to Freddie than she'd intended. The steam from her bath rose around them, shrouding them in their own world of heat. He'd evidently decided on scalding.

"Not gardenia. Too sweet. Not musk. Do you know that comes from a musk deer's . . . ? Oh, sorry. You're too delicately reared to hear something like that. So am I, for that matter. Hmm. I've got it! Neroli!"

He picked up the bottle of pale amber oil, pulled out the stopper, and wafted it under his nose. "This is it, definitely. Distilled from the flowers of bitter oranges. Sweet and spicy and deceptively complicated. Yes, this will do perfectly." He tipped the vial, letting the oil run into the gushing hot water. "There, Miss Kelly. Exactly what you like. Your bath is drawn, and your servant retreats to await your command." He bowed and backed out of the room as if she were an empress.

"You don't have any idea what I like!" she shouted after him.

But he did. All the other perfumes and oils and crystals had been gifts from admirers, accompanied by notes comparing her to this sweet flower or that, or else impulse purchases. Wearing those jarring scents was like acting, pretending to be someone she wasn't. Only the neroli seemed to blend with the person she really was. She had the oil for her bath, and a light splash on her vanity. The spicy smell didn't overpower her; it didn't change her. It made her feel more like herself. That was hard to do in Hollywood.

How did he know, out of all these scents, the one I love?

Lulu closed the door and locked it. She could hear Freddie moving around on the other side. What was he doing? Going through her things? Stealing? Maybe he'd take her money and be gone by the time she was out of the bath. *If he goes, good riddance*, she thought, but she knew she didn't mean it.

Tentatively, she slipped out of her clothes. She'd shimmied in and out of costumes with half the wardrobe department, men and women, fussing over her and hardly given it a second thought. But it felt strangely intimate, somehow, to have Freddie just on the other side of the door.

She stepped into the bath. The water held her, but she couldn't relax in its soothing embrace.

He saved me. Just when I thought everything was over, he saved me.

Her eyes closed . . . then sprang open in sudden alarm.

So what does he want in return?

"Miss Kelly?" he called through the door. "May I liberate a few of your eggs? I make a mean omelet. Are you hungry?"

"You bet I am!" she called back, and winced, chiding herself for not scripting a more cultured response.

Maybe that's all he wants, she thought, settling back into the water. *Food, a better life. I owe him that much, at least.* She swirled the scented oil around with her foot. She had a spare bedroom. Well, two, if you counted the one that was devoted to her clothes and shoes. He could stay for a little while, just until he got on his feet. . . .

No. What was she thinking? That would cause a scandal, and she had enough trouble now. Besides, before long she might not even have a house, much less a spare bedroom.

If she was convicted, or if this even went to trial, she would lose everything.

Freddie could have food, clothes, all the money she had on her. But that was all. She didn't have anything else to give.

Charlie put his paws on the edge of the bath and woofed into the spicy-sweet bubbles. Lulu gave him a damp pat and whispered, "Stop thinking you know what I'm going to do, you mutt." He flashed her a joyous canine smile, and Lulu grinned back, then sank completely under the water so no one, not even a dog, could ask her why she was suddenly inexplicably happy despite the threats hanging over her head.

Freddie was ready with her eggs and toast and two pears cut into slices and fanned decoratively. He sucked in his breath when he saw her, clad in a robe of what appeared to be nothing more than white marabou, her water-sleeked head peeking out from a mass of feathers and fluff. He quickly looked down at the eggs—anything to keep from staring, to keep from *wanting*.

I'm here to help her, he told himself again. *I don't want anything more.*

"You clean up nicely," he said, still not really looking.

"The bath is free if you like." She waved a hand airily over her shoulder.

"No thanks. I don't want our food to get cold. And I know you'd be too polite to eat without waiting for me. Sit down." He pulled out a chair for her.

Lulu eyed the meal. "I don't usually eat so much," she

said, but wasted no time picking up a slice of thickly buttered rye. Freddie watched her eyes close as she relished the first bite. He couldn't imagine Violet enjoying such a simple and delicious thing as buttered bread. Peasant food, she'd call it. He'd tried to make an omelet for her one late night after her cotillion ball, and she'd just laughed and rung to wake up the cook.

"And I hate to break it to you, but that isn't exactly an omelet." Lulu took a bite of the ragged eggs. "An omelet is fluffy and folded. These are scrambled at best." But she took another bite, and another, eating with all the enthusiasm of a guttersnipe at the soup kitchen.

"Maybe you'd prefer hard-boiled?" he asked.

She looked up at him sharply. "Are you referring to my personality?"

He shrugged noncommittally, still smiling. She was so easy to tease. It was like having a little sister, he told himself. A little sister naked under a cloud of marabou. He gulped and poured them each a cup of coffee from the percolator.

They both started talking at once.

"When you've washed up . . . ," she said.

"When you've finished eating . . . ," he said.

They both stopped short.

"Go on."

"Ladies first."

"Age before beauty."

"Pearls before swine."

Lulu slapped her fork down on her empty plate.

"Oh, all right," Freddie said, chuckling. "We can get started on the investigation. I've made a list of suspects. Well, people who handled the gun, at any rate." He placed a leather-bound book on the table.

"My diary!"

"Don't worry. I didn't read a word." He ducked to avoid the napkin she threw. "Sorry. It was the only paper I could find. Look, I put your name first, just to be polite."

He leaned over Lulu's shoulder while she peered down at the list. Some were names, some descriptions, written in a bold, sure hand:

Lulu Kelly
Freddie Van
Ruby Godfrey
Blake Tanner
The acting coach
The ginger-haired prop supervisor
The man in the suit whom Lulu is afraid of

"Why are you doing this?" she asked, looking up at him. Her eyes were big and luminous with unshed tears, her unpainted face a sweet pale heart.

"It's always helpful to start with a list," he said quietly.

"No. I mean why are you helping me?"

"It didn't seem like the cops were going to do their job. They rarely do, unless you push them. I figure if you solve this yourself, you can hand them their case on a silver platter and walk away with their thanks. If you leave it to them to investigate, things might go differently."

"No!" Lulu burst out, standing suddenly so that they were face to face, very close. "You don't understand! Why are *you* helping *me*?" She laid heavy emphasis on those two words and waited.

Freddie had a hundred reasons, some of which had to do with him, some with her. He settled on the one that made the deepest impression.

"That fellow from the breadline, Rocco. He's a bully and a swindler and probably worse. But you felt sorry for him when he was down. You saw that he could be better. So you gave him that bracelet. That's enough for him to get a room for a month, a good set of clothes, hot food. You gave him a chance."

He saw her lip tremble, but she bit it and then said, "So what? That was nothing to me—like giving a nickel to a beggar." She tossed her head like he'd seen her do on set when she was playing Jezebel. But now her hair was slicked back and wet, and a lock only snaked free and hung, damp and infinitely charming, against her cheek. With a supreme effort, Freddie didn't tuck it behind her ear.

"What do I care if that sap gets a few of my things?" Lulu added. "I've got a ton of jewels—a jewelry box full of 'em."

"No, you haven't," Freddie said softly.

"What would you know?"

"I went through your jewelry box."

"Why, you—"

"A little gold cross, a couple of combs set with aqua-marine, and an old-fashioned cameo brooch I bet came from your mother."

Very quietly, Lulu whispered, "My mother never had any jewelry. Not one piece. But the woman in the cameo looks like her, a little. I found it in an antiques shop."

"You don't have all that much money, Lulu. Giving Rocco that bracelet wasn't nothing. They probably pay you well at Lux, but this house costs a pretty penny, and I bet you send plenty back home. Almost everything in this 'roost' of yours is rented and could be gone tomorrow. And you don't accept gifts from men. There's a dozen who would load you up with diamonds if you let them, but you don't take them up on their offers."

"How dare you! You don't know me, Freddie," she said, sad and bitter, with an undercurrent of hope. "I don't have a heart of gold."

"Never said you did. Gold's soft, Lulu. You strike me as stronger . . . and more precious." Freddie finally gave in to impulse and curled the stray tendril behind Lulu's ear. "I think maybe you have a heart of platinum."

Lulu was feeling tender and a little breathless when Veronica and David showed up a moment later with a smor-gasbord of smoked salmon, thinly sliced dark brown bread, and capers.

"I thought maybe you'd be too balled up to feed your-self," she said, barging into Lulu's house in her familiar, proprietary way. Veronica had become Lulu's best friend in Hollywood, and even when the publicist wasn't scheming to bring her greater glory, they often palled around, with or without David. "Besides, since it's two days until payday, Mandelbrot and I needed a cheap date. And, of course, we had to satisfy our curiosity about . . ." She suddenly caught sight of Freddie and performed a staged double take. "Oh. Well, what d'ya know? Curiosity satisfied."

Lulu went pink, looking utterly abashed at being discovered in her feathered dressing gown alone with a man.

"Lulu, my pet, are you sure you want to invite the vulture-like glee of the paparazzi by having an unknown, unattached young man in your house?" Veronica asked archly. "Especially one so handsome and young you can't possibly pass him off as an uncle."

"Veronica!" both Lulu and David protested at the same time.

Veronica winked at Lulu but answered David. "Well, he *is* handsome. There's no denying that. If I own a pooch, I can still be a judge at a dog show, can't I? I don't complain when you ogle starlets' chassis while they sign their contracts, do I?"

"I'd never . . . ," he began, but didn't have a chance. Lulu loved watching the exchanges between Veronica and David. Someone who didn't know them so well might think that Veronica was domineering, David henpecked, and make dire predictions about their future happiness if they ever got married. But Lulu could see the beautiful dynamic in the way Veronica teased and David protested, the way Veronica seemed to sometimes carry both sides of the conversation, leaving David with scarcely a word, but with so much that was devoted and loving passing unspoken between them in the slightest glance. They understood each other completely and perfectly. Lulu could clearly see them sixty years from now, still together, David offering Veronica his arm as they hobbled to the neighborhood deli, Veronica finishing all of his sentences for him to save him the trouble. They were happy, and they would be happy, no matter what, as long as they had each other.

Lulu could only dream of a relationship like theirs. Every other love affair she saw in Hollywood seemed to be just that: an "affair." Either there was something clandestine and illicit about it, as if love were a decadent treat best eaten on the sly, or it was an event, a big premiere carefully planned and orchestrated with the perfectly curated guest list.

They sat around Lulu's kitchen table, planning a strategy and going over the suspect list again and again, trying to see who could possibly have a motive to either shoot Ruby or frame Lulu.

"Well," Veronica said, "I'm just going to assume for the time being that neither of you are guilty of anything but being in the wrong place at the wrong time, though I know you, my favorite client and pal of pals, wouldn't shed much of a tear if Ruby was out of the picture, and Mr. Face over here, well, I'm sure if I investigated enough, I could come up with some sort of secret, not that I'd mind probing—"

"All right. Knock it off, Veronica, will ya!" David said.

"We get it already. The kid's got a nice mug!" David moaned as Lulu finally laughed, and Freddie's cheeks flushed with color.

"Fine," Veronica went on, running her finger down the list, "but I just don't get it. Why would any of these people want to actually off Ruby? Or take you down, for that matter?"

"I can't for the life of me think of anyone in Hollywood who even *likes* Ruby," said David. "I've seen her be a real monster to pretty much every person she's come into contact with!"

"As far as I can tell, the question is, who *didn't* want to see her gone!" Freddie chimed in.

"Well, Blake certainly can't stand her," Lulu said. "He practically turns purple every time she walks into a room. It's always obvious. He's not *that* good an actor."

"And how!" Veronica guffawed. "And why would Vasily or those crew people go that far?" Lulu suddenly remembered that Ruby knew more about Vasily than perhaps Vasily cared to have anyone know. But Lulu knew it, too, as did Veronica. So it couldn't be too much of a secret. Of course, she'd come to understand the difference between what everyone in Hollywood knows, and what everyone knows.

"It doesn't add up," said David.

"And who's this guy in the suit that you're so afraid of?" Veronica asked Lulu, all eyes turning to her.

"No one!" Lulu said, holding up her hands. "I have no idea who Freddie is talking about. Must have been a figment of his imagination—or mine. I never know what I'm thinking when I'm acting. You know how goofy I am like that!"

Veronica and David just nodded, and David started work on another slice of brown bread and salmon as Lulu jumped up to fetch some more coffee. Freddie looked at her suspiciously, wondering why, in this dire moment, she would choose to lie to the only safe people in her life. *There must be some secret. Some terrible, frightening secret*, he thought. He understood such secrets, though, so he chose not to press her.

As they talked, Lulu kept a sidelong watch on the perplexing young man who had entered her life so suddenly and so completely. He was at ease with lively, verbose Veronica, matching her quip for quip. He brought David out of his natural diffidence, and for a while a surprised Veronica fell uncharacteristically silent while Freddie and David talked politics.

Lulu was mostly quiet, exhausted from the upheaval of the past day. Freddie didn't try to bring her into the conversation, but his eyes were attentive and eloquent. He looked at her often, sometimes openly, sometimes with a secret glance that the others didn't see. It was a look just for her, caring, concerned . . . and something else, too. These looks made her heart flutter.

When David and Veronica finally left, there was a long, heavy silence between the actress and her vagabond savior. Abruptly, Lulu told him, "You can stay here tonight."

Then she fled to her room before she lost her nerve, and didn't emerge until the next morning.

TWENTY-TWO

They say as a place to be invited, Pickfair is only slightly less important than the White House," Lulu said as she and her maid, Clara, put the finishing touches on her coiffure.

"And Pickfair is a lot more fun, I bet," Freddie said, peeking into Lulu's boudoir in time to see the maid pin a feathered fascinator onto Lulu's carefully arranged waves. "Some of those White House parties can be deadly dull."

"And you've been to so many, I'm sure." Lulu still didn't know what to make of this strange young man, but with each passing hour she was becoming more and more attached to him. He simply fit her, like a sublimely comfortable pair of shoes that she just never wanted to take off. She was getting used to him, and that made her nervous. But not so nervous as to send him away.

He didn't talk about his past, but she had him pegged for a teacher's son. Maybe he had a decent background and was orphaned before he could make a start in life. Or his parents had lost everything in the crash, a common enough story. He was clever, and he'd obviously read enough newspapers and books to make all those jokes about speaking Latin and mingling in high society sound convincing. He might always seem as if he was making fun of her, but she found she didn't mind as much as she should. And she gave as good as she got.

"Too many," Freddie said. "Herbert was always a bore, talking about his Stanford days as if they were yesterday. Lou was a treat, though. She taught me a little Chinese."

"Herbert and Lou Hoover? Of *course* you're on a first-name basis." She laughed and stood, smoothing the skirt of her crushed strawberry gown.

It was the day after Lulu's release from jail. Clara had been called at home and offered double her usual pay to stay. It wouldn't do to have male company overnight without a chaperone who could vow to the tabloid journalists that absolutely nothing happened.

Throughout the day Veronica called Lulu every half hour, updating them on the investigation. Ruby was still unconscious. Sometimes the doctors thought she might pull through. Other times they weren't so sanguine.

The police were continuing to interview everyone who had been on the set, and Veronica was asking plenty of questions herself, but so far there were no solid answers. They'd pulled the day rushes, but though the rough film clearly showed who handled the gun during the takes, the cameras weren't rolling beforehand, so there was no evidence to be found there. Nothing revealed who had opened the cylinder and inserted the bullets.

Tonight Lulu was scheduled to attend a gala event at Pickfair, the lavish home of Hollywood's most glittering couple, Mary Pickford and Douglas Fairbanks. Usually the studio arranged for a suitable escort—one of the unattached young male stars in the Lux stable, or maybe a handsome older actor, recently divorced, whose arm she would cling to and laughingly insist they were "just very, very dear friends." But the studio informed her that her date had the flu and suggested that perhaps she'd like to stay home to nurse him. Lulu suspected they might try to spin the Florence Nightingale bit into a publicity ploy to show Lulu's good character and get the public's sympathy. Maybe they'd even send cameras into the sickroom. Lulu declined their offer.

They couldn't quite uninvite her—that was up to Mary Pickford—but they made it clear that due to her current suspect state, she might do better to keep a low profile.

"Nothing doing," Lulu had said, and promptly invited Freddie to accompany her. "I can tell the press that we're 'just very, very dear strangers,'" she'd told him. "Some of the suspects will be there, and I want to look every last one of them in the eye. Blake Tanner will be there for sure. He finagles an invitation to every major party. And believe it or not, I know for a fact Roger King will be there."

Freddie had looked at her blankly.

"The head of props. He's married to Velma King, who has been making wigs for Mary Pickford and everyone else in this town for years. Mary invites her everywhere so she won't ever mention that little bald spot."

"But you know about it," Freddie had pointed out.

"Oh, there are no secrets *here*. Only in Ohio and Kansas. We can know all the dirt, as long as *they* don't." She made a sweeping gesture eastward to include all of America and the rest of the world.

For Freddie's clothes, Veronica came to the rescue, borrowing a complete white-tie ensemble from Lux wardrobe on the pretext of a photo shoot. He was worried about dressing in something so fancy, knowing it increased his chances of being spotted. But he felt he had to risk it.

Now, as they were about to leave for the party, Lulu looked him over.

"Your tie isn't straight," she said, cocking her head.

Freddie bristled. All his life people had been telling him to straighten his tie. He had taken it from Mugsy, who'd had only his best interests at heart. His fiancée had gone so far as to straighten it herself. It should have been a loving gesture, but it had always grated, having other hands trying to paw him into perfection.

He braced himself for Lulu's interfering touch, but she only said, "That's good. Casual. You want to look like you don't care what you're wearing. Some of these actors, they run to the powder room to make sure their hair is perfect and their tie is straight, just in case someone snaps a photo. It makes me sick."

Freddie let out a sigh from the breath he hadn't realized he'd been holding.

"Isn't it your job to care about how you look?" he asked.

"That's just what it is—a job. It isn't *me*."

The taxi pulled up to the mock-Tudor house near eight. "It's not as grand as I'd imagined," Freddie said.

"Wait till you see the inside. They enjoy playing at country life, like Marie Antoinette, with geese in the swimming pool and romping Alsatians on the lawn, but inside it's all gold leaf and floor-to-ceiling mirrors."

Freddie handed her out of the car, and they walked together to the front door.

"Wow," Freddie breathed as they stepped into the otherworldly splendor. The walls were paneled in deeply burnished mahogany. They shone in the glitter of electric lights and reflected ghostly images of the mingling guests so that Charlie Chaplin had a wraithlike double on the wall behind him and Joan Crawford's wide-set eyes flashed in duplicate, all-seeing. The Barrymores didn't need artificial multiplication—there were already so many of that famous acting family in attendance. Freddie saw people he recognized from movies—Jean Harlow, Norma Shearer, Gary Cooper, Spencer Tracy—but luckily, no one he knew personally. That was fortunate. His father loved having the Hollywood elite around him, and the van der Waals's parties were usually glittering with stars.

Lulu smiled at him in sympathy as she saw him look around in apparent amazement. She remembered what it was like to be a kid from the slums suddenly thrust into all this splendor. Freddie might come from a slightly higher social strata than her, but it still must be almost overwhelming to him to see these riches.

"They're just people," she reassured him in a whisper. "Most are nice, some aren't very smart, and a lot of them aren't even all that good-looking when you see them close-up in real life. Don't worry. Just stick with me."

She was wrong about his amazement. Freddie was thinking that after a year on the road, after all the hardships and heartache, here he was again, in white tie, surrounded by glitter and money, with a waiter (who hoped one day to be an actor) handing him a flute of champagne. *I might as well be home again*, he thought.

But no, these weren't crooks and industrialists, bankers and businessmen who had made their fortunes on the sweat and misery of the poor. They were today's Scaramouch and Harlequin and Columbine—entertainers paid to delight. For all their foibles, it was as innocent an occupation as being a brickmaker or a ditchdigger. They produced a product the world needed, and were paid for it. Acting, for all its inherent falseness, was an honest trade.

Five steps into Pickfair, he felt like he belonged there.

Not just here, he thought. *In this town. In this business.*

He looked at the girl on his arm.

With her.

☆ ☆ ☆

Lulu made her rounds as blithely as if she'd not recently spent a night being interrogated in jail. Though she knew that everyone at the party knew, and watched her in curious fascination, she laughed and chatted, flitting here and there with butterfly grace and just as fleeting an attention span, making sure she said hello to everyone. Freddie was introduced simply as a new Lux actor. He got a few admiring glances, but no one treated him like he didn't belong.

He enjoyed a particularly amusing conversation with a wild actress named Tallulah Bankhead and her date, director George Cukor. They had just had success together with *Tarnished Lady* and were regaling Freddie with stories, before inviting him to a small after-party at Tallulah's house on Stanley Avenue. As they walked away, Tallulah gave him a dangerously flirtatious glance and mouthed, "See you later."

Before moving away, Cukor whispered in his ear, lips brushing against Freddie's flushed cheek, "Beware. Tallulah's parties have no boundaries, my handsome young fellow." Lulu swooped in, took Freddie's arm, and pulled him protectively toward her, knowing full well that these two lions were both licking their chops for a taste of the fresh meat before them.

"There's Vasily," Freddie said, pointing discreetly. A golden-haired young man was talking to him in a dim corner. Lulu recognized him as one of Vasily's students. The young man seemed to be importuning the acting coach, while Vasily demurred, gently at first. Lulu wasn't close enough to hear what they were saying, though, and took Freddie by the arm to angle closer.

Suddenly there was no need to get any nearer. Vasily's voice rose, loud enough to make conversation around him fall quiet. "I can't!" he all but shouted. "It's too late for that. You don't have any idea what I've done."

He looked around, aghast at the room's attention, and quickly pulled himself together. "And that, dear boy, is how the scene should be performed."

There was a smattering of applause, the producer Irving Thalberg asked Vasily for a copy of the script, and the party resumed.

Freddie and Lulu exchanged glances. "That was odd," Freddie said.

But when they looked back to the dim corner, Vasily was gone, and they couldn't find him for the rest of the night.

All through the party, Lulu heard the whispers behind her back . . . and annoyingly, the ones to her face.

"My dear, how too, *too* ghastly," gushed Lolly, giving her a pair of air kisses and then taking Freddie's arm in a proprietary sort of way. She led them into a large, much quieter room decorated in a Wild West motif. Appropriately, Will Rogers lounged on a rawhide sofa, while newcomer John Wayne tossed a lazy lasso at a set of bullhorns.

In that relative privacy Lolly went on. "She had it coming, but surely, darling, you could have found a less obvious way of removing Ruby from the picture."

"Lolly!" Lulu gasped. "You can't mean to say you think I put the real bullets in that gun?"

"Oh, my dear, I believe anything—simply anything!" she shrilled in her little-girl voice. "My reputation depends on it. Didn't you do it on purpose, then? Not even an eensy-weensy bit on purpose? Oh well. I'll scrap that copy. Though it *would* make a sensational story, wouldn't it? I could spin it so that—"

"Lolly!"

"Very well. It was an accident, then. You put the bullets in just to scare her, and—"

That time, Lulu's warning look was enough to quiet her. She hoped the cowboys weren't taking notes.

Freddie chimed in. "Mrs. Parsons, I noticed you were on the set when the shooting occurred." He gave her the smile he reserved for aunts and grandmothers.

"I certainly noticed *you*, you charming boy," she simpered. Lulu rolled her eyes, but since Lolly was practically nibbling at the bait, she let Freddie continue to fish.

"Did you see anything suspicious?"

"*Everything* I see is suspicious," she replied, pinching his cheek. He managed not to grimace. "Suspicion is my stock in trade. Max, the head of makeup, was wearing a tie that doesn't suit him at all, so that means he's having an affair with someone at Lux. It's a present, you see, and a tacky one at that. He hates it, but he's enamored of the giver, so he has to wear it because they'll be watching. Oh, and Niederman was absent from the set. He never fails to walk by all of the occupied stages to make sure his money is being well spent, but he didn't that entire day. Do you know why? Some people he owes money to have come collecting, and he was locked in his office, hiding from them. He lost his shirt, tie, and tails at the racetrack in the last few months. A cool million at least. Lucky he didn't lose Lux. Best thing he could do is set the whole place on fire. He has every inch of Lux insured for a mint. Poor man, everyone taking his money. If it ain't the horses, it's the whores. Oh, excuse me. I came up with that one last night, but of course, I can't print it, so I had to get it off my chest."

Lulu managed to interrupt the monologue. "Did you say that Niederman has insurance on Lux?"

"Of course! And a separate policy on every new film. Every star, too."

"Thank you, Lolly. As soon as the police get to the bottom of the shooting and I'm cleared, I'll make sure you get an exclusive. That's a promise."

"Speaking of which," Lolly asked as Lulu dragged Freddie away, "are you two exclusive? My readers would *love* to know. . . ."

TWENTY-THREE

Lulu took Freddie's arm and hustled him out to the back lawn. Mary Pickford kept the grounds fairly dark, for those guests who wanted the privacy a wall of night could provide . . . and those whose faces wouldn't hold up to the scrutiny of electric glare. The only light came from a few torches near the pool. Freddie and Lulu sheltered beneath a potted palm, and Lulu, feeling paranoid under so many watching eyes, kept the conversation low.

"I never even thought of Niederman, because he didn't handle the gun," Lulu said. "But it *could* have been him."

"Sure," Freddie agreed. "He could have paid anyone there to put the bullets in. But would he stoop so low?"

Lulu shrugged. "I've heard some stories. And I've seen

some things. Oh!" Her hand went to her mouth. "No, that wouldn't be possible."

"What?" Freddie asked.

"Well, I once saw Ruby in an, er, compromising position with Niederman. She thought she'd get a career boost afterward, but he wouldn't help her out. If anything, I think it held her back. Poor Ruby's ambitions seem to always lead her down the worst possible path. It's a shame, really, because she's a talented actress."

"I got the impression there was no love lost between the two of you," Freddie said.

"There's not, but I can still admit she's got the chops. She might be under contract to Lux, but she hates Niederman. She could have put the bullets in herself, just to discredit him and his studio."

Freddie considered for a moment. "No, she would have known that someone in that group would probably wind up shot, and it could have been her as easily as anyone else. She might have wanted to cause trouble for Niederman, but she wouldn't have deliberately put herself in danger."

Lulu stroked the palm tree's smooth trunk. "You're right. We can cross her off the list." She pounded the palm with her balled fist. "In fact, we can cross all of 'em off but one. This a waste of time. I already know who did it."

"You do?"

She sighed and turned to lean her back against the trunk. "How did you put it? 'The man in the suit whom Lulu is afraid of'? That about sums it up."

Freddie stepped closer and put a hand on her bare shoulder. It felt warm and comforting, impossibly sweet. But it was no use. "That man wants me," she said.

"Wants you to . . . Oh. Wants you. Who is he?"

"Never mind. I'm just sure he set the whole thing up. He wanted me in trouble so he could swoop in and rescue me."

"That's a pretty sleazy kind of knight who puts the damsel in distress on purpose."

"He's more of a dragon than a knight." She shuddered in the chilling air.

"I saw him slip money to the first policeman on the scene. I'll happily testify to that. If you know, then why can't you expose him?"

"It's not that easy," she said, covering her face with her hands. "You don't know who he is."

"Only because you won't tell me. Lulu, look at me." Freddie gently took her hands in his, uncovering her face. "Let me help you."

"You shouldn't. I don't know what he'd do to you if you got in his way. Oh, Freddie! Just . . . just leave me alone. You shouldn't be involved in this." She gave a hysterical little laugh. "It won't be the worst thing in the world. He's rich. He's powerful. He can give me a good life. At least, it would look like that to everyone else. Then someday he'll get sick of me and I'll be free." She felt beaten, defeated. She expected Freddie to walk away.

He put his arms around her. "Do you love him?"

Her eyes flew open. "No! I hate him."

"Then you'd be a prisoner either way. It doesn't matter how much money someone has, or what the rest of the world expects you to want. If there's no love, or trust, or respect, it's better to be a bum." Lulu thought he sounded angry, as if this all affected him much more personally than she realized. "There are too many strong, rich men in this world, taking whatever they want. If you let him win, you'll be nothing more than his slave. Better to go to prison than to give in to someone like him."

"Freddie, I *can't* go to prison. I'll lose everything. Oh, I don't care about that for myself. I'd rather dig ditches than let him touch me. But my family will lose everything. You don't know how it was before I made it to Hollywood. I can't let them fall back into that."

Freddie thought again of his vast fortune. How easy it would be . . .

"Come away with me," he said impulsively, to chase off those billions of temptations.

"What? Where?"

"Anywhere!" He grinned fiercely, and she thought she'd never seen someone look so passionate, so free. "I almost hopped a boat to Russia the other day. We can go to Hong Kong, India—anywhere you like."

"Freddie, I . . . We just met."

"So? I'm not asking you to marry me. I'm not thinking about you that way at all." He could have kicked himself when he saw a little light in her eyes flicker and die. "I mean, you're right, we just met, and that would be . . . Look, that part doesn't matter. We can still run away. Change your name, get a job, live a whole new life. You'll be safe from him. Whatever happens next, you won't have to worry about the law or what's-his-face in the shiny suit."

"Sal," she murmured.

"What?"

"His name. Sal Benedetto."

Freddie's heart skipped a beat. "Oh."

"You've heard of him?"

The memory came back to him, of his father sitting in his office, smoking a cigar with a man Freddie recognized from the papers: Cosimo Benedetto. Freddie, then sixteen, had burst into his father's sanctum to share some piece of news, a good grade, a smart new tie. His father had introduced them. He'd shaken the man's hand, accepted his compliments and congratulations. Weeks later, he'd seen the man's picture in the paper. "Crime Lord Cleared of Tax Fraud." But when Freddie showed it to his father, sincerely believing he had no knowledge of this particular business partner's shady dealings, Jacob van der Waals had explained that business was business and what one administration called illegal, another would condone. A successful man follows his own rules and waits for the laws to catch up.

"Besides," his father had reassured him, "you know I'd never do anything wrong."

In all his stupid innocence, Freddie had believed him.

Freddie vaguely remembered reading that Cosimo had been gunned down and that his murderer had escaped. In some scrap of paper he'd used to line his slap-soled shoes, he'd seen a story on another trial, dismissed almost before it began. Cosimo's murderer shot himself, and his son, Sal, once a suspect, was innocent, as an on-scene witness could testify. He recognized Sal's face now. It had grinned at him smugly in black-and-white newsprint.

"I've heard of him," Freddie confirmed in a grim voice. A heartless businessman like Freddie's own father . . . a ruthless, brutal, murdering thug like those men who had attacked him in the barn. Sal was everything Freddie hated, the worst of humanity. He would never let Lulu fall into that man's clutches.

With renewed determination, Freddie took Lulu's cold hands again. "Listen to me and listen good. It doesn't matter whether it was him or another person on our list or someone we haven't even thought of yet. We still have to do the same thing—clear your name. We're a team in this now, Lulu. Until the end."

She looked up at him, her face pale as the moon in the darkness. Something about Freddie made her feel comforted, safe . . . even, to her amazement, happy. *It makes no sense*, she thought, as giddy as if she'd downed three glasses of champagne. At the worst possible moment of her life, she'd fallen for this poor boy, this bum. *It can't be love*, she argued with herself. *I've only known him for two days.*

But then, in her world, a romance never took more than ninety minutes to be fully realized. Two days was a lifetime.

He moved closer. *He's going to kiss me*, Lulu thought. *And it's going to be perfect. The darkness, the torchlight, the fear and the comfort. And him. Wonderful, infuriating, glorious him.*

She tilted her face, stood on tiptoe. . . .

Freddie glanced over her shoulder. "Well, look who's there."

TWENTY-FOUR

The tingling that had filled her body at the anticipation of Freddie's kiss seemed to sink into the pit of her stomach, where it fluttered like a bird trapped in a bedroom. She followed Freddie's gaze and saw two figures in the shadow of a marble statue of Artemis. The torchlight glinted on red-gold hair, and Lulu recognized the Lux prop master Roger King. But who was that he was talking to?

"I know that double chin!" Lulu said. "That's Joe Schenck, the president of United Artists."

"Mary Pickford's studio, right?"

"So that's what Hoover's doing to combat poverty—a free subscription of *Variety* to all forgotten men?" She felt Freddie close to her back, protective. She could do anything with him at her back—anything! Even tease him.

"You know an awful lot about, well, everything."

"I keep my ears open. Why is a Lux man talking to the head of United Artists?"

Lulu shrugged, feeling the moiré silk facings of his lapel brush her shoulder. A little shiver, novel and delightful, traced its way down her arms.

"We can talk to Roger when he's finished. Oh! Did you see that?" Lulu gasped.

"They shook hands?"

"Open your eyes, lughead. Joe just passed Roger some money. I've seen people make that kind of exchange a hundred times. The numbers game was big in my neighborhood. Look, he slipped it into his inside pocket."

"You're a woman of hidden depths, Lulu."

"You don't know the half of it," she said, adding in her head, *And if I'm lucky, you never will*. After the brief exchange, the pair parted. Joe went back inside, and Roger lit a cigarette. Lulu slipped away from Freddie's delicious warmth and charged up to him, even as Freddie called softly for her to wait.

"You have some nerve, mister!" she said, shaking her finger in Roger's face. The flummoxed man tried to duck out of the way, but her finger stabbed him in the chest. "How much did United Artists pay you to jinx Lux? Because what I just saw could guarantee you a one-way trip to Sing Sing. Didn't you think about the consequences? Ruby might die, and I'm set to take the fall."

"What are you talking about, my dear?" Roger looked

like he was making some effort to keep his calm, but his voice was shaky.

"My friend and I just saw you take money from Joe Schenck. Don't even try to deny it. It's your word against two witnesses. *You* put real bullets in the gun. You handled the gun before it went off."

"Not *right* before," Freddie interjected, but Lulu ignored him.

"You better tell me the truth now, mister, because I'm going to go to Niederman and the police about what I just saw, and you're going to prison for life!"

"Lulu," Freddie tried again, "I don't think Mr. Schenck could have passed him enough money to make it worth-while. . . ."

Lulu half heard this, and grabbed Roger by the lapels. "If you had to sell me out, you could have at least held out for a lot of money." Freddie was right. Even if it was hundreds, it couldn't have been a very large stack to fit so neatly into a palm and a pocket. She felt insulted that her life and future were apparently worth so little. "How much did he give you, you rat?" She fumbled at his pockets. "Aha—I found it!"

She pulled out . . . a slip of paper.

"What does it say? Your lighter, Freddie."

"Sorry. I don't smoke."

"So? Neither do I, but lighting a lady's cigarette is every man's job. Roger, give me a light!" He mumbled something about not smoking either, ignoring the swirl of smoke coming from the coffin nail between his fingers. "Oh Lord, the things I have to do." She reached into Roger's pockets again and found a matchbook, black as Japanese lacquer with a gold-embossed figure of a ram's head, the horns curling back to its shoulders. Lulu struck a match and read the faint penciled writing on the scrap of paper.

"Lemon Squash?"

"Thanks, but I'll stick with champagne," Freddie said.

"No, that's what the note says." The flame neared her fingertips, so she shook the match out and tossed the book to Freddie so he could light another.

"Maybe it's his shopping list," Freddie suggested as he peered down at the paper.

"Yeah, that's it," Roger blurted out. "Now, if you'll excuse me . . ."

"Not so fast, mister. Where's the money?"

"There is no money," he squeaked, pointing at the scrap. "That's all Joe gave me."

"What does it mean, then? No, don't give me that baloney," she said when he sputtered something about drink orders.

"King," said Freddie, stepping up, "you're in cahoots with United Artists. What gives? I know you were involved in the shooting in some way."

"You better tell us," Lulu added, "or I'm going to scream my head off and tell Lolly every last thing." She was pleased to hear Roger gasp. "And we both know Lolly can ruin anyone she chooses."

This threat seemed to scare him more than telling either Niederman or the police.

"All right already," he whined miserably. "Just please, I'm begging you, promise you won't tell anyone."

Lulu nodded, though she had no intention of keeping that promise if it saved her from a murder rap.

"Lemon Squash is the name of a horse. He's racing down at Agua Caliente next week. Joe just had a hot tip for me."

It sounded reasonable, Lulu thought. But why was Roger still so nervous? There had to be something more to it.

"What else?" Lulu asked, unconsciously slipping into a role. She was a hardened girl, a tough cookie who would never take no for an answer. As soon as she started pretending, it came much easier. Inside, she was shaking. Outside, she shook Roger by his jacket.

"That's all, I swear!"

"Lolly!" Lulu called into the flickering torchlight. "I have a scoop for you!"

"Shh! Okay, jeez, Lulu, you win. I'll tell you. Niederman thinks I'm getting hot tips on the horses from a jockey I know. But really, Joe's been feeding me names of horses that look great but are bound to lose. He's hoping to push Niederman into bankruptcy so he can buy out Lux. Everyone knows Niederman's a sucker for the horses. A few more big losses and he'll have to sell Lux for sure."

"You dirty, no good . . . ," Lulu said. "How could you?"

"Hey, I don't make him bet on the ponies. He's digging

his own grave. Joe promised me a job at the new conglomerate as soon as it happens. Twice the pay."

"See," Lulu said over her shoulder to Freddie. "Everyone does it for the money." She turned back to Roger. "If I ever hear about you doing this again, I'll make sure Niederman fires you. Got it?" She gave him a little shake.

"Okay, okay! Man, you're one tough broad. Not like that sweet little Ruby."

Lulu clapped her hand to her forehead. "Good grief! Are you joking? Sweet?"

"So you really had nothing to do with that?" Freddie asked.

"Heck no. That girl's a peach. I wouldn't ever risk hurting her. *You*, on the other hand . . ." But he saw Freddie step forward with a cocked fist and stopped. Lulu, who didn't notice Freddie's menace behind her, was quite pleased when Roger changed his tune and said with exaggerated politeness, "Thank you for being so understanding, Miss Lulu, and if there's anything I can do to help you, just let me know."

"There is, in fact," Freddie chimed in. "You can let us see the gun."

"I can't. The police have it as evidence."

Lulu's heart sank.

"I *do* have one of the bullets, though. I thought I should make the gun safe until the police arrived, so I unloaded the revolver and slipped the bullets and casing into my pocket. But I had a hole in the lining and one fell through and got wedged inside my jacket. I meant to return it. . . ."

"But you were too busy scheming to destroy Niederman," Freddie finished.

"It's in my desk drawer. I'll leave a door unlocked for you. Now, if you'll excuse me, I have some serious drinking to do."

Before he could escape, Lolly materialized out of the shadows. Her ears were as keen as a fox . . . and she wore the pelts of two of the glassy-eyed beasts tossed carelessly over her shoulders, making her look like a sequined barbarian. "Did I hear my name?"

"You did," Lulu said. "Roger here was *dying* to give you his recipe for homemade lemon squash."

She took Freddie's arm and sailed back into the mansion.

TWENTY-FIVE

believe him," Lulu mused with a furrowed brow. "Niederman has every actor and every shoot heavily insured. Maybe a payout from a tragedy would be enough to clear his debts."

"So that's two names off the list," Freddie said as they walked back into the cacophony of the party. "Cross off Ruby and Roger and add Niederman."

"Aren't you going to cross your own name off?" Lulu asked.

"Nah. I'm pretty suspicious."

"You sure are. A man with no past."

"But what a future," he said, looking down at Lulu in a way that made her flush. "Can you think of any other suspects?"

"Well, there's Vasily, who looked a tad suspicious. What

did he mean, 'You don't have any idea what I've done'?"

"Could be anything," Freddie said. "Or he could have really been demonstrating a scene."

"He's the studio's acting coach," Lulu went on, "and Ruby certainly knows his secret. But then, so does nearly everyone else in Hollywood." She filled him in on Ruby's disastrous attempt to seduce Vasily. "It wouldn't matter so much if that got out. They only care if it's a handsome leading man. No one outside of this town knows who Vasily is, so it wouldn't hurt his reputation at all. And yes, though he is quite literally a queen of drama, I seriously doubt he's dramatic enough to kill. It can't be Vasily. That's just too absurd."

"She really tried to seduce him, too?" Freddie asked. "That Ruby sure has a lot of cracks in her plaster."

"I feel sorry for her. She's a good actress, and she's so determined. Too determined, I guess, and in the wrong ways. She thinks if she gives away enough of herself, then someone—directors or the world—will want more."

"She might pull through," Freddie said. "Last we heard, the doctors said she seemed to be stabilizing."

"I hope so."

"In the meantime, we have to get you in the clear. Now think: Who else might have reason to hate Niederman, or Lux, or Ruby?"

"Or me," Lulu said. "I shot the gun. I think I must have been the target. No one could guarantee Ruby would get hit. There were so many last-minute changes to the script. I wasn't even supposed to aim for her."

"Let's focus on finding Blake. He's the only other one who handled the gun."

"Except for Sal," she said morosely.

"I know, I know, but before we start unraveling him, let's tie up all the other loose ends." Freddie stopped suddenly and turned so they were very close. "Hey, beautiful, don't catch the glooms again. We'll figure this out. Together."

"That word alone is enough to make me feel a thousand times better," Lulu said, leaning against him.

"Which word? 'Beautiful'?"

"No," she said with a little sigh. "'Together.'"

What have I gotten myself into? Freddie wondered as they wandered around the party, looking for Blake. But it felt so right that he didn't want to question it. Not right as Violet had been right—a girl everyone would approve of, someone of his education and social standing. Violet had been a perfect match . . . in theory. He and Lulu had nothing in common on the surface. But deeper down he knew their hearts were in accord. They *fit*.

All this time I thought I was running away, he mused, looking down at the pale silver-gold of her hair, the dark blue eyes, the mouth that curled in happiness in spite of all her travails. *I was wrong,* he realized. *I was running toward something.* Her.

He could stay in her world, or they could leave together to begin a life in a new world. Either one would make him happy. With her, he could travel the rails and still feel like a king. But no, Lulu wasn't cut out for poverty. He'd work—honest work—to provide for her. He'd . . .

All at once he saw a pair of smoldering dark eyes regarding him from across the room. A woman with dark hair and a painted rosebud mouth held his gaze, then slithered out from the pack of men who surrounded her with expressions of devoted fascination. "Yoo-hoo!" she called, and wiggled a little paw at him.

"Come on, Lulu. We have to get out of here."

"Why? What's the matter?"

Freddie's heart began to race. How could he tell her that after a year on the road he'd finally been recognized by none other than Clara Bow, the silent film star who was still a major box-office draw? Rumor had it that she was going to quit movies and move to a ranch with her new husband. Why hadn't she moved a month ago, instead of popping up here to pick Freddie out of a crowd?

Clara Bow, a New York native, never shed her lower-class accent but was happy to rub shoulders with the people who would have despised her in her days of poverty. She visited her hometown often, and whenever she did, Jacob van der Waals was eager to secure her presence. Some of the classier stars might shun that kind of fawning, but Clara knew the importance of rich friends and always showed up at his parties.

She'd taken a particular shine to Freddie ever since, as a starstruck fifteen-year-old in the grip of his first real crush, he'd presented her with an astonishingly rare orchid—growing in a pot of dirt. Clara, to his mingled horror and delight, had immediately snipped the priceless flower from its stem and stuck in into her hair. "Silly boy," she'd said. "You only give a woman *cut* flowers." Then, to make sure only the delight remained, she'd kissed him lingeringly on the cheek.

If Clara saw him, she'd be sure to tell his father. He immediately averted his eyes and hoped she would think she'd been mistaken.

"Come this way," Freddie urged, pulling Lulu with him. "I thought I saw Blake."

It was all a fiction, of course, but when they were safely down a corridor, they found someone else they knew. First, a woman at that awkward age—too old to be young, too young to be old—came out of a room discreetly fixing her lipstick. Her cheeks and throat were flushed. She greeted them absently and walked down the hall, fanning herself with her handkerchief.

A moment later the door opened again, and a familiar face emerged.

"Rocco!" Lulu squealed.

He was a new man, clean and clear-eyed. He wore a light gray lounge suit that fit his big frame perfectly. His cuff links had that muted shine that might be steel . . . or might be platinum. He was recently barbered, and he smelled fashionably of bay rum.

His manner wasn't as suave as his clothes. "Oh, it's . . . um . . . you," was about all he managed before Lulu said sweetly, "Glad to see you looking so well. Are you a friend of Mary's?"

He looked down the corridor after the older woman. "Er, I don't actually know the broad's name," he said, watching the retreating backside.

"Not her. Your hostess, Mary Pickford."

"Look, lady, I don't want any trouble. . . ."

"And I've got enough of it already."

"Yeah, I heard. Listen, about the other day in the alley-way . . ."

"Consider it forgotten."

"Yeah, thing is, it *is* forgotten. I mean, I woke up and I had a bracelet in my pocket and I think it might be yours. I was pretty stewed and all. You know how it is." He rubbed his jaw, where the stubble was already starting to show through his shave. "I hope you won't be calling the police, but I can't give it back to you. I already sold it." He gestured to himself, from top to bottom.

"You don't remember what happened?"

"He thinks maybe he stole it," Freddie said.

Rocco shifted uneasily from foot to foot.

"I thought it might look good on you," Lulu quipped. "If my style sense was off, I'm glad you traded it in for something more to your taste."

"It's just that I hadn't had anything to eat for a while, and I'd been tootin' up for a couple of days. My last job fell through. I was an, um, assistant to an elderly lady."

"*Assistant*," Freddie repeated with heavy emphasis.

"Hey, old ladies need love too," Rocco insisted. "Most guys won't give them the time of day." With an air of pride he added, "I appreciate their finer qualities."

"Yeah, like their bankbooks," Lulu said. "So who are you here with?"

"A Mrs. Daniels brought me. She's an old friend."

"How old?"

"About ninety, but her hips are in good shape."

Freddie suppressed a snort, and Lulu pinched him. "And you ditched her for Mrs. What's-Her-Name?"

"She got talking to Douglas Fairbanks and told me to toddle off and enjoy myself. So I did," he added with a self-satisfied smile.

Lulu noticed something sticking out of Rocco's pocket. She snatched it, and the rope of pearls snaked through the air. "Rocco!" she said, dangling them reproachfully in front of his strong Roman nose. "From Mrs. What's-Her-Name?"

Rocco hung his head. "Aw, nuts. You know how it is. Old habits die hard. Are you going to turn me in?"

Lulu considered, then shook her head. "I don't want to be interviewed by one more policeman—even to put away a crook like you." She couldn't quite condemn Rocco. It was like being mad at a puppy for chewing up your purse. Well, maybe more a full-grown bull terrier than a puppy. In this case, it was the leathery old bag's responsibility to keep safely away from him.

"You're A-OK, Lulu Kelly," Rocco said. "If there's ever anything I can do for you, just ask. I get around. I know a lot of people. You need a piece, I got a friend unloads trucks at Bighorn Sporting Goods." He lowered his voice. "You need someone roughed up, terminally or otherwise, I got pals who can do that, too. For a price, of course."

"Thanks, Rocco," she said, "but I don't think there's anything you can do for me. I seem to be in too deep."

"Don't you know who set you up?" Rocco asked.

She could have kissed him—almost—for not voicing any doubt about her innocence. "We can think of a few possibilities," she began.

"Oh, it's 'we' now?" Rocco said with a twitch of his brows, eyeing Freddie. "That's okay, I guess. I do better with broads over sixty, anyway. Still, Lulu, if you ever—"

"She won't," Freddie said firmly, taking Lulu's arm again. "Ever."

Rocco held up his hands in mock surrender. "Hey, I saw you talking with that gossipy dame. The one with half an ostrich on her hat. Be careful of that one. She ain't on the up-and-up."

Everyone had to be careful with Lolly; that was nothing new. Still, coming from Rocco . . .

"Why?" Lulu asked.

"Well, I was taking this hothouse tomato out on the town, a real looker, great drumsticks for seventy-five. She had a couple of cocktails and started telling me all these stories about Hollywood scandals. This actress was caught with her boyfriend by her husband. She thought he was out of town, see. So I said some chumps have all the bad luck. This lady, she just laughed and said it was no accident that the husband came home when he did. She said your friend in the hat actually called him and told him when to drop in, then perched by the front door to catch every detail of the fight and get a photo of the wife's black eye, the boyfriend hanging out the second-story window with his trousers around his ankles."

"You mean, she set up a scandal just so she could report on it?" Lulu was aghast . . . but knowing Lolly, not all that surprised.

"That's not the half of it," Rocco said. "While I was finishing helpin' her get comfortable, the dame keeps squawking. Tells me at least that time the cheating was really happening. This lady told me that a few years ago Lolly forged a purple letter addressed to John Gilbert and slipped it to Greta Garbo. That's why she stood him up at the altar."

"No!"

Rocco shrugged. "So she told me. Just be careful. I wouldn't put it past her to have set you up, just for the sake of a story. She's a hyena, and you starry types are all just meat to her."

TWENTY-SIX

After Lulu returned the woman's pearls, they searched all over Pickfair but couldn't find Blake Tanner. When Freddie suggested they go to his home, Lulu agreed. After all, it was only midnight, still early by Hollywood standards.

Blake lived in the Hollywood Hills. As the taxi wended its way up the winding roads, Lulu and Freddie fell silent, losing themselves in the spectacular view and the not-so-secret pleasure of sitting so closely knitted together as they hurtled through the night.

When they pulled up to a large Mediterranean-style home, Lulu told the taxi to wait in the street and they stepped out into the fragrant night air. All the lights were out, but there was a wine-colored Model A Ford roadster in the driveway with Iowa plates, and she caught a flicker from the back of the house.

"That's definitely not Blake's car. He drives an obscenely garish Rolls that I'm positive he can't afford."

Freddie shot her a look. "You're a rather pretty pot to be talking about his kettle."

"Oh, everyone lives above their means out here. Don't give me that look. You and those eyebrows! They'll be the death of me. There, did you hear voices? Let's check the back. Maybe he has a private party going on."

As they passed through a break in a thick wall of privet shrubs, Lulu caught voices, low and intense, arguing. She put a hand on Freddie's chest to stop him.

"This can't go on forever," she heard a female voice say. "I'm telling you, I can't take it!"

"It won't be forever, darling, but I'm still establishing my career. The studio . . . well, they expect certain things from me." That was Blake's voice.

"Sure, for you to have a new floozy on your arm every night." The woman's voice was bitter and deeply sad. "What about me? How can you leave your own wife in Des Moines while you gad about with every starlet in town?"

"Baby, listen to me. They want a playboy, so I have to be one. If I'm nothing but a drab husband with an ordinary wife . . ."

"Ordinary!" Her voice rose to a hysterical pitch. "Who worked her fingers to the bone while you went to acting school? Who gives your mother a bath every damn day?

Who has to sit alone with the laundry and the cat reading stories in *Photoplay* about your latest conquest? Ordinary? I'll give you ordinary."

Lulu heard the sound of a smart slap.

"Darling, I'm begging you. Just give me one more year. I promise after that we'll stage a meeting. Picture it: small-town girl on her first trip to California wins the heart of dashing screen star. It will make all the headlines. We'll get married again with a thousand camera lenses focused on us. Ethel, wait!"

A petite woman in slacks bumped into Lulu and gave her a glare. "Are you his latest girlfriend? Good luck, honey." She stormed away and got into the car, driving off with a screech of tires, almost hitting the parked taxi.

Blake followed, hangdog. When he saw Lulu, he whispered a coarse word Lulu hadn't heard since she'd left the slums.

"I guess you heard all that? My career's over." His shoulders slumped under their carefully constructed shoulder pads.

"You're *married*?" Lulu asked. Blake was one of the most dashing young male stars and had—or had been given—the reputation of a dangerous ladies' man. Lux set him up with a new girl every few months, and the magazines claimed he left a trail of broken hearts in his wake.

"For five years now. Ethel and I agreed I would come out here alone and give it a go, just for three months. If nothing happened by then, I'd go home to Iowa and take over my father's refrigerator-repair business. When Lux picked me up, it was like a reprieve from up above. But when they wanted to set me up with one of the starlets, I never let on that I was married." He rubbed his forehead. "You know how it is. They make up a story for you, and you have to play along. You can't buck the system if you want to be a success."

"I won't tell anyone," Lulu said.

"And I have no one to tell, so your secret is safe with me," Freddie added.

"It's no use. Someone else knows." His breath was coming fast, and he pulled a flask from his pocket and took a swig. From his stagger and bloodshot eyes, it obviously wasn't his first. "I thought it might be all right, but the doctors say . . . Oh, damn! It's all going to hell, isn't it?" He strode through the backyard and into the house. Exchanging looks, Lulu and Freddie followed him.

"What did you mean by doctors?" Freddie asked Blake.

"Ruby's doctors. I got a call from Sassoon. The doctors say she's awake. They think she's going to live. I know it's terrible to wish anyone dead, but for one brief moment I thought my problem was solved."

"You mean Ruby knew about your wife?"

"She found a letter from Ethel in my . . . well, in my bedroom. She threatened to tell the press if I didn't help her get a starring role. How can I do that? I can talk to people, but it isn't up to me. When you beat her out for the lead in *Girl About Town*, I thought I was done for sure, but she gave me one more chance. I'm supposed to get her the lead in *The*

House of Mirth, but that will never happen. I tried to offer her money, but she nixed that. She said fame is the only thing she cares about."

"So you're the one who put the bullets in the gun?" Freddie asked.

"Me? God no, but I almost wish I'd thought of it." He sank heavily onto his sofa. "My fans are going to tear me apart when they find out. If she lives, she's going to expose me. I'm through, Lulu—through."

"Do you think he did it?" Freddie asked when they were back in the cab.

"Why would he tell us about Ruby knowing his secret if he had done it? That would be pretty stupid, to incriminate himself like that."

"He is pretty drunk," Freddie said. "And not too bright, I think."

"Still, I think we can rule him out. Probably. The only thing we can do now is talk with Ruby. Maybe she saw something. Unless we can find hard evidence or get someone to confess, she might be our last hope. The police have talked to everyone else."

"Well, we can't go now." He lifted her wrist to check her slim gold watch, then used it as an excuse to keep hold of her hand, which nestled, warm and content, within his. "It's two a.m."

Fifteen minutes later they found themselves tucked into a booth at LA's most popular late-night haunt, Canter's

Delicatessen on Fairfax Avenue. The joint was jumping.

"Oh, I really shouldn't," Lulu said when the waitress handed them a menu. "Maybe just coffee . . ."

One hot pastrami sandwich, three pickles, and a plate of French fries later, Lulu was still in the booth across from Freddie, her stomach comfortably expanded, talking like she had all the time in the world. Sal and the police loomed over her like the sword of Damocles, but sitting in this tawdry diner with Freddie, she felt as if the moment could stretch happily on forever.

"I could live here," she said dreamily, and ordered a strawberry shake.

"I wonder if they have delicatessens in Hong Kong."

"Oh, they have *everything* in Hong Kong," Lulu said with absolute certainty, letting herself daydream about an all-night restaurant with queued chefs and waitresses in high-necked silk gowns serving dim sum on dragon-festooned plates.

"I don't think we'll be able to afford to eat like this every day," Freddie said, bringing unpleasant reality into her fantasy.

"Oh, yes, we can. We'll discover gold or write a best-seller and dine on caviar every night. No, forget caviar. I want burgers and fries . . . and ice cream . . . and scrambled eggs. When we move to Hong Kong, I'm going to get so fat it will take two rickshaw drivers just to haul me through the streets!"

"You'll be just as beautiful as ever," Freddie insisted.

"But I won't always," she said, suddenly earnest. "What about when I'm old? It doesn't take much to make a woman old, you know. Just a couple of years and a little bad luck. What will happen then?"

"Do I really need to answer that?" Freddie asked, looking at her with what she knew, suddenly and unequivocally, was love.

"No," she said softly.

The waitress brought Lulu's milk shake and asked, a bit amused, if there would be anything else. "Oh, yes! A big plate of bacon, please." Luckily, the place wasn't kosher. The stout waitress gave her a quick sympathetic smile and went for another portion of food.

"Do you know, one thing hasn't changed at all since my poor days. When I lived in the slum, I'd lie awake dreaming about bacon. We could rarely afford meat, you see, and if we got a little bit, we usually couldn't just *eat* it. It had to be stretched, so it went into the soup. I never got to eat bacon in my life, not real sizzling, crispy bacon. Just a chewy little lump of it that had been boiled in three nights of soup in a row. We couldn't eat the bacon pieces as long as they had any flavor to give to the soup."

She felt Freddie's ankle stroke hers in sympathy under the table.

"Then, when I got to Hollywood and had some money, I thought I'd be able to eat all of those nice things. But the first day I signed my contract, they sent a woman over to weigh and measure me and give me two lists, one of things

I'm allowed to eat, one of forbidden foods. One's a footnote, the other's a novel. So here I am, a working actress, still lying in bed and dreaming of bacon." She sighed.

"When we move to Hong Kong, I promise I'll serve you bacon for breakfast in bed every day."

She held out her hand and they shook, another excuse for contact. "It's a deal," she said. "Except on your birthday. Then I'll serve *you* bacon in bed."

She suddenly realized they'd been talking about beds, when they hadn't so much as kissed yet, and she flushed.

It's just a joke, she told herself. *An impossible dream. But such a nice one.*

They talked until five o'clock in the morning, sometimes laughing and teasing, then falling into moments of somber seriousness. Lulu let herself believe that it was possible— either that they could expose the truth and clear her name, or else run away together.

She paid the bill (noticing a pained look from Freddie as she handed over the cash), and they took a taxi to the hospital to see if they could visit Ruby.

"Then, if she has nothing new to offer, we can go back to the set and snoop around," Freddie said.

Even in the predawn hour, the hospital was a mob scene of media and rubbernecking tourists. Lulu belatedly wished she'd stopped home to change as the cameras turned on her in what was clearly last night's gown. They'd see her with a man in the morning, wearing yesterday's clothes, and make nasty assumptions. And she knew she must be disheveled, and probably greasy from her bacon indulgence. She ducked her head and let her hair partly conceal her face as the flash-bulbs exploded.

"Lulu! Did you shoot her?"

"Hey, Lulu, is this a publicity stunt?"

"This way, Lulu! Give us a smile!"

"Do you think they'll let you have a couture prison jump-suit?"

The spirits of Veronica and Mrs. Wilberforce rallied her, and she gave them what they wanted. She adopted a sad little smile and said, "My only thoughts are for the health of my dear friend Ruby." Then, in the classic, ironic plea of famous people throughout the ages, she added, "Please respect my privacy during this difficult time." Privacy was the one thing she was paid not to have.

It was quieter in the critical-care wing. There were only a few dozen of the top paparazzi and twenty or so stars who either cared deeply about Ruby or hoped to piggyback on her dramatic story. Lulu's publicist and agent met her in the waiting room.

"She's awake!" Veronica said. "And how on earth do you manage to look so good at six a.m.? It just isn't fair. Anyway, they say Ruby's going to be fine. Well, she'll still have her old personality, unfortunately. I'd hoped cutting off the oxygen to her brain might have made her a changed woman, but we can't have everything, can we? Oh, and she'll have a scar on her chest, so no more provocative décolletage for old Ruby.

Of course, when you throw the gals in peoples' faces, they're more inclined to flinch than stare, so it might be all for the best. She'll have to be demure now."

Lulu looked at her friend, a little shocked. "Veronica, you are the limit! Still, it's nothing that a headshrinker and the love of a good man won't cure. Can we see her?"

"Not yet," David said. "We've been trying. She's supposed to be making a statement to the press at any moment. We can all go in for that."

"Good," Lulu said. "Maybe she'll have some information for us. I'll try to talk to her in private after the press statement."

A few minutes later the doctor stood in front of the corridor, his hands clasped together prayerfully. "My patient desires to make a short statement about what happened to her. Though she is out of danger, she is still very fragile, and I must ask for complete silence while she addresses you. There will be no questions. Hospital security is standing by to remove anyone who does not comply with these instructions."

Then he led everyone to a large private room. A few people managed to squeeze inside, but most, including Lulu and Freddie, were in the hallway, craning their necks to see Ruby.

She sat propped up against fluffed pillows, her face pale but carefully made-up, even to the false eyelashes. She wore a pale champagne-colored bed jacket, which, while perfectly modest in what it covered, was of a hue to suggest uninterrupted bare flesh. A white bandage peeked out from the loose folds below her shoulder. The room was stuffed to the gills with flowers.

Ruby, pale and interesting, let her eyes roam around the crowd. She nodded and smiled to one or two people, but it wasn't until she found Lulu's face in the back of the crowd that her eyes really lit up. It was a look of pure malice.

"Thank you all for coming," Ruby said. "The good wishes of my friends are what pulled me through. My road will be difficult, but my doctors tell me that I may hope, one day, to make a full recovery."

("She looks like she could hop out of bed and dance a jitterbug," Veronica said in a loudly whispered aside.)

"I know you're all wondering what happened that fateful day," Ruby went on. "I'm here to tell you that I know exactly who put real bullets in that gun."

Lulu felt for Freddie's hand, and he clasped it tight. With just a few words, it would be all over. She'd name Sal—or someone else, but Lulu was sure Sal was responsible—and the police would rush out and make an arrest and she'd be free. She'd have her acting career . . . and Freddie. Her heart surged, but she trembled now that they were on the cusp.

Ruby picked Lulu out of the crowd again and fixed her with a steady look, her cat's eyes narrowed. "Just as the second take began, I saw Lulu Kelly open up the gun and put bullets inside. Lulu Kelly was the one who tried to kill me."

TWENTY-SEVEN

Lulu **turned and ran.** She didn't even think about defending herself to the mob. It was too late for that. Ruby's damning words hung in the air like a dead man hanging from the gallows. Or a dead woman. Lulu knew all too well the power of a well-acted scene, and Ruby's had been a doozy. It was worthy of an Academy Award. No one present in that room would doubt its truth.

Lulu's heels clacked on the hospital linoleum as she ran. The corridors were confusing. The multicolored lines painted on the wall to guide visitors to different wings seemed to mock her, sending her past the sick, the dying; past children with bald heads, sitting up, bewildered, in bed; past old people in wheelchairs hooked up to tubes and bags. Where was the exit? She had to escape, from the hospital, from Hollywood, from her life. . . .

She heard footsteps behind her and turned in a panic, her arms up, ready to ward off whoever was coming for her.

"Freddie!" she cried, and collapsed against his chest. "She's lying! You know it's not true. Tell me you don't believe her!"

"Never!" he swore, and would have kissed her, but she pulled away from him and ran on.

"We have to get out of here," she insisted. "The press! They'll crucify me." At the moment they frightened her worse than the police. At least the police—the real police— would take her away, keep her in isolation while they questioned her. The press would be like jackals picking at a baby gazelle, holding her in place and ripping bits off of her.

"This way," Freddie said, and hustled her toward a back exit. But the press were there, too. She could hear their mutters and growls from around the corner, so she tried to turn tail. Freddie pulled her into a room marked NURSES ONLY. Luckily, it was empty.

Freddie rummaged through lockers until he found a white uniform with TILLY in neat pink embroidery on the pocket. "Put this on."

"But that's stealing!"

"On the road you have to use a different morality. Leave her your dress. She can pawn it for a dozen new uniforms. If it bothers you so much, you can always send hers back to her afterward."

"If there is an afterward," Lulu said grimly.

But Freddie would have none of that. "Chin up, girl! There's always a next scene. Life doesn't have fade-outs and closing credits."

"Don't be so sure," she quipped. "It's called an obituary."

He turned his back while she stripped off her gown and put on the uniform, complete with white leather shoes far more comfortable than any she'd worn in the last year. They made her think what her life could be if she left everything behind. Comfortable shoes, a little farm . . . even factory work, with a nice fella to come home to. A man who was always there for her, who would never believe she was capable of wickedness.

"They'll never recognize you," Freddie said when he checked her disguise. "You look positively frumpy. In the nicest possible way, of course. Just tuck your hair up under your cap, like this." She shivered at his touch. "There. Now you go out the back. Look like you're in a hurry, but still interested in what's going on. If you just sail by all the excitement, you'll look suspicious." He laughed. "Listen to me, giving the actress advice."

"Thanks, Mr. DeMille. It's much appreciated," she managed to joke.

Then he did kiss her, tenderly, lingeringly.

"Where should we meet?" he asked when he released her.

"Meet? You're not coming with me?"

"It will attract less attention if you're just a nurse heading home alone at the end of her shift."

She didn't like it, but she had to admit he was right.

"There's a movie theater around the corner to the right and down a few blocks."

"Will they be open at this hour?" he asked.

"This is Hollywood. The movie theaters are always open. At least, this one is. Family movies in the afternoon, risqué ones at night, and a show for the kiddies in the morning. Oh, Freddie, I'm scared!"

"But you're strong, too. We both know you're innocent. You'll get through this. No—*we'll* get through this."

It was the worst acting of Lulu's life. She felt stiff and wooden as she shuffled toward the crowd, not at all convincing. Vasily said she had to *become* the character, to feel everything as the character would feel it. But for the first time she found she could not escape herself. Why? she wondered as she maneuvered through the throng of visitors and press and curious gawkers. There was always so much she wanted to escape from. It was freeing to become someone else, even a nurse for just a few minutes. *I can keep the costume, go to Mexico, and keep right on pretending*, Lulu thought desperately. *If I believe I'm a nurse, I can be a nurse, and leave everything behind.*

That, she realized, was why she couldn't get into this role. There might be things in her life she was desperate to abandon, but there was one thing, one wonderful thing she would never let go, no matter what. Her love for Freddie made her cling to herself. She could be no other than Lulu, the girl who loved Freddie, the girl Freddie loved . . . even if being Lulu came with its own host of problems.

She never thought it would work. She felt their stares

boring into her. But it was only her imagination. The crowd was alive, hunting like a hungry thing, like a single animal with eager eyes. But they looked at everything with equal intensity, searching for a scoop or a scandal. After a tense few minutes, she was out the door.

She walked briskly until she came to the movie theater, still aware of the astounding comfort of her feet in the soft, sensible shoes. For one panicked moment she thought Freddie had abandoned her. But no—he'd run ahead, and there he was, beckoning to her from inside the smoky glass doors. "Got a quarter for a pair of tickets?" he asked, looking a little sheepish. She handed over the money and they sat down in darkness.

The theater was almost empty. One man, who looked like a hangover from the night crowd, was slumped in a corner seat, asleep. Harried mothers and nursemaids caught a few winks in the center aisles, while kids sat fidgeting in the children-only section. There were many more children than guardians; some had evidently been dropped off to be entertained by the continuous cycle of shorts, newsreels, and double features that played on repeat. Though mostly unsupervised, the kids could take care of themselves. When a man came in and tried to sit next to a little girl in the children's section, she announced in a penetrating shrill voice, "I have a hatpin!" It was enough to make the man leave the theater entirely, under disapproving glares of all the children.

Lulu and Freddie hunkered in their seats and conferred in low voices.

"Hong Kong is looking better and better," Lulu said. Before them on the huge screen, little Emil was confronting the man who stole the money he had pinned to the inside of his jacket. He proved the money was his by pointing out to the police where the pinholes had pierced the bills.

"See," said Freddie, catching the scene from the corner of his eye. "Even a tiny pinhole can prove innocence or guilt. There has to be something out there that will show you didn't put those bullets in the gun. We just have to find them."

"But how can I, when all of Hollywood is out for my blood?" Lulu asked. "If anyone spots me, I'll be arrested right away."

"Then you just lie low. Go to a hotel, check in under another name, and I'll do all your digging for you."

The feature faded out, with Emil's grandmother slyly pronouncing the moral of the story—never send cash. A newsreel began, and while the announcer talked about the situation in Europe, Lulu and Freddie made their plans. He would check out Roger's bullet and try to get alone with Ruby to ferret the truth out of her. He would talk to the chief of police again.

And if worst came to worst, he would arrange passage on a westbound ship.

"I'm so tired, Freddie. So very, very tired. Maybe we could just stay in here for the rest of our lives," Lulu daydreamed as she leaned against his shoulder. "Once you pay your quarter, you never really have to leave. We can live on popcorn and chocolate nonpareils."

"I like your way of thinking, sweetheart," he said. "At least, we can stay here for a few hours, until the furor dies down a bit."

Suddenly the newsreel changed to affairs closer to home. Freddie gasped softly as his own face came up on the screen, larger than life, then mercifully faded as the film cut to an earnest-looking man interviewing Jacob van der Waals. Freddie glanced down at Lulu. She was nestled against him, eyes closed. "The saga of the missing millionaire continues," the announcer said, favoring alliteration over accuracy. And then Freddie's father began to speak.

"There is no grief greater than that of a father who has lost his son. I know my boy is alive, somewhere out there. Please, son, come home."

Freddie felt a pang of grief for the man he once thought his father was. Not for his old life, but for the old comfort of a life unquestioned.

"We have to go," he said at once, interrupting Lulu's drowsy question about whether there were milk shakes in Hong Kong.

"Whatever for? I thought we were staying here for a while."

"I just saw someone I know. Knew." He all but dragged her out of the theater before she could notice what was happening on the screen.

They weren't more than a block from the movie theater when Lulu heard the wail of sirens from very nearby. "Someone must have spotted me," she cried. "Hurry!"

Together they dashed down one street, then the next. She couldn't see any squad cars, but the sirens grew closer, seeming to surround them. The sound became overpowering, and she pressed her hands to her ears as she ran.

Then a black car blocked their path. Lulu wheeled around, Freddie right alongside her, and doubled back. Another car skidded to a stop at the next cross street. They were trapped. She clung to Freddie, certain it would be the last time she would see him. They would drag her away to jail.

From the east, where the rising sun hung glaring and blinding, came three figures from one of the cars. She squinted in their direction, trembling.

"Good-bye, darling," she whispered to Freddie. "You've made me so . . . so . . ." Then the men were on them. She tensed, waiting for their hands. But not one of them touched her.

Two seized Freddie by the arms, jerking him away from her. He struggled, and they threw him to the ground. Within an instant they had him wrapped up in a white coat, his arms strapped across his chest, the sleeves securely buckled behind him.

The third stood serenely with his hands loosely clasped. He had gold cuff links with little winking diamonds peeking from the sleeves of his gray morning coat and a heavy gold watch chain across his waistcoat.

He ignored Lulu completely. She might have been a puddle in the gutter.

"Isn't it about time you quit this silly charade, Frederick?"

Without another word, the man walked calmly back to the car. The other two hauled Freddie to his feet and followed.

"Lulu!" Freddie shouted, struggling desperately. "I'll come back for you. I swear! I'll never let you down!"

Then one of the men upended a small bottle into a cloth, clamped it over Freddie's face, and he became limp and yielding, his eyes closed.

It all happened so fast she scarcely had time to react. "Freddie!" she cried, and tried to run after him. But another man appeared behind her, from the other car, and caught hold of her, gently but firmly.

She whirled and began pounding on his chest. "Let me go! Let me go!" She might as well have pummeled a brick wall.

"Easy there, Miss Kelly," he said, his voice soothing.

"How can I be easy?" Lulu wailed. "What's happening? Why are they taking Freddie away? It wasn't him! I'll confess, if that's what it takes. Let me go to him!"

"There's nothing you can do for him now," the man said.

"But I have to do something. Won't you tell me what's happening?" She turned her red, bewildered eyes up to him.

"I said there's nothing you can do *now*." He patted her head, which had an oddly calming effect, though if anyone had asked her before, she would have been sure there was nothing more condescending. "But there is something we can do *soon*." He held out his hand. "I'm Murphy B. Murgatroyd, but most people call me Mugsy."

She recoiled, then looked at him with a combination of

amazement and delight. "You mean Freddie's nursemaid? The philosopher who taught him to box?" She wrapped her slim arms around him in a crushing hug. She had no idea exactly who or what Mugsy was, but she knew unequivocally that he was on Freddie's side.

"It wasn't him who put the bullets in the gun, you know. It wasn't me, either. I know Freddie's only a poor boy, but they can't railroad him like that. I'll sell everything I have to get him a lawyer. Just because he's poor doesn't mean he shouldn't get a fair shot."

Mugsy looked her sympathetically. "Kiddo, I think maybe there's a couple things Freddie neglected to mention to you."

TWENTY-EIGHT

Freddie awoke to whiteness. White walls, white ceiling, and a glare so bright it pierced him even when he squeezed his eyes shut again. An antiseptic tang tickled his nose. He forced his eyes open a sliver and saw menacing shapes lurching through the brightness. A wave of panic flooded him, and he tried to marshal his thoughts, but he felt groggy and stupid. He tried to shake his head, but it didn't seem to move properly.

"Ah, good," said a pleasant voice that grated on his ears. It was far too measured to be trustworthy. "Our patient is awake."

Freddie felt cold fingers on his wrist, his own pulse throbbing against them. He convinced his uncooperative eyes to loll to one side, but he still couldn't see clearly. There was a bitter taste in his dry mouth. What had happened to him? Everything was fuzzy, indistinct, within his head and without.

When he tried to speak, his tongue felt thick, and only a moan emerged. One of the shapes came closer, and he felt a jab in his arm. All at once he felt a surge of adrenaline as his awareness sharpened and his memory returned. He was strapped to a bed, with cloth-lined leather restraints holding down his wrists and legs and thicker leather belts strapped around his waist and chest. He struggled against them, but they only cut into his flesh.

There were four other people in the room: a doctor, two burly orderlies . . . and his father.

"Settle down, young man," the doctor said in a voice that sounded almost drugged, so calm and even. "This will be much more pleasant for you if you don't fight it. Then afterward you will be right as rain again."

Freddie's father stepped forward. "I thought we agreed that this should *not* be a pleasant experience for him," he said sharply.

The doctor shrugged. "Pleasant is all relative. The unsound mind is not capable of properly evaluating pain and pleasure, and in any event, when the process is over, he will likely be unable to remember any of it."

"How unfortunate," his father said, looking at his son with a peculiar smile.

The doctor began to fix a horseshoe-shaped object onto Freddie's forehead. It pinched against his temples. He tried to shake it off, but his head was strapped down, too, and he could only twitch.

"Father, what's happening here? What are you doing to me? Tell me what's happening, damn it!"

His father ignored him, as did the doctor.

"As I explained in my office," the doctor said to Freddie's father, "the preferred method is to administer electroconvulsive therapy only to a patient who has been sedated and given a muscle relaxant. But some of my fellow psychiatrists are of the opinion that the . . . shall we call it the discomfort factor? . . . is a deterrent to relapses in those whose psychoses may be self-induced or even artificial. However, the medical complications associated with unsedated electroconvulsive therapy are such that—"

"Extreme pain?" Jacob van der Waals said. "Possible broken bones, chipped teeth. Yes, you told me all of that. The risks are perfectly acceptable. Doctor, before you begin, I want a moment alone with my son."

"Of course," the doctor said, and backed out of the hospital room with a little bow, as if Jacob van der Waals were royalty.

"Father, don't do this," Freddie pleaded as soon as the door eased shut.

"Some people, when they find they have made a substantial investment in a company that fails, cut their losses and sell out. You know that has never been my philosophy, Frederick. When something disappoints me, I *squeeze* it." He held up his hand and made a tight fist in front of Freddie's immobilized face. "I do whatever is necessary to make it pay. It takes a lot to make me give up on a foundering company. Do you think I would do any less for my son?"

He flexed his fingers.

"You are my heir, Frederick, my scion and my legacy. I don't love you because you are my son. I love you because you are *me*. You've read your English history, haven't you? Those dukes never have names of their own. They're the Seventh Duke of Somewhere. They might as well be the same person through the centuries. We're American nobility, my boy. You must follow me, and your sons after you, and so on, building our empire for time immemorial."

He leaned close to Freddie's face. Up until then, his voice had been pedantic, a stern, quiet lecture. Now he roared, spittle hitting Freddie's cheeks.

"But you can't follow in my footsteps if you've lost your mind!" His eyes were bloodshot and bulging. "You have willfully blemished the family name. You've broken Violet's heart and spat in the face of everything I raised you to stand for. You're a disgrace!"

He took a deliberate deep breath. "But all will be forgiven. Eventually."

"I'll never forgive you for what you've done!" Freddie growled.

"Me?" his father asked in all apparent innocence. "You mean you won't forgive me for giving you every privilege a young man could ask for, the best education, a happy home, a mansion, a car, more money than you could spend in three lifetimes?"

"You killed Duncan's father!"

"Is that what you think, you poor deluded child?"

"Don't bother lying to me. I was there! I saw it all!"

For a moment Jacob van der Waals looked taken aback. Then he collected himself. "As the police clearly found, Mr. Shaw was shot by his son. If you were there, you no doubt saw Mr. Shaw threaten me with a gun. Duncan killed his own father to stop him from committing a horrible crime."

"You didn't pull the trigger, but you killed him all the same. How many men have shot themselves or jumped off of skyscrapers after you ruined them, Father? How many old women starved because of you? How many widows sold themselves on the streets to feed their children because you beggared them to get a few more dollars for yourself?"

"You're talking nonsense, Frederick. I'm just a business-man. Don't fault me for being a good one. Communists and radicals have gotten ahold of you and filled your head with rubbish. But don't worry. A few sessions with the doctor and your head will be sorted out."

He patted Freddie on his strapped-down arm.

"I'm not insane, Father," Freddie insisted. "I left because I saw everything clearly for the first time in my life. I want nothing to do with you or your dirty money."

Mr. van der Waals leaned closer to Freddie. "Just between you and me, I know you're not really insane," he whispered with a little smile. "But we have to give the papers something.

Imagine the scandal if they knew the truth. A little insanity runs through the best families, though, so no one will mind that. You had a nervous breakdown. A few electric shocks, and you'll be good as new."

He smiled, and Freddie thought he'd never seen anything so corrupt and vile.

"And if it doesn't work, we can always go ahead with a lobotomy. Then you'll be nice and amenable. Marry Violet—she won't mind if your bulb is a bit dim. Leaves her more time to shop. Then I can try again with the next generation. You can make more little van der Waals and spend your days weaving baskets with a nurse." He stood up. "Just remember what will happen if you ever disappoint me again." He opened the door and motioned for the doctor to come back in. "Enjoy your therapy. I'll be watching."

He sat in a chair in the corner while the doctor put a rubber bar, like a horse's bit, into Freddie's mouth. "Bite down on this," he said. "And don't worry. It will only last six seconds or so."

From the corner he heard his father's voice. "Make it seven."

It was the longest seven seconds of Freddie's life.

Despite what the doctor had promised, he remembered it all. The doctor's placid face looming over him. The hellish agony as every muscle in his body seized, the way mind seemed to explode as if every nerve was flying off into space, the terror, the leaden lungs, the absolute belief that this suffering would last forever.

His father's silent presence in the corner.

Then he was breathing again, deep ragged breaths, and tears were streaming down his face.

He was seventeen, a minor. His father could buy anyone's cooperation. Freddie had thought he'd escaped, but he was trapped.

"Another session tonight, I think," the doctor said. "I'll send in a nurse to clean up all that drool."

Freddie lay in bed scheming. But no matter how he looked at it, he couldn't see any way out. He was underage; the law was against him. He was his father's property until he was twenty-one. He could be held for involuntary psychiatric treatment or virtually jailed in his own home or in a private institution. His father was serious about the extreme measures he would take to keep his son in check. Freddie thought it was the embarrassment of having a defiant son that bothered his father the most, as if he couldn't keep his investments in line.

All I can do is endure, he thought, sinking into depression like quicksand. *Submit to the shock therapy, act like an obedient son . . . and then when I'm twenty-one, I can leave forever.*

It was such a long time, though, and he had no stomach for lies and hypocrisy. He didn't think he could do it.

And then there was Lulu.

He couldn't give her up. Not for a single day. Maybe if he played along, his father would . . . No. That was impossible. For one thing, he wouldn't rejoin his father's world even to have

Lulu. For another, his father would never allow it. He might like to hobnob with movie stars, but he was as class-conscious as a Brahman, and Lulu, for all her rising fame and sparkle, was by her origin an untouchable.

Freddie closed his eyes and tried to think. But all he could manage was to picture Lulu's face floating over him, her lips curled in a delightful smile, torturing him with her absence, her impossibility.

The door creaked. He opened his eyes, and there she was, in the flesh.

He closed them again and turned away. The shock must be playing tricks with his mind. The nurse faintly resembled Lulu, but she had caramel-brown hair peeking out from under her nurse's cap in tight curls. Her cheeks were plumper, her nose more narrow, and there were dark circles under her black-lashed eyes. She walked differently too, shuffling wearily, a little hunched as she pushed a wheeled chair across the room. No, he might never see Lulu again. She was lost to him.

"Ready for your sponge bath, Mr. van der Waals?" the nurse asked.

Freddie's eyes sprang open. She had disguised everything else perfectly, but her voice betrayed her. "Lulu!"

"Hush," she whispered, and was at his side, tenderly touching his face, his chest, his hands, as she unbuckled his restraints.

"But how . . . ?"

"Later," she said, and helped him sit up.

"There's a guard outside, one of my father's men."

"Don't worry," she said, and helped him into the chair. "Now, just let me sedate you."

She kissed him, and after that it was easy for him to act as if he were in a contented drugged delirium.

"He's not supposed to be unsecured," the guard said when Lulu rolled Freddie into the hallway.

"I gave him enough to knock out an elephant," Lulu-as-nurse said. "He'll be loopy for hours."

"Why can't you give him his bath in there?" The guard jerked his chin toward the room.

Nurse Lulu shook her head in a schoolmarmish way. "Don't you know that electricity and water don't mix? Mr. van der Waals wants his son cured, not killed." She winked at the guard flirtatiously.

Freddie, gazing blankly into the middle distance with an idiotic grin on his bobbing face, wasn't entirely certain about that.

"Okay, Nurse, but I'll be right at the door."

"Outside, if you please," she said primly. "We value our patients' privacy."

The man stood watch at the door, making sure Freddie didn't try to escape. Unfortunately, he didn't know about the back door to an adjoining room with an exit outside, and by the time he realized that most baths don't last an hour, Freddie and Lulu were long gone.

"How did you manage it?" Freddie asked from the passenger seat of Mugsy's black Duesenberg. Lulu was wiping away the contouring makeup that had changed the shape of her face.

"Well, it was surprisingly easy," she said as she stripped off the caramel-colored wig and fluffed her platinum waves. "Thanks to you I already had the nurse's uniform. Beyond that, I just had to pay off the real nurse to let me take her place."

"How much?" he asked grimly.

"I asked her how much a doctor makes in a year," Lulu said. "She told me about three thousand dollars, so we settled on that. Really, that poor girl makes a paltry amount, considering she actually has to *bathe* people. You're not bad, but imagine all those unappealing mounds of flesh she has to scrub." Lulu was delighted with her success, but she sensed a certain stiffness from Freddie. "Darling, what's wrong? I would have saved you faster, only . . ."

"Three thousand dollars," he said slowly. "I know you don't have that kind of money. Not on short notice, maybe not even if you sold all of your things. Who gave it to you?"

"Why, Freddie, what does it matter? You're free now, and Mugsy booked passage on a ship to Macao, which isn't quite Hong Kong, but close enough."

"Was it Sal?" he asked through clenched teeth. "Did you agree to . . . to . . . ?" He couldn't choke the words out.

"No! What do you think I am?"

Freddie relaxed visibly. "I think you're a brave girl who would sacrifice yourself for the people you love, if you thought that was the only way. But I wouldn't let you. You know that, don't you?"

"Look here, mister. If this fling is going to last, you have to stop with the 'I won't let you' garbage. I make my own decisions, and you just have to live with them."

He grinned at her, then sobered. "So where did the money come from, then?"

Lulu looked at Mugsy uncertainly.

"Tell him, kiddo," Mugsy urged her.

"It was your father's money," Lulu confessed.

Freddie drew in an angry breath, furious. He'd sworn never to touch that money, those wages of sin. He hadn't when he was in jail, not even when Ben died. Not even to get Lulu the best team of lawyers money could buy. And now, while he lay helpless, those proceeds of blood and tears and suffering had been put to use for his benefit, the last thing he would ever want, ever allow.

But he looked at Lulu's anxious, loving face, and let his breath out. "How did you get it?"

Mugsy answered with an embarrassed little shrug of his hulking shoulders. "I've been handling your school fees and bar tabs and tailor's accounts for years, boyo. You think by now I can't forge your signature or your old man's? How do you think I got it? I *stole* it. Your pop's involved with plenty of criminals. What's one more?"

Using his father's money was anathema. Stealing it, though—that was another story. Freddie burst into laughter and put his arm around Lulu, squeezing her tight.

TWENTY-NINE

He wouldn't accept passage to Macao, though. Not yet, anyway. "We have a job to do. We have to clear your name."

"Oh, Freddie," Lulu said. "I don't care about that! What will it matter when we're living under assumed names with fake mustaches in Macao? Won't I look adorable in a Fu Manchu?"

"You love acting, Lulu. I won't let you give up your career to run away with me."

"There's that bullyboy 'I won't let you' again. I'm not asking you what I *should* do. I'm telling you what I'm *going* to do."

Freddie shook his head. "I'm not leaving until you're cleared of attempted murder. We have to find out who put the bullets in the gun. Then, once you're off the hook, you'll be free to make the choice for yourself. I don't want you with me just because you're running away."

"But if you stay, your father might catch you again," Lulu said.

"Maybe," Freddie admitted, "but now we have Mugsy on our side. My father thinks Mugsy's helping him, but really he'll be looking out for me."

Mugsy had hidden Freddie in a seedy hotel room he'd rented under an assumed name on the outskirts of town. Lulu contacted Roger and made arrangements to see the overlooked bullet.

"Don't worry," Roger said over the phone. "I won't let the police know where you'll be. I know if I did, you'd blab my secret to the world."

"Why, Roger, I'd never . . ."

"I'll leave the alley door to studio C unlocked," he said, and hung up.

He was leaving the bullet in his desk drawer. They were to go to the studio after dark, once most of the crew had cleared out.

"But what are the odds that one bullet will tell us anything?" Lulu wanted to know. "Every minute you stay here makes it that much more likely your father will catch you. What do we do after that?"

"I'll kiss you, and we'll go out for ice cream," Freddie said, making good on the first part of his threat.

"Freddie! Be serious!"

"I'm always serious when it comes to ice cream. And kisses," he added, taking her in his arms again.

That night Lulu, Freddie, and Mugsy crept into the deserted studio. Mugsy held the flashlight, but Lulu took the lead, moving silently by memory through the dim halls. It seemed like Lux was empty.

They locked themselves in Roger's large windowless office before shutting off the flashlight and turning on a lamp.

"Here it is," said Lulu, pulling out a paper bag with its top secured with a rubber band.

"Don't touch it," Freddie cautioned. "They might be able to get prints."

"Never mind about that," Mugsy said. "Maybe they coulda got prints from the bullets fresh from the cylinder, but this one's been kicking around in this guy's pocket and who knows what else."

Lulu dumped the bullet on the table, and they all looked at it.

"It looks . . . like a bullet," Lulu said helplessly. She leaned heavily against Roger's desk. "I don't know what this was supposed to accomplish. One bullet looks exactly like any other. There's nothing we can learn from this."

"Don't be so sure," Mugsy said. He picked up the bullet and let it rest against the calluses of his meaty palm. "This ain't your ordinary bullet."

Lulu leaned forward eagerly.

"I carry a gun, and I've been shot a time or three, so I

made it a point to learn something about ballistics and gunshot wounds," Mugsy said.

"You've been *shot*?" Lulu and Freddie asked at the same time.

"Sure. You don't know *all* my secrets, whippersnapper. Once as a kid in the Great War, once during a robbery, and once when a couple of kidnappers tried to swipe you when you was three years old."

"I never knew," Freddie said.

Mugsy shrugged. "Didn't want you to think you owed me one."

"Mugs, I owe you about a million."

"Nah. Your pop already paid me that, and more. How do you think I'm driving a Duesenberg? Protecting you pays well. Too bad your pop never figured out I'm really working for you, not him. Anyway . . ."

"What about the robbery? When were you robbed?"

Mugsy fixed Freddy with an even stare. "Who says I was the one being robbed? Maybe I was the robber. Now," he said decisively, "to stick to the matter at hand. You might not think it, but when a bullet hits you, it's the speed that takes you out."

Lulu asked, "You mean, a fast bullet does more damage?"

"Not at all. It's when a bullet slows down that it tears a real hole in you. Think of a bullet as a bunch of energy. When the bullet is moving, the energy is in the bullet, right, giving it speed. But when it slows down, that energy has to go somewhere. Where does it go? Into your flesh. A slow bullet rips a much bigger hole than a fast one, and does a lot more damage."

"Mugsy, I do believe you just quoted one of the laws of thermodynamics," Freddie said. "Never knew you had it in you."

"What does that have to do with Ruby?" Lulu asked.

"Most people buy bullets that have a lot of stopping power. When they shoot something—a deer, a person—they want it to go down and stay down with as few shots as possible. See this bullet?" Mugsy held it up for their inspection. "It comes to a perfect point. Since they started making hollow-point bullets, almost no one uses these anymore."

He set the bullet down on the desk and twirled it so it spun like a dervish. "It's jacketed, too."

"Meaning?"

"It won't fragment. It's designed to be fast and clean—to go straight through something without expanding or breaking up. Sometimes you see these in large-caliber hunting ammunition, for big game, something with a lot of flesh and fat around its vital organs. If you want to stop a charging rhino, you need a bullet that will go in the neck and come out the rear end. A bullet that stops after six inches is only going to tickle him. But I've rarely seen it in small caliber handguns. It would make a wound like being poked with a big pencil, clean and straight through. It will do damage, but all things considered, a neat in-and-out is less likely to kill a person."

Lulu scrunched up her forehead. "So you're saying that

whoever put the bullets in there didn't want someone to die?"

"That doesn't make sense," Freddie said. "If you don't want someone to die, why do you shoot her in the first place?"

Lulu's eyes were opened wide. "It makes sense if you're the one getting shot!"

Freddie gasped. "You mean Ruby . . ."

"Shh!" Mugsy hissed, and flicked off the light. There was a sound from the hallway.

"Probably a janitor," Lulu whispered. She thought she heard the hushed *swish-swish* of a broom.

They stood together in silence until the sound of sweeping subsided.

"So it was Ruby after all," said Lulu wonderingly.

"Maybe not," Freddie said. "It could have been one of the others, and they just didn't want to kill anyone."

"Seems to me the next thing we have to find out is where this bullet was bought," Mugsy said. "It's unusual enough that the shop owner will probably remember whoever bought this kind of ammo in the last few weeks. Only problem is, ammunition must be sold in a dozen sporting goods stores in the city and probably another hundred within a day's drive. Whoever did it was probably too smart to buy locally."

"Don't be so sure," Lulu said. "Actors aren't always the sharpest tacks. I guess we just drive around and ask everyone?"

"Only thing we can do," Freddie said. "Let's take the bullet and get to work first thing in the morning. Ow!" He hit his shin on a chair.

"Let me put the lights on," Lulu said.

"No." Mugsy caught at her in the dark. "Someone might still be out there. Use the flashlight." But when he hit the switch, it flickered just long enough to make them see spots and then died.

"Wait a minute. I have a matchbook here somewhere." Freddie struck the match and retrieved the bullet by its orange flame.

As he was shaking it out, he heard Lulu's startled cry. "Let me see that matchbook!" she said, fumbling for his hand in the darkness. She opened it and struck another match, then bent to read by its light. "Bighorn Sporting Goods. They must sell bullets there. Oh, Freddie, do you remember? This is the matchbook I took out of Roger King's pocket. He must be involved."

It came back to Freddie then: the bustle of the set the chaotic day of the shooting, the props man asking for a light, the dark-haired, green-eyed girl tossing him a matchbook that spun through the air, shining black and gold. . . .

"No. It was Ruby's matchbook," Freddie said, telling them about the memory. "I'm sure of it."

"Next stop, Bighorn Sporting Goods," Lulu said, her eyes glowing with excitement.

"But they won't be open for hours."

"Then we'll go back to Mugsy's hotel."

"I won't be able to sleep a wink," Freddie said.

"Who says I'll be letting you sleep?" Lulu asked with a roguish grin.

Before Lulu could recover from being shocked at her own

outrageous flirtation, they heard a crash of shattering glass and a man's demented voice shouting, "What have you done with it? Is this what you want, you tramp? Ruby Godfrey, I swear that one way or another, I will finish this *now*!"

THIRTY

Lulu and Freddie raced down the hall in the direction of the uproar, while Mugsy—the only one of them actually armed and prepared for a fight—tried to hold them back from what was clearly the hysterical confession of a would-be killer. He grabbed at their shoulders to slow them down and managed to stop them in the hallway before they could burst into the dressing room where a confused commotion was still emanating. He dragged them next door instead and hissed, "Stop and think! I ain't havin' neither of you gettin' hurt on my watch, and this guy sounds bent outta his tree. Let me handle this."

"Listen!" Lulu whispered, and they pressed their ears to the adjoining wall. They could hear pacing and a slurred voice saying something indistinct about lies and blackmail.

They were in the female dressing room section. Lulu looked around her, recognizing the chamber belonging to Elizabeth Holdridge, the faded silent film star who was playing her fading and anything but silent mother in *Girl About Town*. So the next room over was Ruby's.

"I know that voice . . . almost," Lulu said softly. It was tantalizingly familiar, as if someone she knew very well was acting a part. It came to her suddenly: It was the right voice, the wrong accent.

"Vasily!" she breathed in astonishment. His Russian accent had vanished.

"*He* put the bullets in the gun?" Freddie asked.

"I have no idea. But Ruby knows his secret," Lulu said.

"But you told me *everybody* in Hollywood knows his secret. Why would he . . . ?"

There was a loud *thump*, like a body hitting the ground. "Freddie! Do you think Ruby's in there with him?" Lulu gasped, itching to go see.

"She can't be. She's in the hospital."

"Or someone else, then. Did you hear that? He just said he's going to finish this now. I'm going in there!"

"Lulu, wait!" Freddie tried to hold her back, but she slipped past him and threw open the door . . .

. . . directly into the black cavernous barrel of a gun.

It was a sight she'd hoped never to see again. When Sal had pointed the gun at her face, she'd thought her life was over. Now here was that dark, cold eye staring her down again. *You can never escape your fate*, she thought.

"Vasily, why?" she asked. She heard the others behind her, but there was nothing they could do. One wrong move, and a simple squeeze of the trigger would end her life.

"Oh, Lulu," Vasily moaned. "Oh God . . . I'm so sorry. It wasn't supposed to happen this way." His finger twitched on the trigger.

"Where is she?" Lulu asked, trying to see around him. There was no one, just an overturned leather chair. That must have made the thump.

"Who? What are you talking about? There's no one else here. There's *nothing* else here. It's all over." With his free hand, he pulled a flask from his pocket and took a swig. The smell of the cheap grain alcohol stung Lulu's nose. She saw the glass shards of a smashed liquor bottle next to the makeup table. "But, my dear, now that you and your friends have arrived, it seems we're having one hell of a party. And how gay a time we are having, yes? Well, bully for us! I always say, go out with a bang. BANG!"

He jerked the gun, and Lulu squeezed her eyes shut. But he didn't fire, only gave a strange and piteous laugh.

"Vasily, you don't want to do this," Lulu pleaded, trying to reach through his drunkenness to find out what was really happening.

"Do *not* presume to tell me what I do and do not want to do, young lady! Show some respect! And I'll tell you a little secret: I have wanted this since I was a teenager. You see, it seems that I'm going to hell! Yes, I'm going to hell . . . and all because I fell in love."

Vasily's scarlet-rimmed eyes brimmed with tears. The gun quivered in his unsteady hand.

"I fell in love with a beautiful man, and he loved me back. He was so kind, and he was funny and he saw me for everything that was good about me. Our love was the most real thing I had ever known, and so sweet, and I felt so . . . so honest and so human. But it was forbidden, and the world wouldn't allow anything that true and beautiful to live, so they jailed him, and I'm told he died there. But me? I got off easy," he said bitterly. "My father simply had me put in a mental institution, where I was tortured and told that I was unworthy of love and life, but since I was so young, I could still be saved. Saved with electric shock, and needles, and . . ."

He broke off and, gun or no gun, Lulu wanted to comfort him. She reached up to touch his face, but he jerked away.

"Ruby knew!" Vasily ranted. "She stole my past from my bedroom. She took the proof. Do *not* judge me. I can see it in all your eyes. Yes, I was a fool to keep it around, but I wanted some shred of my past, some connection to the boy I left behind. Now that blackmailing vixen has it, and there's nothing in the world that will fix the mess I'm in—nothing but a bullet to the head."

"I am so sorry, Vasily. Honest, I am. But why involve me?" Lulu asked. "Why put the bullets in the gun so everyone thought it was me who shot Ruby? What have I ever done to you?"

He looked at her in drunken confusion. "Bullets? What

are you talking about? I would never do that. *I'm* the one who needs to die."

He took a step back from her, and in one quick gesture put the gun to his temple and pulled the trigger.

"No!" Lulu screamed, and surged forward.

There was no bang, just a little click.

Vasily, perplexed, looked down at the gun in his hand. "Well, that was terribly anticlimactic."

He tried to open the cylinder, but Mugsy barged past Lulu and snatched the gun from his hand. A second later he'd flung Vasily down in a chair and had him covered.

Mugsy looked down at the gun, frowning. "What the . . . ?" He fiddled with it. "It ain't even closed right." He started laughing.

"Somehow, I don't think this sap is the one you're looking for." He held the gun out for Lulu's and Freddie's inspection. Even Lulu, with her limited knowledge of firearms, could tell that the bullets were inserted backward.

"And they're not even the right caliber," Mugsy added. "Even if he loaded them right, he'd get a misfire."

"And our suspect knew a lot about ammunition and guns. Or at least, they made it their business to find out." Lulu sighed with relief. "So it can't be Vasily."

"Then what's going on here?" Freddie asked sternly.

Vasily began to weep silent tears, and Lulu decided the best course of interrogation would involve compassion. She gently put her arms around him and let him cry on her shoulder.

"Vasily, we're just trying to figure out who put the bullets in the gun. If you didn't do that, you have nothing to worry about. No one really cares about . . . that other thing."

"Maybe not," Vasily said, "but they will undoubtedly care that I've escaped from a mental institution."

"We have something in common, then," Freddie said dryly, but Lulu hushed him as Vasily told his terrible story.

The great Vasily Anoushkin was born a mere Willie Bednarski in Providence, Rhode Island, to devout Polish parents who lived solely for their faith. The only reason they didn't steer Willie toward the priesthood, like his brother, was because they needed grandchildren to carry on the family meatpacking business. But Willie had other ideas.

From an early age he loved to act but was regularly beaten for raiding his mother's closet for costumes and putting on shows for some unseen but appreciative imaginary audience.

When he was older, he defied his father and won a role in a community theater production. His father had refused to attend the performance, but he'd showed up to retrieve him afterward and caught Willie in a compromising position with the young manager of the theater company. The manager was jailed, while Willie's father had him committed.

"But I escaped," Vasily said. "I ran as far away as I could, changed my name, and took up my parents' old-world accent, the one I worked so hard to lose as an actor. For a while I toured with the vaudeville circuit, but eventually I came to Hollywood. Russian acting coaches were all the rage, so that's what I became. Vasily Anoushkin, the debonair Russian."

"But you made a good life for yourself. And you are the best acting coach a girl could ever ask for," Lulu said earnestly. "You've taught me everything, Vasily. You taught me how to find and use feelings inside of me I never knew existed. You taught me how to find goodness and truth in any and every character. I owe you so much."

He looked up to Lulu's eyes with teary gratitude, then shook his head. "Thank you, my angel. You are so very special. So gifted. But it's over for me. Ruby came to me a few weeks after her ridiculous attempt at seducing me, and she had my identity card from my time in the asylum. I stole it when I fled so they'd have a harder time finding me. It had my photo on it, and I thought if they couldn't show my picture, I could better slip into obscurity. But she found it in my things and threatened to expose me if I didn't get her the leading part in *Girl About Town*. So I tried! Oh, Lulu, I tried. She just wasn't good enough. *But you were.* Sassoon ignored my protestations and gave you the lead in *Girl About Town*, so Ruby was going to expose me."

"But you didn't shoot her?" Freddie asked.

"I couldn't even shoot myself." Vasily gave a mirthless laugh. "I should have tried poison."

"No!" Lulu said. "You can't think such a terrible thing. You are a brilliant acting coach and a splendid man. Whatever happens, you have to fight through it. I'll help you, however I can."

"That's sweet of you, Lulu. But what hope is there for me in this world? I have had to deny myself my truth and any chance for love that I can be proud of like every other living person. I just don't think I can carry on anymore. Not if Ruby exposes me. I am an escapee! Even if they don't drag me back to the institution, my career will be over the minute they all learn I'm a fraud. I only came here tonight to see if she might have hidden the evidence in her dressing room, but I couldn't find it. I'm doomed."

He hung his head. Lulu stood up resolutely.

"If it is here, we'll find it. And if it's not . . . I'll think of something. Just promise me, Vasily, *promise* you won't ever think of hurting yourself. Your students love you very much, you know."

He wiped the tears from his eyes and held her close.

"Where have you looked for the evidence?" Mugsy asked, businesslike. "Tossing rooms is an old hobby of mine."

"The drawers, the boxes . . . pretty much everywhere."

"Maybe it's in the broad's house," Mugsy suggested. "I can perform a little B and E, and—"

"No," Lulu said firmly. "If she was blackmailing you, she would have kept it close. She wouldn't have left it home."

"Then it's at the hospital with her, and we won't be able to get it," Freddie said.

"No. She was wearing her costume. Remember that dress? There weren't exactly pockets on that little number. No, she would have had it in her purse."

"Which is right on that table," Freddie said. "I searched it myself."

"So did I, first thing," Vasily said.

Lulu bit her lip. "Let me see, just in case."

She dug through the black alligator purse. It contained only a woman's standard arsenal: lipstick, compact, handkerchief, a little mad money, and a spare pair of stockings. She looked for hidden compartments and felt for anything concealed in the lining, but found nothing.

Then she had an inspiration.

All of those things in Ruby's purse were essentials, but what among them was the most important to her? She remembered how Ruby was always checking her face in her compact, as if to reassure herself that her beauty was still intact.

With a feeling of certainty and triumph before she even opened it, Lulu pulled out the compact.

"Checked it," Mugsy said.

"Somehow I don't think a gentleman of your background will know the ins and outs of a lady's compact," she told him. "It might be more complex than you think." The compact opened in three parts, not the usual two: mirror, a space for the puff, and . . .

"Bingo!" Lulu said. She dug her fingers into the loose powder in the third compartment and pulled out a dusty folded identification card, worn and yellowed with age, bearing a picture of a much younger but unmistakable Vasily.

Freddie handed him the matchbook from Bighorn Sporting Goods. "Go on," he said gently. "Say good-bye to your past. It's hard, I know, but who needs the past when you've got a future?"

With hope shining in his eyes, Vasily struck a match and burned his old identity to ashes.

They saw Vasily safely to his home, leaving him in bed with two aspirin on his nightstand. Then they headed to Bighorn Sporting Goods. They met the owner as he unlocked the door. "Do you sell these?" Lulu asked, holding up the bullet.

"What is it, some kind of club?" he asked. "You're the second dame to come in looking for one of those. Usually I sell maybe a box a year to some schmo who doesn't know what he's doing, but suddenly everyone wants them. What gives?"

"Who was the first girl?" Freddie asked.

"A blonde, like you," he said, almost salivating at the memory. Lulu's face fell. Ruby was dark-haired. "Real curvy, dressed to the nines, which was funny, considering she came in almost as early as you three. Asked me if I was here alone and dragged me to the back room. Started asking all these questions about guns and ammunition, cuddling up to me like I might get lucky."

"What kind of questions?" Lulu wanted to know.

"Funniest thing. She wanted to know what kind of bullets I might have that were least likely to kill someone. I think she was an actress. Asked her why she wanted to know, and she said she was rehearsing for a part. Said it was sure to be the part of her life. I showed her those." He gestured to the bullet Lulu was holding up. "She seemed tickled pink. Well, I offered to close up shop so she and I could get a little more comfortable, and she grabbed the box of ammunition and hit the road. I didn't much care, since the whole box wasn't worth more than two bits. But I was a little sore to be led on."

"Sounds like Ruby, except for the hair," Lulu said.

"She could have been wearing a wig. Do you remember anything else about her?" Freddie asked the shop owner.

The owner closed his eyes. Lulu and Freddie exchanged a look, guessing what parts of the girl he might be remembering. "Great gams. Nice big . . . er." A lascivious little smile drifted across his face, and he opened his eyes. "No, nothing else. Oh, she did have a beauty mark, like a little heart right by the corner of her mouth. I thought it was a muffin crumb and tried to brush it away, and she slapped me and called me fresh. I ask you, isn't a guy allowed to get a little fresh when a doll like that wiggles into his back room at seven o'clock in the morning?"

"Well, *hello*, Ruby," Lulu whispered under her breath, as Freddie pulled her into an impromptu waltz.

THIRTY-ONE

Mugsy, would you please take the new evidence and this charming and ever-so-eloquent shop owner to the police and clear my name?" Lulu was suddenly all bustle and efficiency. "And if it's not too inconvenient, drop Freddie off at your hotel on the way."

"And where, may I ask, are you going to be?" Freddie inquired.

"Oh, arranging my things for the Far East. Freddie, is it still the Far East if we have to travel west to get there? It's all awfully confusing."

"You mean, you're still thinking of going with me? What about your career? Now that you're safe from arrest and from Sal . . ."

She took his face in her hands. "Let's put it this way: I'm

going to be with you, no matter what. Just . . . well, just wait a while. I have an idea."

"What is it?" he asked.

She put her hands on her hips. "Freddie, let's get one thing straight right now. I'm not going to be a slave to my man. I might be your girl, but I'm always going to have a life of my own . . . and a little bit of privacy. How dull would I be without an air of mystery?" She mugged a look of glamorous inscrutability. "Just cozy up, dream of me, and I'll let you know if it all works. If not, we're off to Macao!"

She kissed him fleetingly and ran out of Bighorn Sporting Goods, hailing a cab with a street urchin's whistle.

It was really far too early to visit anyone in Hollywood. At nine a.m., people were either sleeping off the previous night's excesses or still enjoying them. But, she rapped insistently on Blake Tanner's door until he opened it, dressed only in his silk pajama bottoms.

"I need to ask you a favor," Lulu said.

"Here it comes," he said with a cynical huff. "What do you want, money? I'm in debt up to my ears already. Help getting a part? I might be a star . . ." Lulu raised her eyebrows. What an ego! He was just a notch above her, on the stellar scale. ". . . but I don't have as much pull as you might think. Go ahead, cough it up. What do I have to do to keep you from spilling the beans about my wife?"

For a moment Lulu didn't say anything, only looked at him in quiet disgust until he started to wither. At last she said, very slowly and clearly, "Your secrets are your own, Blake. I'm asking you this as a friend. You can say no and still nothing will happen."

Blake furrowed his brow like a confused hound. "I guess you better come inside and have some coffee." He looked over his shoulder as he led the way, as if she were some sort of alien species, probably benign but perplexing nonetheless. *Is it really so hard to believe that a person won't resort to blackmail, given the opportunity?* Lulu wondered.

Then she remembered what city she was living in.

Over coffee and brioche from Van de Kamp's Bakery, Lulu told him about her plan.

"Do you mean to tell me that vagrant you wrangled to play the bum is one of the richest people in America?" Blake asked. Lulu caught a gleam of avarice in his eyes.

"He's poor as a church mouse. He gave it all up."

"Sucker."

"Blake, none of that. Now, will you help me?"

"Oh, all right," he said, and she surmised he still thought she planned to tell the world about his wife if he didn't. *Well, whatever gets the job done,* she told herself. *It isn't blackmail unless I mean it to be.* "Do you really think it will work?" he asked.

"I sure hope so," Lulu said. "Because to tell you the truth, I don't really know where Macao is."

She went to Vasily next. Now that the evidence of his secret past was destroyed, he seemed like his old self again. His gray eyes dancing with excitement, he pulled her into his house and said, quite forgetting his Russian accent, "Are they after you, my dear? You did it after all, didn't you? What a marvelous actress you are! Do you need a place to hide out from the coppers? How thrilling!"

"No. That's all being cleared up, thank goodness." She told him of her discovery about Ruby and the bullets.

"How very bizarre, and terribly, terribly sad," Vasily said.

"I just can't see why she would do such a thing," Lulu confessed.

"I can, clear as day," Vasily said, arranging himself on his white leather fainting couch. "She wants fame, my dear, and anyone who wants fame for the mere sake of it is more than a bit insane. Don't you agree? She desperately needs to be seen, and adored, and desired far beyond rational thinking. Everything she does is in service of that obsession. You saw how she would have ruined me to advance herself. She wants fame as other people want breath. She needs it—and without it, she perishes."

"I thought maybe she just wanted to ruin me," Lulu said.

"A pleasant side effect, no doubt, but make no mistake. This was all about Ruby. Everything Ruby does is about Ruby. Do you remember that day? How she seemed to move herself in front of the gun? I recall thinking afterward, what dratted bad luck for her, to forget her cues and miss her mark on the floor. She never was good at hitting those little Xs. But in this case I'm sure it was deliberate. She wanted to be shot."

Lulu shook her head in wonder. "Because being shot

would get her some attention? How . . . how horribly sick!" She felt physically ill at the thought. "What a twisted place this is, Vasily. Why does anyone come here?"

"Come, now, you feel it too, Lulu. Maybe not as strongly as Ruby, but you crave the spotlight, the camera, the adoring eyes on you."

"No, not like that. I want to be good at my job, to . . . to transform people, somehow, to transform myself! Not at all for people to see *me*, but for them to see people far more interesting than I could ever possibly hope to be. And, if I'm any good at it at all, then to help people escape their lives too. Even if for just a little while. To not have to cope with what's just *too real*."

Vasily looked at her as if he knew her better than she knew her own self. "I see. Well then, if you say so. That's very honest, my dear."

"There's something so terribly wrong with poor Ruby," Lulu said, veering away from that uncomfortable subject. "What if she had died? Didn't she think of that?"

"Oh, no doubt she did. Maybe she even hoped to. Her career is stalling. She's getting older. . . ."

"She can't be more than a little bit older than me!"

"She's over twenty-five if she's a day. Ancient for a starlet. A male star can age, but a starlet only has a couple of years to catch her break. No, Ruby feared she was all but washed up. Her name would have been forgotten as utterly as if she'd never lived. If she'd been killed on set, though— instant Hollywood legend! People would talk about her for decades. Her ghost would haunt Lux, and Louella Parsons would swear she was the brightest young thing of her generation. Death makes angels, darling."

Lulu shuddered, then set herself back to her purpose. She had to try to save Freddie from his father. She asked Vasily for a favor.

"What fun, my dear! I've never been a tycoon before."

Veronica and David were easy to convince. "I'll model myself after Anita Loos," she said. "Do you think spectacles make me look more serious?"

David looked a little nervous, but luckily, he was just playing an agent, so it wasn't much of a stretch.

That afternoon, Lulu placed the call to Jacob van der Waals's suite at the Ambassador. "Hello, sir. Pardon me for disturbing you, but this is Lulu Kelly. I'm the young lady you saw with your son the other day. I was hoping to . . ."

"Where is he, you little tramp?" he bellowed.

Lulu held the receiver away from her ear.

"I know his whereabouts, and I was hoping to discuss things with you this evening. Can you come to my place, say around seven o'clock?" That would give everyone enough time to go over their parts and settle nicely into their all-important roles in what was to be the most vital scene Lulu had ever tackled.

"How much money do you plan on extorting from me?" Mr. van der Waals asked bluntly.

Good Lord, Lulu thought, *is that all anyone thinks about?*

"I just want to talk to you, sir. I want to explain something before you take Freddie home with you."

"You think you've gotten your grubby little meat hooks into him, don't you? You might have tickled his fancy for a while, but he'll remember his place soon enough. You'll be just another one of a hundred sluts he's left by the wayside. He's going home and getting married to the right kind of girl, and if you think for one minute that a cheap little gold digger like you can . . ."

Lulu really couldn't take any more, so she hung up, rang the Ambassador's front desk, and asked them to send the busboy up to Mr. van der Waals's suite with her address.

"And . . . action!" Lulu whispered under her breath when she heard the heavy knock at five minutes after seven. Her little makeshift cast of players was ready.

Clara opened the door and admitted Mr. van der Waals to Lulu's foyer.

He looked so ordinary for a monster. Well dressed, of course, of middling height, with the slightest paunch and his hairline beginning to recede in a widow's peak. But not the sort of man who would beggar thousands to put a few more dollars in his bank account. Not one who would destroy the lives of his son's best friend and his father and then be indifferent to their tragic deaths.

Certainly not one who would order a doctor to hook electrodes to his son's brain and torture him until he was nothing more than a compliant menial.

But he had done all that and more, both Mugsy and Freddie had assured her. "He said he would lobotomize me if the shock treatments didn't work," Freddie had told her. "He'd rather turn his son into a vegetable who could still produce heirs than let me live my own life." She shuddered, and slipped into her character.

She was playing Lulu Kelly that night. Not the weak Lucille who had submitted to a mobster's threats and lied under oath. Not the battered Lulu who had trembled in a police station. She wasn't poor. She wasn't meek. She didn't seek money, or fame, or even security. This Lulu Kelly had only one goal—to be with Freddie.

If a screenwriter had written the part, she would never have auditioned. A woman who wants nothing more than to be with her man? How shallow, how one-dimensional, how old-fashioned! But she knew what love was now. It was just like in those preposterously romantic movies.

"What's all this?" Mr. van der Waals asked as he strode in, standing like he owned the house. "Who are these people? Where is my son?"

Before she could answer, Vasily rose from his chair and slowly walked very near to Mr. van der Waals. "Fascinating," he mused aloud, peering uncomfortably close at the tycoon. "I wonder what's behind all of that marvelous bluster. So much anger and brio. I'd love to know what dark wounds that fantastic bravado is masking. So much delicious entitlement! Absolutely fascinating. Lots to chew on here. Quite a meal . . ." He sank back in his seat to make some notes.

"Where's Frederick?" Mr. van der Waals asked again.

Blake spoke up. "What was Freddie like as a baby?" he asked, cocking his head to one side. "None of the backstory will actually be in the script, but I like to go to the very beginning of things when I play a part. Was he fussy? Did he eat strained prunes? What was his first word? I imagine it was 'Bub-Bub,' which was the name of his favorite stuffed elephant. In the backstory I'm creating, of course."

"What is all this nonsense?" Mr. van der Waals demanded.

"How would you characterize your relationship with your mother?" Vasily asked. "I want to gain a firm hold on the source of your greed. Did it arise from loneliness? A feeling of inadequacy?" He leaned forward, studying Mr. van der Waals intensely. "Has money become your mother, Jacob? Or your father? Would you say you were oedipal?"

Mr. van der Waals sputtered. From a nearby desk, Veronica said, "Oh, never mind about that. It's not in the script—the page count would balloon far too large if I threw that in. The audience doesn't care! They just want to see that crazy, savage face leering down at a little old lady as he tears her house deed from her hand. They want to see him kicking blind men's dogs and knocking kiddies down with his juggernaut of a car. We're just giving the people what they want, for cripes sake!"

Mr. van der Waals was speechless.

"Don't forget the Shaw case," David said. The others murmured in agreement. "Those are the scenes that really aced the script for me. Imagine what all of America will say when they're sitting in a darkened theater, watching him ruin his son's best friend's family, see a man die . . . and call his lawyer. Classic American tragedy. Mr. van der Waals, it's gold, I tell you! I've got three studios salivating for this."

"And we have our lead actors cast already, sir," Lulu said quietly. "Blake here will play Freddie, and—"

"And I will play you," Vasily interrupted. "God, what a chance for an actor! To play one of the world's unsung villains! I could be *nominated*."

Mr. van der Waals's mouth worked in silent fury for a moment. "Do you mean to say you've written a screenplay based on . . . me?" Mingled with the fury, Lulu thought she saw a note of pure terror.

David piped up. "Well, sir, the names will be changed, of course. Heaven knows we don't want a lawsuit on our hands!" With that they all erupted in laughter, causing the dark red of Mr. van der Waals's face to deepen further.

David went on. "But the facts are pulled straight from life, and who it's based on will be a very open secret. Your son was remarkably candid, and we have a few other sources willing to speak about the ins and outs of your corruption and greed. In Hollywood, these stories are the stuff dreams are made of."

"You can't do this!" Mr. van der Waals shouted, and stepped toward Lulu menacingly. She held her ground.

"Sure we can," Veronica called from her corner. "Got half the script written already and studios lining up."

She shuffled the pages and handed them to Lulu, who

began to read. "Scene opens on a huddled beggar, a little girl holding out an empty cup at the foot of the Pierre. Then the camera climbs, pointing downward, until the little beggar girl is just a speck, all the way up to your balcony, Mr. van der Waals. Tricky shot, some effects like they did in *King Kong* to be sure, but gosh, it's powerful imagery. Chock-full of symbolism. Look how far you are above the masses! Look how far you have to fall! We all know what will happen to you after this movie comes out. You're rich, Mr. van der Waals, but you can't buy the entire movie business. Not when there are always stories like this to be told. The public loves it."

She lowered her voice. "And public opinion is a mighty powerful thing. How many houses will be open to you when the world knows the truth? Oh, no doubt plenty of your friends and business partners are almost as bad as you, but they managed to keep it a secret. You haven't. How many investors will abandon you? I'm sure you'll salvage plenty of your fortune—but your name, Mr. van der Waals! That name you are so proud of, that you mean to pass on to Freddie and his children. That name will be tarnished beyond repair. You'll be the most hated man in the country. What happens to your grand empire then?"

He ground his teeth together. Then, after a long, bitter pause, he asked, "How much will it take to make this go away?"

"It *never* goes away, Mr. van der Waals. It's your life." Was that a flash of remorse she saw on his face? If so, it was fleeting. "But I promise you, the only way this movie won't be made . . . is if you emancipate Freddie."

Mr. van der Waals was shaking. She had him.

Or so she thought.

He turned on his heel, and she thought he was leaving. But he only opened the door and called out into the hall.

"It's time!"

He turned back to Lulu. "I'm afraid your little ploy won't work. I would have been happy to pay you off with a few thousand, but you got greedy. Luckily, I made an arrangement for such a contingency. You have a very pretty face, Miss Kelly. For now. Allow me to introduce a gentleman of my acquaintance, one I've used to help with some of the, shall we say, rougher business negotiations I've had to deal with."

In walked Sal Benedetto.

Lulu suppressed a scream, and Sal looked almost as startled to see her. She felt her knees tremble. But Sal made no move toward her.

"If you please, Sal, teach this young lady what happens when someone tries to blackmail me," Mr. van der Waals said.

Lulu pressed her lips together to keep them from quivering. She wanted more than anything to run. But she had to be strong and see how this played out. It was the only way she could help Freddie.

Sal stood regarding Lulu for a long moment, a look of amused respect on his face.

"Not her," he said at last. "Deal's off."

"What? You're paid to take care of problems. Now take care of this!"

Sal crossed his arms. "If I was you, I'd give the lady what she wants."

"Why, you dirty, no good . . . ," Mr. van der Waals began, but Sal uncrossed his arms, letting his jacket fall open to reveal his gun. Mr. van der Waals backed down.

"You win," he snarled. "Freddie can stay or go." He stalked out to the hall. "But don't you think for a second that he'll stick to you, you trashy little—"

Sal slammed the door in his face. The group erupted into triumphant cheers. All except Lulu.

"Nice little scam you have going here, Lu," Sal said. "I gotta hand it to you. You can lie like a champ. Is he worth it, though?"

She didn't answer, but the glow on her face said it all.

"Heard you're all square with the law now. Shame. You and me, we could have been something. Might be, still. You never know. We're both street kids, Lu. That Freddie, he's just slumming. You know his father is right—he'll go back where he belongs someday. They always do, baby doll."

She still didn't say anything and didn't move when he stepped forward and kissed her cheek in a brotherly way.

"No hurry. I'll be sticking around Los Angeles for a while. Big things happening here. There's plenty of time for us. You don't rush a good thing." He tipped his hat. "Be seeing you, Lu."

When he was gone and the others had finished congratulating her on her success, Lulu sank down on her sofa, looking so radiant, so incandescently happy, that no one noticed the tiny nubbin of fear nestled inside her. Freddie wouldn't leave her for his old life . . . would he?

THIRTY-TWO

Lulu had almost everything she could have dreamed of. Her freedom, her good name, her rising career. Who could ask for more? She looked joyously down at the kaleidoscope of colors in the remains of her Cobb salad. *What a world this is*, she thought. *I can honestly tell my physical culture trainer that all I ate was a salad, but look—bacon!*

But the seemingly bright sky of her life, despite its myriad splendors, had a cloud. One that threatened a deluge of tears. This would be the hardest thing she'd ever done. To have found what she didn't even realize she'd been looking for and then give it up . . .

She raised her eyes and let her gaze rest on the handsome boy sitting opposite her in the Brown Derby booth. Outside, it was uncharacteristically stormy, but inside the

Derby, it was cozy, alive with chatter and gaiety. Freddie had hardly touched his grenadines of beef in sauce bordelaise, but seemed content to devour her with eyes brimming with love. He smiled and took her hand across the table. Somewhere, a flashbulb flared. Lulu winced.

"I don't mind," Freddie said. "It's a small price to pay for the pleasure of your company." He glanced toward the photographer, who had slipped the maître d' a hefty tip to be allowed to snap pictures of the many actors in the popular restaurant. Despite the veritable Milky Way of stars, the photographer seemed most intent on capturing the notorious Lulu Kelly. Even though she was thoroughly cleared of all charges and the story about Ruby was the national buzz, she was linked to one of Hollywood's most curious scandals, and the press happily served up her life to Hollywood's hungry public. "I'll put up with all kinds of paparazzi to be with you."

Lulu took a deep breath and sighed. This wasn't going to be easy. "About that," she began, as outside the wind blew harder.

Freddie, perhaps sensing what was coming, quickly steered her away from what she was about to say. "Did you read the interview Ruby gave? She said she was delirious from pain medication during her initial interview and had confused a nightmare with real life. She said she realizes now that it must have been just an unfortunate accident, and she wants the world to know that she has no hard feelings against whoever made such a terrible mistake."

Lulu almost snorted out her sip of ginger ale.

"Is that the story she's telling the press? Veronica told me she confessed everything to the police and the studio heads. The police were all for prosecuting her for perjury and criminal mischief at the very least, but the studio convinced them—in their usual way, of course—to let the whole thing drop."

"Lux forgives her, then?" Freddie asked.

"Oh, worse than that! Lux is positively thrilled with Ruby now. Veronica says she's getting three magazine covers in the next week alone. All dolled up in that frilly bed jacket, looking plaintive and suffering. They have her lined up for a top-billing lead as soon as she's recovered enough. Some movie about a nun. Can you imagine? If she pulls that baloney off, she *should* get an Oscar. And rumor has it they're delaying the casting of *House of Mirth* with her in mind for the lead. There goes my break."

"You're better at comedy than melodrama anyway, love." Lulu pouted, and he grinned. "How did she go from criminal to studio darling?" Freddie wanted to know.

"Easy: She became famous. And stopped just a hair short of being infamous. There's no harder trick to pull off. It's an outcome your publicist can't plan for and all the money in the world can't buy."

"And it was all thanks to you, in the end," Freddie pointed out. "No one in the audience will know that she put the bullets in the gun, or practically committed suicide, or that she would have sent an innocent person to prison."

"No. All they see is that she suffered, put on a brave face, and rose like a rouged-up phoenix from the ashes and gun smoke. Almost wish I'd thought of it myself."

"Lulu!"

"Oh, I'm kidding, of course. I honestly hope, for Ruby's sake, that she doesn't do anything to mess up this chance."

"She's lucky to be alive," Freddie said. "When people have a brush with death, it usually changes them."

Lulu sighed. "Knowing Ruby, it will probably only make her more prickly and arrogant. At least now we can hope she won't try to throw herself at everyone with money or power . . . though you know what they say about old dogs and new tricks. Maybe she's bought herself a little dignity with that stupid gamble."

"Let's hope. Say, what are you doing tomorrow?"

"I'm back on the set."

"For *Girl About Town*? You must be joking."

"Can you believe it? Niederman said they're even using the footage of the shooting and writing it into the plot."

"That's ghastly," Freddie said, shaking his head.

"I know. Now I suppose Ruby will probably get top billing for that, too. Niederman says it will likely be the studio's top-grossing film. Everyone will want to see it out of morbid curiosity."

"This business, this town—it's all crazy," Freddie said.

"No. It's the world that's crazy," Lulu said. "If they didn't want it, we wouldn't make it."

"So that accounts for tomorrow." Freddie caught her

hand as she set down her ginger ale. "What about the rest of your life?" He held her gaze.

"Freddie, I . . . I can't." Outside, lightning blazed through the night sky.

His face fell, but he held her hand tighter. "What do you mean?"

"I sold myself once before, Freddie. I can't do it again." She pulled her hand away and clenched her fingers together in her lap.

"Lulu, I'm not . . ."

"We can't be together. You were born a millionaire, Freddie. There's no getting around that. It's who you are and what you'll always be, no matter what kind of momentary detour you've taken. And all that *I'll* really ever be is a kid from the slums, like Sal said."

Freddie's face hardened. "You're picking Sal over me?"

Her eyes widened. "You fool. How can you ask me that? He wanted to buy me too. He just tried to force the sale. But you, Freddie—oh, you're the most wonderful man I've ever met. The most wonderful *person* I've ever met. But I'll never be a rich man's plaything. Now that I know all about your money, even if you say you won't touch it, everything is different. It sounds crazy, but it was so easy to love a bum who couldn't give me anything but love. Someone who knew what it was to do without and to be grateful for what was worked for and earned. But I can't feel that I'm bought and paid for. I can't . . . I *won't* love someone who might feel like he owns me."

"I'd never . . . ," he began, but she interrupted him, tears in her eyes.

"I wouldn't be myself," Lulu said. "I'd just be Freddie van der Waals's girl. The millionaire's baby. Or worse, that horrible name your father spit at me. Every time I earned something for myself, the world would say, 'Sure, of course she got that part. Do you know who she's dating?' Oh, I don't even care what the world would think—*I* would think it. Freddie, I adore you, but I just can't." The tears fell, and she made no effort to hide them.

A waitress in a short skirt, oblivious to the melodrama unfolding at the table, sailed up and asked pertly if they'd like a little something sweet.

"No," Freddie said. "Just the check."

She placed it down next to Freddie.

Very deliberately, he slid it across the table to Lulu.

"I'm broke, remember. This is on you." He moved to her side of the booth, put his arm around her, and dabbed her cheeks with his handkerchief. "*Everything's* going to be on you, Lulu. At least for a while. I swear I'll never touch my family's money again. That life is over, forever. I think I have a job, though. Veronica introduced me to this private eye who's looking for an assistant. The pay isn't great, but I might be able to take you out for an ice-cream soda at Schwab's once a week."

She looked up at him, hope shining in her eyes.

"I don't mind being a kept man," he said with a gentle smile. "I don't mind being owned, as long as you're the one who owns me."

"Oh, Freddie!" She reached for him. It felt like every moment had been leading up to this. Her successes paled beside this instant, and all of her hardships seemed a small price to pay for such happiness.

"Only, I kind of thought we could be a team," Freddie said. "You might have more money than me, but I promise I won't hold it against you."

Lulu laughed, her tears drying. "Hey, Freddie, if I said you had a nice body, would you hold it against me?"

He complied happily, squeezing her closer. "You sure you wouldn't rather be in vaudeville than Hollywood?"

Lightning flashed again, followed closely by a boom of thunder. The restaurant lights went out, and Lulu and Freddie sat, cuddled close in the darkness, while around them women squealed and somewhere a plate fell and broke.

"Is this our fade-out?" Lulu whispered, resting her cheek against his.

The lights flickered back on, and Hollywood life resumed in all its noisy, brazen splendor.

"No, Lulu. If I have my way, this is merely the opening credits."

He took her face in both his hands and kissed her, and distantly, as if from some celestial audience, Lulu heard the faint sound of applause.

ADAM SHANKMAN is the director and producer of the exuberant musical remake of *Hairspray*, the producer of the top-grossing *Step Up* films, and the director of the adaptation of the Nicholas Sparks bestseller *A Walk to Remember*, starring Mandy Moore and *Bringing Down the House*, starring Steve Martin and Queen Latifah. Adam has also directed episodes of *Modern Family*, and *Glee*, and he's a popular personality as a judge on *So You Think You Can Dance*. He also produced and choreographed the 82nd Annual Academy Awards (which was itself nominated for a record 12 Emmys).

LAURA L. SULLIVAN is a former newspaper editor, biologist, social worker, and deputy sheriff who writes because storytelling is the easiest way to do everything in the world. Her books include *Love By the Morning Star, Delusion,* and *Ladies in Waiting*. Laura lives on the Florida coast, but her heart is in England.